THE FERTILITY PROJECT

ISBN: 9798594845138

I would like to thank all my readers who have supported me as an author. Without you, none of this would be possible.

Thank you, Liyuan, for helping me set up Facebook ads. Your assistance helped put my books in front of more readers.

Thank you, Anonymous Military Advisor, for educating me on military affairs.

Thank you, Arijana, for everything. Sometimes it's hard to pick yourself up, and you're always here to assist me in that.

Contents

Prologue
Disaster Night, Part 1

The Lenco Bearcat's engine roared on the desolate road. Now that the vehicle had reached the outskirts of the city, the driver was free to speed up. Up until two minutes ago, the blaring of the passing civilian cars and the horns frustratedly being sat upon permeated the air. Now, it was so quiet that every team members' shifting got discernibly audible.

"ETA, ten minutes!" the driver called out from the front.

Intervention Unit officer Jackson glanced at his teammates and then closed his eyes. He had a routine of blanking his mind and relaxing before each mission. He had been on so many missions even before joining The Company that he had learned how to perfect the technique long since. Some rookies that were assigned on missions with him often wondered how he was able to remain so calm, and sometimes even take short naps when they were dropping into the unknown that might cause them not to be on the chopper or vehicle back home. He'd shrug and tell them the same thing he always told them – *'Don't think about what might go wrong because it will.'*

Some of the rookies took his advice and managed to survive the mission in one piece. Others... Jackson could usually tell which ones were not going to last long in this line of work. If the things they went up against didn't end their lives, then they themselves would, with their own guns in their own homes. He always tried to be a guardian angel to his team members if it didn't jeopardize the mission. Unfortunately, sometimes he had to choose between the lives of his buddies or the mission – and the mission always came first.

"So, what's our mission exactly?" Talker, one of the team members, asked.

"We'll recon the gate at the campus entrance," Team Leader Bulldozer said. "Make sure that the guard stationed there is okay and that nothing escaped the campus. After that, we're on standby."

The Company's Intervention Unit used code names for each member due to the secrecy of the operations they performed. Using real names was so discouraged that The Company started punishing the members right from the selection and first phase of training if they used real names. During the selection stage, Intervention Unit candidates were referred to as numbers, and the instructors would usually give them code names based on their performance or quirks. Team Leader Bulldozer got his name due to his mountain-like build and immense strength. He apparently beat the timed record of The Company in the training for extracting civilians by barging through all the doors so quickly that no one was ever able to even come close to beating his record.

"What about the other teams?" Squarepants asked.

Squarepants got his name on the first day of training. When the instructors addressed him, he responded with 'aye, aye, sir'. He got the code name and a week of eating MREs out in the cold. Jackson's code name was Survivor, and he hated it. When he joined The Company's selection process, he was already notorious for his prior military experience and being the only man to come out of multiple missions alive in his entire team. He'd come under suspicion that he had turned against his teammates, but due to the lack of evidence, he was honorably discharged. Upon joining The Company, the instructors did their best to drill him more than the other members, due to his reputation, but he had already been through hell and high water by then.

Hell, one time, his entire team got ambushed and killed, and he got imprisoned by the enemy soldiers, brought to their base, and interrogated incessantly for days. He managed to kill the guard and escape, making his way through the inhospitable rainforest terrain for five days with no food (except what he managed to catch) and no equipment, having to move constantly and cover his own tracks (including burying his own shit), until he exfiled the hotzone. By then, he had gone with only three hours of sleep in that past week and was a wreck.

There was nothing that the instructors could throw at him that he wouldn't be able to survive. In time, he got used to getting called Survivor until he identified with it more than he did with his real name.

Aside from Bulldozer, Squarepants and Survivor, the Alpha team consisted of three more members – Cougar (he was specialized in infiltration), Talker (talked way too much, and not just in training), and Poseidon (Survivor didn't know how he got that name).

"Bravo Team will secure the South side of the campus. Charlie will infiltrate the science building to find the VIP - Professor Richards - the guy in charge of the experiment, and Delta is on standby," Bulldozer said.

"And HQ doesn't know what we're up against?" Talker asked.

He took a drag out of his cigarette with a reticent expression on his face. The tip of his cigarette lit up with embers before the smoke began billowing up in the air.

"We're on a need-to-know basis," Bulldozer retorted. "All we know is something went so wrong down there that the guards called for a Code Red. HQ classified it as level three."

"Red... *and* level three, damn," Talker said.

Everyone knew what that meant. The highest Survivor had been on was red level seven, and it was hell. He reckoned that level three wouldn't be much better, either. He and the team were playing cards back at HQ when the alarm resounded. They barely had enough time to put their tactical gear on and testfire their rifles before getting loaded inside the Bearcat and sent off on the mission with minimal briefing.

During such missions, the Intervention Unit's job was to infiltrate the mission zone, find out what was happening and, if necessary, neutralize the threat while rescuing any civilians. Unfortunately, that sounded way easier than it actually was because what The Company dealt with was usually much harder to assess and approach than the standard police and military operations.

"I've never even been on a red level three," Squarepants said. "What about you, guys?"

He scanned the faces of his teammates with a timorous and curious glance.

"Level one for me," Cougar said.

He held his head down, revealing the bald scalp riddled with tiny scars. Survivor remembered hearing something about Cougar saying that he got the scars from shards of glass when he was forced to jump out of a window once. Bulldozer raised four fingers to indicate level four.

"Three, four times," Talker said with a toothy grin.

He didn't look like the military type at all, let alone someone for spec ops. He had a kempt, chestnut-curtain hairstyle and a pretty-boy face that made all the men jealous and all the women wet. He was around forty by Survivor's rough estimation, but he looked better than everyone in the Intervention Unit – not gaunt, haggard, harsh, and distant.

"One. Wasn't too bad, honestly," Poseidon shrugged.

He was leaning against the inner wall of the Bearcat, with one leg stretched forward in a relaxed position, his shotgun between his legs.

Squarepants looked in Survivor's direction and laughed.

"I don't even wanna ask about you, man."

Survivor shot him a bemused glance before leaning against the wall just like Poseidon.

"If they sent our team and Survivor's in it, we're fucked," Talker said. "All of us except him, of course."

"Shut the fuck up, Talker. We're all getting out of here alive," leader Bulldozer said.

"I sure hope so," Squarepants briskly responded with a more confident timbre. "I've only been on Orange level Nine, like damn, I'm like a little baby for all of you."

"Don't worry, we'll keep you safe, baby boy," Cougar tousled Squarepants' hair.

"Five minutes!" the driver shouted from the front.

"Check your gear," Bulldozer said.

Everyone on the team began checking if they had everything on them. Survivor placed his Heckler and Koch MP5 on his lap. He pulled out his sidearm – Glock 19 with extended mag – and popped out the magazine to make sure that it was full before putting it back in.

He checked his tactical vest for the magazines he had. There were six magazines in total on the front, each holding thirty 9mm Parabellum rounds. He had two more magazines in the holders on his left leg. He also brought two stun grenades – just in case. Many of the guys from the Intervention Unit liked carrying hand grenades because they were never sure what they would be up against, but if the hostiles needed a frag to be taken care of, they'd most likely have to call in the Fat Guys Unit anyway.

Along with the battle-ready gear, each Intervention Unit had to carry additional supplies, like first aid, a small canteen of water, and an MRE, in case they got stuck on the mission for too long. They also had a radio that was attached with a wired earpiece in case they needed to communicate with HQ. The Company strictly avoided using radios without earpieces to avoid causing any noise on noise-sensitive missions. Along with the main gear, the security members also carried a gas mask, a combat knife, an NVG on their helmets, and thermal goggles – from Survivor's experience, all three could always come in handy.

The rest of the Alpha members had varying weapons and equipment. Each Intervention Unit member had the freedom to use the loadout they were most comfortable with. Survivor checked his MP5's red dot sight to make sure it worked. Over the years, he got acquainted with every and any gun that the special forces used, and he preferred sticking with the MP5 for room-clearing and tight-spot missions.

"Talker, put out the damn cigarette, we're almost at the dropoff point," Bulldozer roared.

Talker inhaled a long drag from his stub, as if to defy the team leader, before tossing the butt on the ground and crushing it under his boot.

"Can never even have a moment of relaxation with you, can we boss?" he winked.

Bulldozer ignored his remark and gripped his G36 tighter.

"One minute!" the driver's voice came from the front.

Bulldozer touched the button on his earpiece and said.

"HQ, this is Alpha Team. We're ETA one minute from the dropoff point."

A voice came into Survivor's earpiece a moment later.

"Roger that, Alpha. Keep your eyes open. Teams Bravo and Charlie are already in position, and they see some suspicious activity on the campus grounds."

"Copy that. Will keep you posted. Alpha out," Bulldozer said.

The Bearcat slowed down significantly, and that was the team's cue. Within seconds, the vehicle came to an abrupt stop.

"We're here! Move it!" the driver shouted.

"Let's go!" Bulldozer was the first one to stand up, and the others soon followed.

He opened the backdoor of the vehicle, and one by one, the team members hopped off with their guns raised. Survivor was the last one to step out, and as soon as he did, he was hit by a waft of the cold night breeze. The driver had stopped in the middle of the empty parking lot near the campus entrance, just between the campus grounds and the forest that the vehicle undoubtedly came through just now. The campus itself was cordoned off by wire fences that stretched in both directions as far as the eye could see. The entrance had a toll gate with a barrier next to a small guardhouse. Although a glance through the windows was enough to tell that the guardhouse was empty, the team still held their weapons raised as they approached it.

"Go!" Bulldozer called out when he scanned the guardhouse's interior from the outside window.

Talker took the lead and went around the toll gate barrier, taking up a position from which he could shoot if any hostiles showed up. The other team members went behind him and around to the entrance of the guardhouse. Survivor used his left hand to twist the knob and push the door open, allowing Cougar and Squarepants to step inside and scout out the room.

"Room clear!" Squarepants called out.

Now that the room was deemed safe, the rest of the team could go inside, except Talker and Poseidon – they would need to stay by the door and make sure no one got the drop on them.

As soon as Survivor stepped inside the room, he could tell that something had gone terribly wrong in there. The rotating chair was overturned on the floor next to a dried splotch of blood. The desk and the monitors on top of it had red droplets here and there. Although the amount of blood wasn't significant enough for the person to have died from it, it was probably a serious wound.

"Alright, where's the fucking guard?" Squarepants asked.

Bulldozer approached the security computer, placed his gun on the desk, and leaned on it without a word. By this time, Survivor had stopped next to him to stare at the screen along with him. A camera feed was displayed, with nine equally divided squares showing different parts of the campus.

"Is that live?" Cougar asked.

"Yeah," Bulldozer responded.

"HQ said the guards called in about an hour ago. Check the feed for that time; we might be able to see something."

"No time for that now."

Survivor squinted just in time to see movement on one of the small squares. Multiple figures were moving in prudent manners through a hallway until they disappeared out of sight. In seconds, they reappeared on another square showing a different section of the hallway with lockers. The image was clearer here, and it became apparent that they had the same tactical gear as Alpha Team and were clearing the building with their weapons raised. Survivor recognized the figures as members of the Intervention Unit, most likely Charlie Team.

"This is Alpha Team. Bravo, Charlie, do you copy?" Bulldozer said after pressing the button near his earpiece.

The team in the live feed stopped in front of a door on the camera, and one of them – the leader most likely – raised a hand up to his ear.

"This is Charlie Team, we read you. Over," a voice responded, a moment later.

"We see you on the camera feed from the guardhouse, Charlie. Give me a sit-rep. Over," Bulldozer briskly stated.

"Alpha, no sign of-," Charlie leader started, but his voice was cut off.

At the same time, the camera feed froze, and Charlie Team was left standing in front of the door in breaching positions.

"Charlie, you cut off. Repeat that last," Bulldozer said.

The live feed unfroze, and Charlie team was nowhere in sight. The door that they stood in front of was open, but no one was in sight. Then, all at once, all the other cameras began glitching out, and pixels covered the entire feed, like a badly buffered online video. Gunshots resounded somewhere in the distance, faint, but loud enough to be heard.

"Boss? We got an issue," Talker said from outside, as he took a peek into the guardhouse.

"Hold on, Talker," Bulldozer hushed him. "Charlie, this is Alpha. Can anyone hear me?"

Static came through, followed by a long, piercing screech. Squarepants growled in pain as he grabbed at his ear, cursing. Suddenly, a voice came through, but it wasn't Charlie.

"Kill the children," it said in a whisper with a trembling voice.

"What the fuck?" Poseidon scoffed.

Bulldozer scanned the faces of his teammates reticently before pressing his mic button once more.

"This is team Alpha of the Intervention Unit. Who is this?"

No response.

And then, a loud, panicked voice came through so abruptly that it almost startled Survivor.

"HQ! This is Charlie Team! The whole team has been wiped out! Repeat! The whole team has been wiped out! Send backup immed-"

The sentence was interrupted by the same loud screech from before. The camera feed began working again at that point, but it was choppy. Survivor saw one Charlie member appearing in the hallway in a running stance before remaining frozen like that for a few seconds and then reappearing elsewhere. The camera was able to catch him in a position where he was standing in front of one of the lockers with his hand on the handle. In the next moment, the hallway was empty.

"Charlie, this is HQ, what's going on out there?" HQ's voice came through.

The cameras began glitching again, and the hallways where the security officer had last appeared was riddled with pixels. It remained frozen.

"Charlie, do you read me? Over," Bulldozer tried again.

Deafening silence ensued for a long moment.

"Can't talk. It's out there," a barely audible, trembling voice came through in the next moment.

Bulldozer tried pressing the Charlie member for more info, but there was no response.

"Bravo Team, this is Alpha. Gimme a sit-rep," Bulldozer said.

"Alpha, this is Bravo Team. We've secured the South side of the campus. No sign of suspicious activity here. Moving North towards the Genetics Center," Bravo leader responded.

"Roger that, Bravo."

Then another voice came through.

"Alpha, this is HQ. You have new orders. You are to go inside the Science building and look for Professor Howard Richards."

"Roger that, HQ. On our way," Bulldozer said.

"We're really going in there, Bulldozer? With whatever wiped out Charlie?" Squarepants asked.

"How about we just call for backup and let the Fat Guys handle this?" Cougar asked.

"Can't. Backup is on another assignment. Looks like someone else fucked up tonight," Bulldozer said.

"Fan-fucking-tastic," Talker shouted from the outside.

Bulldozer leaned closer to the monitor and double-clicked the image where the Charlie member was last seen. The camera was still frozen and pixelated, but now something else became apparent. At the far end of the hallway, peeking around the shadowed corner, was the outline of a silhouette. Survivor couldn't discern any details on the figure from here, except for the featureless head that peeked around, and the hand that grasped the wall, as if curiously staring down the hallway.

"What the fuck is that?" Squarepants asked. "Is it even human?"

"Probably not," Bulldozer frigidly said. "Squarepants, stay here and keep an eye on the cameras. If you see something suspicious, let us know. The rest of you, follow me."

"Roger that," Squarepants placed his gun on the desk, lifted the chair, and took a comfortable seat in front of the monitor.

"Look at you, already getting well-acquainted with the armed security guard duty. Maybe you missed your calling, Squarepants," Cougar mocked him.

"Fuck you, man," Squarepants flipped him off.

"Cut the chatter," Bulldozer said as he moved towards the door. "Alright, let's move."

Chapter 1
103 days until disaster

"We all know about the theory of evolution," Professor Richards said.

The entire auditorium was silent, mesmerized by the professor's lecture, staring at the slide on the wall that showed a Neanderthal with a club standing in the middle of a desolate field. As Assistant Professor Victor scanned the students' faces, he couldn't find a single person that looked bored, unfocused, or sleepy. In fact, the lectures had been so engaging that the students would often offer their own theories and answers. Whenever the professor took short five-second pauses between slides or sentences to allow the listeners to process the information he conveyed, all the eyes were fixated on him - the professor knew exactly what to do in order to grab the attention of his students.

"Now, there have been countless scientific theories that didn't get widely accepted or were outright discredited," the professor continued. "However, we have to take them into consideration when talking about reproduction."

He clicked a button on his remote, which changed the slide on the wall behind him. The slide now showed a couple looking down at their newborn baby with smiles on their faces as the woman cradled it. Professor Richards continued.

"Now, one popular theory posits that you don't need to be the strongest in order to survive and have your offspring survive. You need to be reproductively *compatible*. Think of this."

He pressed the button on his remote again. The slide of the happy family instantaneously disappeared and was replaced with the image of a house from the middle ages, from the perspective of the house's interior. A woman stood by the door saying goodbye to a knight – who was presumably her husband – while a half-dressed man with a conniving grin hid in her closet. The auditorium exploded with laughter. Professor Richards waited until the room calmed down before continuing.

"During the medieval ages, the husband left his wife to go on a crusade and was gone for ten or so years – or, he never came back at all. The wife was then left alone for a very long time, and you can guess how things went from there," he shrugged.

The students laughed briefly again before the professor proceeded with the lecture.

"Now, this is very dependent on mother nature," Richards pointed at a male student from the front and said. "Bryans here could be the most reproductively compatible candidate..."

A whistle and applause ensued while Bryans blushed.

"However. If mother nature decides she doesn't like him and the neon lights above him explode and kill him, he is effectively removed from the reproduction cycle."

Bryans uncomfortably shifted in his seat. Richards pressed the button on his remote to change the slide. It now showed the famous picture of the homo sapiens evolution from monkey to today's human.

"That is called natural selection. But if Bryans gets killed by the exploding light, the rest of you will know to avoid sitting under any faulty lights in the future. Now, Darwin theorized that through this process of elimination, humans would evolve, adapt, and eventually, only the strongest seed would remain. He theorized that this process would take millions and millions of years. We can even see traces of evolution in various species and subspecies, like chickens, various reptiles, etcetera. We, as living organisms, adapt in order to survive the conditions mother nature throws at us. We start living in the water? After some years, we would grow fins, webbings between our fingers and toes for easier diving. Nuclear war? After many generations, our descendants would grow immune to the radiation. And, so on and so forth."

Richards pressed the button again. The slide now showed a community of people celebrating happily on the streets. He glanced at the slide before scratching his clean-shaven face.

"Darwin even had species of animals that he bred generation after generation, specifically for the purpose of proving that his theory was correct. Unfortunately, as I mentioned earlier, it would take a long, long time to prove his theory as accurate with one hundred percent certainty. Now, if mother nature can eliminate us one by one until only the strongest survive, then we have to ask ourselves one question."

The professor clicked the button, and the slide changed into a picture of clones of human males and females standing in rows, with the same, blank facial expressions.

"What is stopping us from *artificially* creating the perfect species of humans?"

A few students exchanged glances with each other. The others continued staring at the slides with rapt fascination. The professor clicked the button once more until the slide changed into a picture of a classroom full of students sleeping at their desks with the caption 'Thank you for your attention' above.

"That's it for today's lecture," Richards said. "Any questions?"

A young woman raised her hand.

"Tara Nugent, was it? Go ahead," Richards said.

"Professor, has anyone actually tried cloning the perfect human?"

"To my knowledge, no. Cloning humans is still considered illegal and unethical. There have been rumors of secret organizations successfully cloning humans, but that's all just conspiracy theory mumbo-jumbo. But we're not talking about cloning here, we're talking about *breeding*. You may be familiar with some of the experiments that the Germans conducted during World War II to create the perfect Aryan race. While we know today that they were on the wrong track due to the physical attributes they sought out in their candidates, we can safely say that yes, it has been attempted in the past. Unsuccessfully."

More students started raising their hands. Richards pointed to a buff, young man.

"Professor, hypothetically speaking, if we were to try to breed the perfect human, say, a person to weather an apocalyptic event, what kind of qualities would that person need to have?"

"Big biceps!" someone shouted from the crowd, much to the laughter of their classmates.

Richards briskly half-smiled before putting his hands in his pockets and replying.

"Well, first of all, it would all depend on what purpose this particular human was bred for. Think of it as a tradeoff. I don't believe that there will ever be something called a 'perfect human', but I do believe there will be humans that will have perfected one area of their focus, whether it be art, math, fitness, archery, surgery, or anything else."

"We already have such humans," someone from the crowd said.

"We have humans who are really good or talented in certain areas. But, are they perfect?" Richards swiveled his head left and right, making eye contact with the people in the room.

A few 'no's filled the room.

"No," Richards confirmed. "They can still make mistakes, even after thousands of hours of practice. We know that based on the area of expertise, certain skills require more genetic talent, which leaves little room for practice," he gestured towards the buff student. "For instance, we have explosive strength, which is used by sprinters, and that skill itself is around seventy percent genetic, and only thirty percent practice-based. In other words, if you have no genetic talent and you work hard, you will still never break a certain barrier. But... combining talent *and* practice can make for incredible success. Even with that combination, though, our skills deteriorate after some time as we get older and cease to practice. So to answer your question, the skillset of the individual would depend on the situation."

More people started raising hands, but Richards raised his tone, before pointing to Victor.

"That's all the time we have for today. You can get your next assignments from Assistant Professor Lukanski. I will see you all next Wednesday."

As the crowds of students began standing up and picking up their things, Professor Richards walked up to Victor and put a hand on his shoulder. Victor looked up with curious eyes.

"Victor, come see me in my office after you are done here."

"Yes, professor," Victor nodded.

The crowd of students started flocking around Victor's desk, until he reminded them to stand in line. Around thirty students were attending the lecture in total, but many of them didn't stay to get their assignments, Victor noticed. Around ten minutes later, everyone was gone, and he was left alone in the lecture hall. Victor packed his notes and folders and headed outside.

The murmurs of students out front waiting for their next lecture in the auditorium filled the air. Some of them greeted Victor, and he nodded back in return. As he made his way through the crowd and reached the bottom of the stairs leading up to the second floor, he felt a buzz in his pocket. He sunk his hand into the pocket of his jeans and pulled out the phone to see a message. It was from Jennifer.

Hi honey, when are you coming home? I made you some pasta.

Always so thoughtful. He typed a message and clicked the send button.

Will be home by tonight, just need to talk to Professor Richards in his office, and I'll be on my way. Love you.

He climbed up on the second floor and turned left towards the professor's office. Professor Richards was one of the more privileged staff members in the university due to his prestigious achievements and academic awards. He had the biggest and most luxurious office on the campus, rivaling that of the principal. Once he arrived in front of the door, Victor knocked gently three times.

"Come in," Richards' muffled voice resounded from the other side.

Victor opened the door, revealing Professor Richards sitting in his swiveling chair with his feet on the desk. His pristine shoes gleamed from the sunlight cast through the window behind him.

"Victor, come on in. I have something important to discuss with you." The professor motioned him to come closer as he dropped his feet down.

Victor sat on the chair in front of the professor's desk, straightening his back and staring at the professor in curious anticipation.

"What can I do for you, Professor Richards?"

"How is the family, Victor?"

"They're fine, professor. It's a little difficult for my wife and me since I can only visit them on the weekends, but we're getting used to it."

"And your daughter?"

"Well, when I'm home, Leah doesn't let me get any sleep. I can't even begin to imagine what it's like for Jennifer."

"Ah, yes. The perks of parenting," Richards cackled. "I remember what it was like when I first had James and Haylee. They never let me and my ex-wife have a good night's rest."

"I suppose that drags on for at least a few years?"

Victor had been a parent for less than a year, but he felt like he didn't learn much during that time. Richards seemed hesitant to answer.

"You get used to it after a while," he finally said after a moment of grimacing.

He leaned forward and intertwined his fingers, giving Victor a serious look.

"Victor, let's talk about business a little bit, shall we?"

"Of course."

"The reason why I called you here is because I have a proposal for you."

28

Victor raised his hand in a stop sign.

"Professor, I have to stop you right here. I have way too much work on my hands right now, and I really don't think I can handle any more projects."

"This isn't just any project, Victor. This is groundbreaking. And you know I don't say these things lightly."

He was right. Victor had known the professor for many years, and they'd become well acquainted. Not only was he an excellent mentor, but he was also a fatherly figure that Victor never had. Somehow, Professor Howard Richards could always sense when something bothered Victor. And he always knew exactly what kind of advice to give him, whether his problems were of academic or of personal nature. Over the years, he had undertaken various projects and experiments under the professor's guidance, either for the gain of personal experience or because he felt honored to participate with the professor.

Richards would often remind him how one day Victor would be the one to teach a new assistant professor in the college, long after Richards was gone. Whenever Victor remarked how he would not come even close to the professor's achievements, Richards dismissively waved and told him it was nonsense.

"You are my scientific descendant. My children are not interested in this. But you, Victor, you are raw talent," he would often say.

If the professor said that this new project is groundbreaking, then passing it up would be a missed opportunity for something big.

"Alright, so tell me more about this assignment, professor," Victor said.

Richards' lips contorted into a gleeful rictus, before he leaned back and opened one of the drawers. He pulled out a thick folder and slammed it against the desk in front of Victor, causing a slight gust of air to disperse in all directions.

"Go on," he said.

Victor reached for the folder and opened it. The first page had three simple words printed in capital letters across the entire page.

THE FERTILITY PROJECT

The assistant professor looked up at Richards for confirmation. Richards gave him a nod of approval as he swiveled his chair to the side and leaned on the desk with his elbow. Victor began going through the documents. The first page briefly summarized an experiment the professor had conducted on mice. Despite being profoundly educated in reproductive science and medicine, there were a few terms from embryology, hormonal infertility, and other branches that Victor didn't understand. The more he read, though, the more his eyes widened in amazement.

"Professor, is this true?" Victor finally looked up at the professor once he finished skimming through the first page.

Richards had a complacent smile on his face. He looked like he was trying really hard not to burst out laughing. Any moment now, he was going to tell Victor that this was all just a prank and that none of it was real. But instead, the professor turned to face Victor and said.

"Tell me what you think, Victor."

Victor looked down at the paper, before flipping to the next page. There were photos attached on a clip along with the more detailed explanations. Victor looked back up at the professor.

"So, if I understand correctly, in layman terms, you conducted experiments on lab rats and made infertile rats fertile?"

Richards spread his arms and bellowed with excitement.

"Can you even begin to comprehend the enormity of such a discovery, Victor?!"

"The experiment was a success?"

"Do you think I'd present you with this file if it wasn't?"

That made sense. Victor looked down at the files again. This was big. Infertility treatment, including IVF had been practiced for years, and although some of the first attempts were as low as twenty-nine percent, the technology improved enough to increase those odds up to sixty-five percent for women under the age of thirty-five. But what Professor Richards presented here wasn't a gamble of a solution – it was an actual, almost one-hundred percent successful fertilization method.

"So, what do you need from me, professor?" Victor asked, breathless from excitement.

"Glad you asked. I need you to work with me as my right-hand man in the second phase of the experiment."

"Second phase?"

"That's right. We're going to test the fertilization method on humans."

Silence permeated the air for a moment, while Victor processed what the professor had just said. As if in a flash, thousands of thoughts rushed into his mind – he and the professor conducting the experiment and helping desperate infertile women conceive, having their names published in breaking news articles, receiving scientific prizes, and going down in history...

"Here's what I need from you, Victor," the professor said, interrupting his train of thoughts. "I need you to find twenty suitable students to participate in this project. I will interview them and select the number we need, and then you and I are going to interview the female candidates for fertilization. I have already assembled a list of suitable candidates. This entire project is funded by the university, and they've cut no corners on it. You can imagine what a PR boost this would be for them. That means that for the duration of the experiment, we won't need to attend the lectures."

"Understood, professor."

"Now, there is one thing you need to be aware of. If you agree to do this, the experiment will last for five months. But during those five months, I will need you close at all times. You will have to stay here on the campus with me. That means that you will need to be focused for five months and your family can't stay with you, nor visit you."

Victor didn't like the sound of that. It was already bad enough that he had to leave Jennifer and Leah alone during the week, but not being able to visit them for five months…

Richards saw the hesitation on Victor's face, so he raised his hand to speak.

"Now, before you say anything, let me be clear here. You wouldn't be working under me as my assistant. You'd be working *with me*, as my equal."

"That's a big job for someone like me, professor."

"Nonsense. You are more than capable of handling it. Think of the path you've gone through to get where you are. Despite the hardships in your life, you graduated top of your class, you got accepted into one of the most prestigious universities for reproductive science and medicine, and not to brag – but you got mentored by me."

Victor reflected on that for a moment. It *was* a long and hard journey. Sleepless nights studying and stressing and working, all so he could be where he was today. He couldn't help but feel a sense of pride now that the professor put it that way. Richard closed the file and spoke.

"Tell you what. Take this file," he slid the folder closer to him. "Go home tonight and take Monday and Tuesday off. Spend time with your family, and when you have the time, read the file. When you come back on Wednesday, tell me what your final decision is. Deal?"

Victor looked down at the file. He was tempted just to say yes right away. But it wasn't right towards his family. He closed the file and nodded to the professor.

"Deal."

Chapter 2
99 days until disaster

"Just don't come in here, alright?" Jennifer's muffled voice came from the bathroom.

"Alright!" Victor responded.

The nursery was on the other side of the house and well-isolated for them to speak in normal tones. Victor was sitting on the sofa with the Fertility Project papers splayed on the coffee table in front of him. Richards made sure to take scrutinous notes about everything in the experiment, including the change in the lab rats' behavior once they were inseminated, the fully detailed process of how the fertilization process worked, etc.

"Okay, just one more minute!" Jennifer shouted from the bathroom once more.

"Take your time!" Victor said, not taking his eyes off the papers.

Truth be told, he couldn't have been less in the mood for sex. He and Jennifer had been sexting throughout the entire week, and she's been sending him nudes, and he couldn't wait to get his hands on her, but now that he was presented with the Fertility Project, sex seemed so irrelevant, so superficial. He had already made up his mind that he would give Jennie a quickie and then continue reading through the notes.

But that left him with another problem.

How was he going to tell Jennifer about being away on a work-related project for five months? He kept telling himself on the drive home that he would keep his excitement in check and go through the notes first to confirm the plausibility of Richards' research before giving a concrete answer to the professor. But now that the notes were in front of him, there was not a shred of doubt about it – he would say yes.

The door of the bathroom opened, and Jennifer's soft footsteps resounded down the hallway. Victor jerked his head up, and in seconds, his wife appeared in front of him. She wore red, two-piece see-through lingerie, with matching thigh-high stockings. She had done her hair too, so that it curled all the way down to her shoulders.

"I've been a bad student, professor. I need to be punished," she said.

Victor forgot all about the notes and the Fertility Project.

***

The weekend was eventful. Victor had finished reading the entirety of the notes the professor gave him on Friday and spent the rest of the time with his family. He and Jennifer even managed to hire a babysitter while they went out for movies and dinner. They hadn't done that in a long time, and it was a refreshing change from constantly sitting at home and catching up on sleep.

The extra two days Professor Richards gave him were exactly what Victor needed. He had no idea what to do with all the extra time, and he found his mind at moments wandering back to the project. It was tempting to go back and reread the notes over and over, but he promised himself that he would not touch anything work-related while he was home. On any normal weekend, Victor would barely have enough time to absorb and give the love and attention that his family deserved before having to go back into the throes of work, but now he found himself counting down the hours until he had to return to the office.

It was Sunday night when Victor decided to talk to Jennifer about the project. He had already made up his mind about participating, but he now only needed to make his wife see the benefits of the project. She would protest and complain, he was sure of it, but she would concede in the end. The problem was – would she relent because she'd get tired of arguing and spend the next week sulking, or would she see that the experiment was for the greater good and fully support him? He kept going over the conversation in his mind, trying to figure out the best way to break it to her.

I'm gonna be away for five months. I won't be coming home for five months. The project will require me to stay on the campus for five months. If I accept this, I'll be gone for five months...

No matter how he phrased it in his mind, it didn't sound good. Eventually, he stopped overthinking it and just decided to talk to his wife. When he called Jennie to sit and talk, she had a grievous and worried expression on her face. It was the same kind of expression she had whenever there was a serious issue he wanted to discuss with her. It was as if she always expected him to tell her that someone died or that he wanted to file for a divorce.

"So uh..." he started. "Professor Richards offered me a new project to work on."

"That's great, honey. You're learning a lot from him," Jennifer smiled, now visibly more relaxed.

"Yeah," Victor nodded. "The thing is, this is a big one. The biggest one yet. The professor wants me to work on this one with him as his equal. And if we're successful, we'll probably become famous."

Jennie clapped her hands together and grinned in uncontained excitement.

"Honey, that's great! I'm so happy for you!"

She clambered up to her feet from the sofa and hopped into Victor's lap. She grabbed his face with her hands and gave him a long smooch.

"Wait, wait, wait," Victor pulled his head back before she could get even more excited than she already was. "There's a catch."

Jennifer stared at him in anticipation with her arms hanging around his shoulders.

"I won't be able to come home for the next five months."

Jennifer's smile slightly dropped but still remained plastered to her face in a half-grin.

"Oh," she simply said. "Can... Leah and I come visit you, then?"

"I'm sorry, Jennie. The professor is very strict when he lays down the rules."

"I see."

Jennie stood up from his lap and turned her back to him, slowly pacing around the room.

Victor stood up too, and braced himself for the unpleasant conversation.

"Jennie, I know it's long. But if this thing succeeds, we'll be secured for a long, long time."

"So, what's the project?" she asked, as she pivoted to face him.

He hesitated before answering.

"Professor Richards found a way to increase the fertility chance in infertile women. It's similar to IVF, but instead of extracting the ovum, fertilizing them, and placing them back in the uterus, we-" he noticed the blank stare in Jennie's eye that clearly said she was losing focus. "Anyway, it's a new groundbreaking discovery that may help infertile women conceive with more ease."

Jennie looked down and crossed her arms. A moment later, she looked up and said.

"I think that's great."

"You do?"

"I do. Look, you and I never had problems conceiving, but some couples that I know did... and they still do. If this can really help unfortunate parents get children that they desire so much, then who am I to stand in the way of science? I think you should do this."

Victor raised his forefinger and squinted in suspicion.

"Is... is that like, a trap or something?"

Jennie laughed and approached to hug him.

"Honey, no. I really think you should do this. I mean, I obviously don't know your odds of succeeding-"

"Over ninety-five percent."

39

"-nor do I understand the scientific terms for this, but if you believe in it, I think you should do it. Under one condition."

"Okay, name it."

She leaned closer so that he could feel her warm breath on his lips.

"If this by any chance isn't successful, and the professor offers you more projects like these, tell him that you have an angry wife that won't let you leave your family for more than two weeks."

Victor chuckled.

"Deal," he said as he kissed her.

The short kiss turned into passionate making out until they found themselves on the couch, with Victor on top of Jennie. Just as he cupped her breast, a muffled sob came from the nursery.

"Goddammit," Victor let his head slump onto Jennie's chest.

"Looks like the practical part of the fertilization process will have to wait, professor," she said.

***

Richards was ecstatic when Victor told him on Wednesday that he would participate in the project. He clenched his fists and shouted 'Yes, my boy!' before patting him on the back, not so gently. He told Victor to find twenty candidates for the interview by Monday, but the assistant professor was already ahead of him.

Finding the candidates was easier than Victor expected it would be. Out of thirty students that he deemed suitable for the interview, twenty-three responded to Victor's email which he sent out on Saturday, saying that they were more than eager to work on the project with Professor Richards. Of course they were; the professor had this cult-like following in the university. Victor couldn't help but feel a bit of envy for the respect and attention Richards got. He hoped he'd be able to rival that one day, even if it happened after the professor retired – which wouldn't be for another ten years or so.

Since there was a surplus of three students, Victor went through the list and, with a heavy heart, hand-picked the twenty candidates suitable for the interview with Professor Richards. He didn't know yet what the interview would consist of, but he did know that he would be present during it. The whole time, he couldn't help but shake the feeling of piggy-backing off Professor Richards' work. The professor said they would be equals, but Victor only contributed thus far with assistant-like work – and rightly so, because he wasn't as acquainted with the Fertility Project as the professor. He mentioned it to Richards when he visited him in his office, but the professor simply opened his desk drawer and slammed a thick pile of messy notes in front of him.

"Read this, and you will know everything that needs to be known," Richards said.

"But professor, even if I learn all of this, I still lack the experience," Victor complained.

"Victor, you've done all of this during studies, haven't you?"

Victor knew it was a rhetorical question, but he still answered with a straightforward 'Yes'.

"Good," the professor leaned back. "You will see that this process is no more complicated than grabbing a glass of water in the kitchen without spilling it."

"I still think we shouldn't split the credit. After all, you're the creator of-"

"Let me be the judge of that, Victor," the professor raised his palm. "I need you to understand one thing. I've contributed to science a lot throughout my life. Even though I'm not old enough to retire yet - and I apologize for being sentimental here - I see a lot of myself in you. You're going to achieve great things in life, Victor. I'm just giving you a little push to get your foot in the door."

Victor couldn't help but smile. What the professor was doing for him was selfless and fatherly. Victor didn't have the words to express his gratitude. Before he could say anything, the professor huffed and said.

"Alright, enough of this. Don't wanna get too sentimental here, do we? We haven't even started the project. Let me see the list of those candidates."

***

"How do you perform in stressful situations?" Professor Richards asked.

He and Victor were sitting behind the desk, with notes splayed in front of them. They stared at the scrawny, young man with thick glasses sitting across from them. Victor noticed that the boy often scratched the back of his head and touched his neck. An obvious sign that he was uncomfortable. It didn't matter if he couldn't hide his nervousness, as long as he could complete the task successfully.

"Well, I..." he started timorously. "I often have to do things under stress, so I'm somewhat used to it. I mean, I... I haven't um... haven't done any big things thus far, but like, I feel like I'm really good deciding on the right approach during panicked moments."

He finished by clearing his throat and clasping his hands together between his legs. Richards nodded and jotted something down. The sound of a pen scratching against the paper with fervent motions filled the silent air while the student patiently awaited the next question, his eyes as wide as saucers, transfixed on the professor.

"Why do you want to participate in this project?" the professor asked.

"Well, um... I feel like I can uh... learn more from you, and like, you always have something valuable to research. I want to be a part of that, and um, maybe learn something new that I can like, use later in life."

Richards continued staring at the student in silence this time. It was the oldest trick in the book – stare at someone in silence after they've finished talking, and you'll give them the impression that you expect more information. The student got visibly more uncomfortable, so he scratched his shoulder and said.

"That's um... that's the main reason why I want to participate."

Richards smiled, nodded, and looked down at his notes again. He lay the pen down beside the paper and turned his palms upward.

"Alright, Jeremy. No more questions on my end, you can relax now."

Instantly, the student's shoulders drooped down from their tense position, but he continued staring at the professor in anticipation with his hands between his legs.

"Victor, do you have any questions for Jeremy?" Richards asked.

Jeremy's eyes darted to the assistant professor. Victor shook his head.

"No questions from me, either. Let me explain to you about the project," he said as he lay his own pen on the desk and leaned back in the chair. "So, your job essentially would be, along with the other students, to assist the professor and me in performing check-ups on the subjects. You would have the freedom to watch the procedure, but you will not be given details about it due to the secrecy the university required from us. The project will last for five months, and during those five months, you and the five other selected students will rotate in shifts. How you do the shifts doesn't concern us, as long as someone is always on-site in case of an emergency. Any questions so far?"

"Will I have to sign an NDA?" Jeremy got bolder all of a sudden.

"Not an NDA," Professor Richards interjected. "But something of the like. As the assistant professor mentioned, you won't know any sensitive details about the project, therefore even if you happen to leak any of it to an outside source, no harm will be done. However, the papers you will sign are there as proof that you participated in the project, and to give you the extra points, avoid penalizing you for missing classes, etcetera."

"What if I want to drop out earlier?"

"That's not a problem either, but we would need to find a suitable substitute first, and the agreement is then terminated. If you need to leave due to an emergency, then one of your fellow students will have to cover for you until you return or a suitable replacement is found. Keep in mind that if you drop out early, you won't be getting any of the bonuses we mentioned."

"Yes, professor."

"Well, then. Anything else you would like to ask?"

"No, professor."

"Very well. Thank you for your time, Jeremy. We will be in touch with you."

The professor flashed Jeremy a PR grin, signaling that the conversation was over. Jeremy clumsily stood up and awkwardly thanked Richards and Victor before turning around and leaving through the door. Silence fell on the room once more before Richards pivoted his head towards Victor and asking.

"What are your thoughts on him?"

"He's smart. Timid, but smart. And not to mention he's hard-working. He's always the first one to finish the assignments, and he does it so meticulously that I could hardly find faults, even if I wanted to."

"Being hard-working and smart are valuable qualities, but they're not enough. Not for this. Tell me, how do you think he would perform in the project?"

Victor looked down at the meager notes he jotted down about Jeremy. He suddenly felt like he was a student himself, taking an oral exam in Professor Richards' class. If he answered this question wrongly, the professor might think that he's not mature enough for the Fertility Project.

"He's not ambitious," Victor finally said. "He's clever and hard-working but doubts himself. Doesn't often believe in what he's doing until he sees the end-results."

Richards nodded.

"My guess is that he would drop out within the first two weeks," Victor concluded, trying to sound as confident as a doctor giving his diagnosis to the patient.

Richards stared reticently at Victor for a moment, as if searching his face. For a moment, Victor thought that the professor would disappointedly tell him how wrong he was, but then his mentor grinned from ear to ear and said, "Atta, boy. See? I told you that you have what it takes for this. Let's scratch Jeremy off the list."

Richards grabbed the pen and drew a gigantic X across the paper in front of him. The pen whistled a loud *wish-woosh* before the professor put it down and patted Victor on the shoulder.

"Let's get some lunch. We have our first subject arriving at four."

Chapter 3

99 days until disaster

"Amanda!" Wayne shouted louder this time.

Amanda snapped her head in his direction. She was so lost in her own thoughts, staring out the car window that she hadn't even heard him the first time.

"I'm sorry, what did you say?" she asked absent-mindedly.

Wayne averted his gaze from the road to face Amanda briefly before giving her a compassionate smile. He gently put his hand on her thigh and said.

"Hey, don't worry. It's gonna be okay. This is going to work, I'm sure about it."

She squeezed his hand with a warm smile. She wanted to believe he was right, but after everything they'd been through, she couldn't help but be reserved about this. Amanda and Wayne had been trying to have a baby for over two years now, but without success. They spent countless hours in various clinics, trying to determine what the issue was. It was difficult finding out that the problem was in Amanda. She could see the relief on Wayne's face when they got the results, but he never said anything. He never once blamed her for her problem, but was supportive and patient the entire time.

He went with her to all of the doctor's appointments when she underwent various hormonal and other treatments. The doctor kept assuring them that there was a high chance that the procedure would be successful after enough tries, and like a fool, Amanda allowed herself to look forward to having a child of her own one day. It didn't help that most of the other couples who had undergone the same procedures were mostly successful. And then there were the awkward moments at family gatherings when her parents or parents-in-law would ask her and Wayne about getting some grandchildren. Five years ago, she found those incessant questions annoying. Now, they were hurtful.

At one family gathering, Wayne got into a heated argument with his relatives about 'minding their own damn business'. They backed off for a moment, but then one of the women shouted, 'But Amanda is running out of time'. That stung like hell. Amanda simply picked up her purse and smiled at the relatives, saying that she was happy to come to this final reunion before she and Wayne stormed out. They never showed up for family gatherings again, even though they received invitations to plenty of them.

"So, what did you say just before? I kinda spaced out," Amanda said to Wayne as he turned left onto a narrow road stretching forward towards the horizon.

Thin pines and firs encroached on the road on both sides, but they weren't enough to be called a forest. Although they formed around the road like

49

a wall and obscured the sunlight, Amanda could see between them and beyond onto the vast, green plains that stretched all across the horizon.

"I said, are you sure you don't want me to go in there with you?" Wayne repeated.

"No, thank you, honey," Amanda said. "You couldn't go in even if you wanted to. They said that the interview would only be conducted with the female volunteers. But you can wait outside in the waiting room,"

"I don't understand. It doesn't make sense for them to question only you."

"It's not questioning," Amanda chuckled. "And what do you mean it doesn't make sense? It makes total sense. I mean, the problem is... is in me, not you."

Wayne sighed and continued staring at the road. They were alone on the road now, and the beams of sunlight pierced between the branches, intermittently blinding Amanda and leaving her in the shade.

"Well, it still makes no sense that we can't be in touch until it's all over," Wayne protested.

Amanda shrugged.

"I guess they don't want to stress the patients with bad news from home or make them nostalgic or whatever. I had a friend who served in the Marine Corps for a few years, and she said that you couldn't have your cellphone on you in boot camp during some kind of guard duties."

"Why?"

"She said there have been cases of people receiving bad news, partners leaving them, someone dying, and they'd off themselves with their guns."

"Damn." A moment of silence went by before Wayne spoke up again. "But what would you off yourself with over there? A scalpel?"

"It's not abo-"

"Or maybe an injection. Or a bottle of pills... okay yeah, I get it now."

Amanda gave him a playful punch in the shoulder and chuckled.

"It's not about committing suicide, you fool. It's probably about stressing us out and messing up our hormones."

"That's... that's what I thought."

"Uh-huh. And we still aren't accepted into the project, so don't start planning."

"Oh, come on. How many candidates do you think could possibly know about this? I bet they didn't even get enough candidates to sign up."

Amanda scoffed.

"Remember that time when Uncle Joe's was giving a free mug if you tag him on Instagram? Imagine what it's going to be like for free treatment to get a baby."

"Fair point. But a lot of them were probably eliminated during the initial selection. The professor said that your results were adequate for a candidate."

"Adequate. But I still need to pass the interview."

"Who knows, maybe it's just a formality, you know?"

"I hope so."

Amanda leaned her head on the window, allowing the low vibrations of the badly-maintained road to batter her head like a soft massager. She stared at the rows of trees coming into view and disappearing instantly like a quick-moving slideshow. She felt nervous, but at the same time, the tranquility of the road made her feel sleepy. She only got a few hours of sleep last night.

Not only was she unable to fall asleep in the motel in an unfamiliar bed, but the anxiety wracked her. She tried calming herself down as much as possible, but it was like a never-ending cycle. When you stress too much, your cortisol level increases, then you stress about your cortisol, and it grows even higher. She could only hope that the doctors wouldn't disqualify her in the meantime with surprise tests or anything like that. Less than fifteen minutes later, just as Amanda's eyelids started getting heavy, she heard Wayne's voice next to her.

"Here we are."

She looked up and glanced at the wired fences that cordoned off the campus grounds. It looked big enough to hold a small town inside. There were rows of buildings, tall and short. Amanda envisioned the campus of the University for Reproductive Science and Medicine to be much smaller, but she also expected the buildings to have certain signs or names on them in order to be distinguished. The closer they approached the crowded parking lot in front of the campus, the more nervous Amanda got. It just then hit her how real this all was. A part of her wanted to turn around and run back to Seattle, but then she remembered that this was her last option before she and Wayne proceeded with adoption.

She had to do this.

Wayne found an empty parking spot on the left side of the entrance where the guardhouse was, and once the car engine stopped running, it was time to go. Amanda opened the door on her side, feeling the warm waft of air hitting her. There wasn't a single tree around the parking lot, effectively providing no shade from the heat.

"Come on," Wayne placed his hand on the lower part of Amanda's back and gently nudged her forward.

They peeked inside the guardhouse window, tentatively taking steps closer. The guard, a middle-aged man dressed in a simple, blue, short-sleeved shirt with a badge on his chest, and black pants, looked up from the crossword puzzle he was solving and reached across the desk. He slid open the small window and stared at Wayne in rigid anticipation.

"Hi. We're looking for Professor Howard Richards," Wayne said.

The guard leaned back, stood up from his chair, and walked through the door on his left. He went outside to greet the couple and turned towards the campus, pointing toward one of the buildings.

"You'll wanna go to that big building over there. The one shaped like the letter O."

There was no way to miss it. It was one of the widest and tallest buildings on the campus grounds, stretching three floors high. It took Amanda a moment to realize that the guard meant that the building looked O-shaped from a view above.

"Go to the second floor, turn left. You'll see his office on the right side. If you can't find it, feel free to ask anyone in there, everyone knows the professor," the guard finished.

"Thank you," Wayne said.

The guard nodded and strode back inside the guardhouse.

"We gotta walk all the way there?" Wayne asked with a hint of disappointment in his tone.

Amanda shrugged.

"At least you'll do your much-needed cardio," she gently patted him on his jelly-belly, as she called it.

***

"Thank you for your time, Ms. Stevens," Richards grinned courteously to the young woman sitting in his office.

"Please, call me Regina. And you're welcome! I was so nervous before this conversation! I actually rehearsed like I would for a job interview, but then I realized that the questions here might be different, I mean different in a way that they are more medical and less business-like, so I decided to just wait and see what would happen, and I'm sooo relieved that it wasn't too difficult," the woman recited perkily like a machine gun, as she swung her blonde hair behind her shoulder.

She spoke so quickly that Victor wouldn't have been able to take proper notes even if he wanted to.

"Well, I understand the stress of attending interviews," Richards nodded. "This is a step we need to complete in order to ensure the candidate is the best fit for this program. Now, we are past our time here, so before you leave, do you have any questions for us?"

"Yeah. So, when do I get to know if I passed?"

"We'll let you know by the end of the week," Richards politely said.

"Thank you! I also wanna know more about what we'll be doing in the experiment, can you tell me more about that?"

"That's something we can't disclose just yet. If we select you, you will get all the relevant details."

"Okay. And how will we know if the experiment is a success?"

"Again, that's something that will be discussed during the experiment," Richards glanced at his watch in a not-so-subtle way and said with a grin. "Well, we still have a few more candidates to interview, so thank you again for coming in today, Regina."

"You're welcome! Hope to hear from you soon. Goodbye!" with a smile on her face, she pulled her chair back, picked up her purse, and walked through the door.

Richards maintained the fake grin on his face all the way until the door closed, and once it did, he puffed loudly and said.

"Wow. She sure is a talker."

"I suppose she was just nervous, professor," Victor smiled.

He couldn't imagine what these women were going through, but he tried putting himself in their positions. As if reading his mind, Richards said.

"It's not our place to judge whether they are nervous, but how suitable they are. In the case of our subjects, confidence is not an important factor. Remember that tradeoffs must always be made if we want to achieve a higher goal. Now tell me, what do you think about her?"

Victor repeatedly tapped the pen on the desk, staring at the half-blank paper in front of him. He looked at Richards and saw him staring at him with rapt fascination. This has become a regular occurrence in the past week since they started the project. Richards would ask him surprise questions – questions of more importance than the usual chit-chat – and would expect Victor to give a well-elaborated and analytical answer.

"She really wants to do this," Victor finally said. "Of the three women we interviewed so far, she was the only one that showed no hesitation over anything we told her about the project. She is determined to go through this."

"You think she wouldn't drop out during the project?"

"I'm sure she wouldn't. If not because of the baby, then because of herself. She's somewhat self-centered, and I can guarantee that her ego would not allow her to quit before the project concludes."

"Alright, Victor. Let's put her on the top of the list until we find more suitable candidates. If we don't, she's in."

Richards took some notes on the paper on his side of the desk. Once he was done, he pinched the edge of the paper between his thumb and forefinger and gracefully placed it on the pile of documents on the right. He looked at the page that was under the paper he just scrawled on and raised his head.

"Amanda Weaver!" he called out loudly.

Victor stared at the door. In seconds, it opened, and a woman in her early twenties with chestnut hair peeked inside.

"Good afternoon. Doctor Richards?" she timorously smiled.

"Professor. Please, come in," the professor corrected her as he motioned for the woman to step inside.

Amanda cracked the door open wide enough to squeeze inside the office, before gently closing the door behind her. As she strolled towards the chair in front of the desk, Victor could already see the tension in her body language. She was scared.

"Have a seat, Amanda," Victor took the initiative to help ease her discomfort when he realized just how nervous she was.

"Thank you," she uttered quietly, as if afraid to break the deafening silence in the room.

She hung her purse on the chair and sat down, placing her hands in her lap. Victor had his nose buried in the notes on the desk, but he could feel the woman's gaze on him. He suddenly felt uncomfortable, like he was a member of some sort of committee deciding the fate of the person in front of him. That hit him even harder when he realized that he was, in fact, doing exactly that.

"Ms. Weaver," Richards started. "The results are phenomenal. Of all the candidates we've had so far, these are the most ideal numbers I've seen."

"Thank you so much, professor," Amanda shyly smiled.

"It's true," Victor interjected. "We've seen candidates who were just at the threshold, and we've seen some that have had some numbers disproportionately higher than they should be. Yours are... exactly where they are supposed to be."

He looked at the woman and gave her a reassuring smile. Amanda smiled back, but before she could say anything, Richards began again.

"Now, Amanda. Tell us a little about yourself."

Amanda jerked her head in the professor's direction with somewhat wide eyes, before clearing her throat and starting.

"Well... I'm twenty-three years old, and I work as a hotel desk clerk in Seattle. I graduated from-"

"Oh, we don't need the academic education, we already have it here. We want to know more about *you*," Richards dismissively waved his hand and smiled.

"Oh, um. Okay," Amanda looked confused.

She looked at Victor briefly with confusion on her face before averting her gaze back to Richards.

"Well, um... I have a husband named Wayne, who I've been married to for three years now. I used to attend calligraphy classes, but I stopped recently. I plan to get back to them in the future, though. I like doing yoga and Zumba. I also speak four languages besides English; French, Turkish, and Spanish."

"Wow," Victor nodded in amazement as he wrote down what Amanda said.

"Excellent," Richards also scribbled something down with his ugly, doctor-like handwriting before looking back up at Amanda. "Now, I can see that aside from your test results, you also have a squeaky clean record. No history of mental illnesses in your family, you don't smoke, you don't drink, you are moderately active in sports... It's safe to say you are physiologically speaking, the ideal candidate."

Richards leaned on the desk and crossed his fingers.

"Tell us why you want to have a baby."

Amanda's face contorted from confused to something that looked like she had bitten into a lemon. She tried masking it by smiling, but Victor could already tell how uncomfortable she was. Amanda let out a sigh-laugh before clearing her throat and saying.

"Well, why do any of us want to have children? I mean, I never really thought about the reason, but um..." she cleared her throat again. "I want to have a family. I want someone who Wayne and I can give our unconditional love to and to have someone to wake us up in the morning and... run around the house and... call me mommy-"

Her voice trailed off, and she put her hand over her mouth. Her eyebrows rose in a sad expression, and Amanda gasped, her eyes welling up with tears.

"Ms. Weaver..." Richards started compassionately, but it was clear that he didn't know what to say.

Victor was faster. He stood up and went around the desk to approach her. He pulled out a paper handkerchief from his pocket, offering it to her. She grabbed the handkerchief and wiped her eyes, apologizing.

"It's okay, Amanda. Do you want to take a break or drink some water?" Victor asked.

He happened to look in Richards' direction and saw the professor shooting daggers at him. He suddenly became aware of what a mistake he made, so to mitigate the damage he just caused, he gently placed one hand on Amanda's shoulder and uttered a low 'take your time' before returning to his seat. Even after he sat down, Richards had the same stern expression on his face that followed Victor.

"Well, anyway. Ms. Weaver," Richards said in the next moment as he turned to Amanda.

She was sniffling and wiping her remaining tears, apologizing over and over for her breakdown.

"No, no. It's fine, Ms. Weaver. This is a sensitive topic, I understand," Richards said with sudden compassion in his voice. "I apologize for having to ask these questions, but I can assure you, they are imperative for us in order to assess who the right candidates are."

"I-I understand," Amanda uttered through the remaining sobs.

"I'm going to tell you more about the Fertility Project and then ask you a few more questons. Is that okay with you?"

Amanda nodded fervently. Richards leaned back in his chair, which squeaked in protest. He proceeded to explain to Amanda how the experiment had not yet been done on humans, but that there would not be any major risks to health. He told Amanda how she would need to stay in one room inside the genetics building for five months, and that there would be tests, checkups, and other things conducted every day. By this time, Amanda had calmed herself and was listening to the professor attentively.

Richards further explained that visits from family members would be prohibited, there would be no outside communication, including internet, but that she would have an assortment of books, movies, TV shows, etc., to pass the time. Once he made sure that Amanda understood everything thus far, he proceeded to explain that the selected subjects will be given one final chance to opt out before the experiment starts. However, if any of the subjects decided to drop out once the experiment started, they would need to compensate the college for the funds provided for one subject – and it was a hefty sum.

"Do you understand everything so far, Ms. Weaver?" Richard scrutinized Amanda.

"I do, professor," she nodded with a calm voice. "I already knew all of this before coming here. I can assure you, I won't be dropping out, no matter what."

Victor searched her face in an attempt to detect signs of lying or hesitation, but if there were such gestures in either her facial or body language, Amanda managed to hide them well.

"Perfect," Richards grinned. "Now, do you have any questions for us, Ms. Weaver?"

"I already know everything relevant to the experiment, but I just have one question."

"Go ahead."

"The documents said that the success rate of conception is expected to be over ninety-five percent. Is that true?"

"Absolutely," Richards raised his arms. "Although this hasn't been tested on humans yet, this method is guaranteed to have a high success rate. It takes a few treatments sometimes, but it is extremely rare that the ovaries reject the treatment."

Amanda smiled, looking as if she was trying to not start crying once again.

"Thank you so much, professor," she said with gratitude in her voice.

"If that is all, then we are done here today. We will be in touch with you and you will know by the end of the week if you've been selected for the project."

Amanda thanked Richards again. The professor gave her a courteous smile and said, "Thank you for coming down here to meet us, Ms. Weaver."

Amanda thanked both of them before standing up, picking up her purse, and walking out the door with one final sniffle. The door closed, and Victor sighed.

"She definitely seems-"

"What were you thinking, Victor?!" Richards' voice abruptly cut him off.

Victor looked at Richards and saw him staring at him with an intent gaze.

"I'm sorry, professor?" Victor asked, unsure what Richards meant.

"Rushing to console the potential subject like that, do you realize how detrimental it can be for the project?"

Victor opened his mouth, but didn't know what to say. He couldn't believe that such a ridiculous statement came out of the professor's mouth.

"I... professor, I literally just gave her a handkerchief. She was distressed."

"You can't show any sympathy for the subjects, Victor. It's unprofessional."

Victor frowned, now getting a little irked.

"With all due respect, professor, not showing sympathy toward the patient can be just as detrimental to the experiment."

Richards let out a gasp and smiled before rotating his chair to face Victor. He put a hand on Victor's knee and said.

"Listen to me, Victor. These women haven't even been selected, yet. We are not psychologists, and it's not our place to deal with their emotional baggage. They are distressed because they can't conceive, I understand that, and you can probably

63

relate to it immensely since you have a child of your own. But if you spend your energy showing compassion to the subjects during the experiment, they will begin trusting you as more than a medical expert. Do you understand what I'm saying?"

Victor tentatively nodded. Richards continued.

"If they start trusting you, they will talk about their problems with you. And then, say after two or three months of the experiment, one of them may ask you to let her outside the room, just to the building entrance, just for two minutes, because her husband is there. She hasn't seen him in months and misses him a lot, and she wants to share her experience with him, possibly even some good news. She begs you to let her see him, promises she will come back quickly. Would you be able to say no to a pleading woman you were well acquainted with, Victor?"

Victor hung his head down. He understood now what the professor was trying to say. Richards leaned back in his chair and said.

"Now, let's say you show that compassion and let her outside. She says goodbye to her husband and, after returning to her room, starts feeling nostalgic, depressed even. Her hormones go haywire, and the fertilization is rejected. Out of the four subjects, she was the ideal one, but now it's ruined because of an outside factor, and we can't attempt the process again until her hormones are fixed. Do you see the point I'm trying to make, Victor?"

Victor wrinkled his nose and awkwardly scratched his cheek. Now that the professor put it that way, it made total sense. Suddenly, he felt really stupid for trying to console the woman.

"You're right, professor. I'm sorry. I didn't look at it that way."

"There will be time for compassion and congratulations, Victor. But only after the Fertility Project is complete. Remember that in order to achieve scientific greatness, sacrifices must often be made," he leaned towards the notes on his side of the desk and said. "Now, what do you say we compare our notes and call it a day? We have more candidates arriving tomorrow."

Chapter 4
97 days until disaster

The past few days had been hectic for Victor. He and the professor interviewed a number of women who showed up at the campus. There were a lot of good candidates, and the competition was fierce. It would be hard to decide which five candidates would be going through with the Fertility Project. Frankly speaking, most of the interviewed candidates were excellent, with the exception of two that didn't show up and three that looked reluctant during the interview.

It was Friday afternoon, and Victor and Richards were in the office, looking through the candidates' papers. The decision had to be made today. After that, Victor would go home for the weekend, then he'd come back to the campus on Monday, and that's when the Fertility Project would officially start – at least, according to Richards. When Victor asked him when they would do the preparations of the experimental rooms, Richards told him that he would take care of everything over the weekend. Victor suggested staying and assisting him, but Richards dismissively waved the suggestion away and told him to spend these last two days with his family before the project officially started. Victor didn't protest.

Although Howard Richards had an ex-wife and kids, he lived alone in the city relatively close to the campus. He didn't have a toddler and a wife waiting at home for his return to spend the weekend with them. He told Victor a few times that his devotion to work was the final nail in the coffin for his marriage, but that he never regretted it. He even justified not having a close enough relationship with his children, stating that 'time with your family is limited, but scientific discoveries are timeless'.

Although Victor wanted to achieve greatness one day in scientific contributions, he didn't want to neglect Leah and Jennifer. He thought many times if he had to choose one, which one he would go for. The answer came without a shred of hesitation. His wife and daughter were his reason for living, and if he one day had to quit the job he was doing and find a new one just to pay the bills, he'd do it in an instant.

That's why he admired Richards even more. He portrayed an insurmountable dedication to his job and scientific research.

After almost two hours of brainstorming and bouncing suggestions off of each other, the two of them finally made a decision. Richards pushed the papers of the eliminated candidates to the right side of the desk, and had the five winners in front of him and Victor. There was also a paper pile of five other candidates that would serve as a replacement in case any of the five women dropped out before the project started. The professor tapped his forefinger on the desk rhythmically, transfixed on the papers.

"Five women," he said. "Over three hundred women applied to participate in the Fertility Project, and only five passed the initial selection. And more will be eliminated, most likely."

"Who knew that there would actually be a competition one day for having a baby," Victor said sardonically.

Richards gave him an aloof smile and responded.

"It's a shame that the university hasn't provided more funds so that we could get more test subjects, but we will have to go with what we have. If all five subjects drop out, we are royally screwed, Victor. We can get the replacements, but then we would need to request more funds and extend the project."

"I understand your concern, professor. They won't drop out, I'm sure of it. These women want to have babies more than anything."

It felt strange giving the professor a piece of information and not being on the receiving end.

"You're probably right, Victor," the professor leaned back in his chair and spread his arms victoriously. "This is a big step! We need to celebrate, my boy!"

He reached into one of the lower drawers and rummaged through it. A moment later, he brought out a small brown box, which he promptly placed on the desk. Before Victor could read the letters on the top, Richards opened the box, turning it so that the contents faced the assistant professor.

Cuban cigars.

"Oh, professor. No, I really can't-"

"Come on, it's a one-time opportunity, Victor. I always save these only for the most special of occasions," he gently took one cigar out, before leaning into the drawer and taking out a double-edged guillotine cutter. "It would be my privilege to celebrate with you."

Victor stared at the professor and the Cuban cigar that he had his index finger wrapped around. He was dead serious, but more than that, he had a facial expression that Victor knew all-too-well. It was the one he had when he didn't intend to back down until Victor agreed. The assistant professor looked down at the box of cigars. There were three more remaining, squeezed in the box like neatly sliced sausages.

What the hell, why not?

Victor snatched one cigar from the box and tried mimicking the professor in holding it – with a lot less grace.

"Atta boy," the professor let out a triumphant laugh, before reaching into the drawer and pulling out a Zippo lighter.

***

The days were going by slowly. Amanda tried occupying herself with whatever shows she could find on Netflix, but she found her mind wandering back to the interview she had with professors Richards and Lukanski. She chided herself over and over for screwing up so badly. How could she allow herself to break down in the middle of such an important interview? Now that a couple of days had gone by, she cringed every time she remembered how she had broken down in front of the two men. She was almost entirely sure that she would not be receiving a call from them with any good news, but she still couldn't help but hope.

Tell us about yourself. Why do you want to have a baby? The questions repeatedly crept back into her mind over and over, and when she didn't find herself scrutinizing her answers, she'd imagine giving different, more coherent, and eloquent responses.

Wayne was busy with work these days, so she had to spend a lot of time alone with her thoughts. Although she enjoyed some alone time from time to time, these last few days she found herself constantly checking the clock and eagerly waiting for his return. She didn't have many friends to talk to anymore, either. Most of them already had their own families and were too busy.

It was Friday evening, and Amanda was sitting in front of the TV in a curled-up position, watching *The Queen's Gambit*, but not registering what was going on. She had somewhat managed to get herself out of the perpetual cycle of self-pity and was coming to terms with the fact that the Fertility Project would be out of the question for her. So, that meant that she and Wayne would have to resort to something else, and they only had one more option – adoption.

Would that really be so bad, though? Having a child that wasn't her blood? Her family would frown upon her for such a decision, but who cared what they thought? They didn't know what it was like trying to have a baby and not being able to – and knowing that it was her own fault for that. No, adopting would work just fine. She would love that child as if it came from her own womb. And it might bring her and Wayne closer again. They had started drifting apart over the past two years, and having a child would help them reconnect. She feared that if a solution was not found soon, she would end up not only childless, but husband-less, too.

A buzzing on the coffee table reverberated so loudly that Amanda nearly jumped out of her skin. Her phone was ringing. She hastily reached for it and looked at the screen. Unknown number. She paused the TV show just in time for the main actress to make a close-up grimace on the screen, and slid the green button to answer the call, ironically thinking to herself how it was going to be one of those annoying marketing agencies.

"Hello?" she answered with a voice cracking from hours of not being used.

"Good evening, this is Professor Howard Richards. Am I speaking to Amanda Weaver?" an authoritative male voice resounded on the other end.

Oh shit, it's him!

"Professor! Good evening, yes, it's me." She quickly stood up, trying to hide the sudden trembling in her voice.

"Ms. Weaver, I'm calling about the Fertility Project you applied to."

"Yes?" Amanda swallowed.

71

"I am happy to inform you that you've been selected to participate in the Fertility Project. I will need-"

Amanda didn't hear the rest of the things the professor said. After hearing the first sentence, she clasped her hand over her mouth and firmly shut her eyes. She wanted to scream, jump, dance, run around the block...

"Ms. Weaver, are you still with me?" Richards asked.

"I'm sorry, professor. I'm still here. Please, go ahead," Amanda said with an audibly emotional timbre now.

She didn't care anymore if the professor could hear her excitement.

"Alright. I have already sent you an email with everything you need to know before the project starts, but I will explain it now to you, as well."

"Yes, please."

"Okay, so you need to be at the university on Monday at 3 pm. Earlier is okay, but just don't be late. You need to bring a sample of your husband's sperm, and you don't need to bring any personal items of your own, because they will be provided once you get settled in. You will have your own room, with various forms of entertainment to pass the time, like movies, TV shows, books, video games, artistic requisites... you mentioned you like calligraphy, right? Well, you will have enough time to practice it over the course of the next five months. Is everything clear so far?"

"Yes."

"Good. Now, I must inform you, as I mentioned in the interview, that outside communication will not be allowed, so as to prevent the subjects from stressing out, etcetera. That means, no visits from family members either until the project is complete. No phone calls, no internet. Do you understand, Ms. Weaver?"

"Yes, professor."

Amanda didn't care about any of that. It was a small price to pay to finally have a baby of her own. The professor continued.

"Very well. Then I need to inform you of one final thing. If you happen to drop out of the Fertility Project, you will be required to compensate the university for the funds provided. That also includes emergency situations, like deaths of family members, and such. If this doesn't work for you, you can still opt out before signing the papers on Monday. But once you've signed them, you have to stay on the campus for the duration of the project until it is complete, which means five months. Is that understood, Ms. Weaver?"

"Perfectly, professor."

"Good. I know that I sound repetitive, but I need to lay everything down before we start, to avoid any confusion and potential issues like we've had in the past. Now that we've cleared that up, I have one final question for you, Ms. Weaver."

Amanda held her breath.

"Do you want to proceed with the next phase of the Fertility Project?"

"I do," she said before the professor even finished his question.

"Excellent. In that case, we will talk again more on Monday. You can ask the guard at the gate where to find me, since the experiment will be conducted in a different building than the one where we met. Allow me to congratulate you once more for making it to the final phase of the project, and I am looking forward to working with you, Ms. Weaver," the professor's voice turned perkier towards the end.

"Thank you so much, professor. I won't let you down, I promise. Thank you," Amanda didn't have the words to express her gratitude.

"You're welcome, Ms. Weaver. I'm sure you'll do great. You have a great weekend and see you Monday."

Amanda thanked the professor once more and said goodbye. As soon as she hung up, she became aware of how much she was trembling. She was literally shivering, even though it was warm in the apartment. She exhaled slowly with her quivering breath and gently placed the phone down on the coffee table. Just then, the euphoria started hitting her in full power.

She put both hands over her mouth and rocked back and forth, maniacal laughter creeping out of her, as she tried not to allow the burst of happiness to overtake her entirely. She couldn't wait to tell Wayne the good news.

***

"Congratulations, baby!" Jennifer wrapped her arms around Victor's neck, giving him a smooch on the lips.

Victor couldn't believe how enthusiastic she was about the entire project. He expected Jennifer to start giving him the cold shoulder, and then after a while to tell him that she was bothered by him having to leave for five months, but the entire time since he first told her about it, she was nothing but supportive. He felt guilty for expecting such a negative reaction from his wife. He was tempted to ask her why she wasn't angry, but he felt that it might cause Jennifer to get passive-aggressive. He wasn't sure if she harbored any grudge against his decision but refused to tell him so.

"Do I smell pizza?" Victor asked when the savory aromas coming from the kitchen wafted to his nose.

"Yes. Homemade. And I got your favorite chocolate pie for later," Jennie said enthusiastically.

"Where's the catch?" Victor cocked his head suspiciously.

"There's no catch, silly. I just missed you," she said as she peeked inside the oven.

Yellow light and a low-whirring noise came from the device.

"Pizza will be ready in a few minutes, but you'll have to wait for it to cool," Jennifer said.

"Alright. And where's the little devil?" Victor asked as he slumped his backpack on the floor.

"Ah-ah-ah!" Jennifer pointed to the backpack reprimandingly.

Victor rolled his eyes before picking up the backpack from the floor and carrying it over to the foyer, where he hung it on the coat hanger.

"See? Not that hard, is it now?"

"No, Mom."

"Now, that's just creepy."

Victor glanced inside the nursery towards the crib. The lights were on, and he saw his daughter sitting spread-legged in the middle of the crib with various toys of random shapes messily splayed about. When Leah heard Victor coming in, she curiously jerked her head in his direction with an open mouth.

"Hey, baby girl," he approached the crib and smiled down at Leah.

In turn, his daughter produced a happy moaning laugh, jovially swaying her arms up and down, causing the plastic giraffe to drop out of her hand.

"Yeah, I missed you, too. C'mere," Victor bent down to pick her up, feeling a slight pang in his lower back.

I'm getting old.

He picked up Leah and held her in his arms as she made yet another happy sound.

"Yeah, I know. I'll visit the chiro for that once the project is done," he started walking towards the door, listening to Leah's many sounds, acting like they were responses to his words. "Yes, I know it's a long time. But daddy's gotta work, honey. Hey, you wanna try some pizza with me later?"

"Are you talking to her again like she's an adult?" Jennifer shouted from the kitchen.

"What? No!" he leaned closer to Leah and whispered. "Don't tell her I lied, she'll kill me. Alright?"

Leah swung her arms towards his face and produced another short sound.

"Okay, pinky promise?"

Victor brought forward his pinky, but rather than grabbing it, Leah curiously observed it and touched it with her tiny hands. Victor walked into the kitchen and saw the steaming pizza on the kitchen counter. His stomach growled at the realization that he hadn't eaten in almost six hours.

"How about some pie while the pizza cools off?" he asked.

"Dessert before dinner? Do you wanna give that example to your child?"

Victor looked at Leah, who was mesmerized by the colorful contents of the pizza.

"Give her to me. I need to feed her, anyway," Jennifer gently took Leah from Victor and returned to the kitchen counter.

She displayed amazing proficiency in handling everything one-handedly while holding the baby. Victor felt a sudden wave of sadness at the realization that he wasn't here enough for his family. He saw them every weekend, yes, but he was away five days a week and missed all the little important things that Leah did. She would soon utter her first word, walk her first steps, do something cute, and so on, and he wouldn't be here to see it. He suddenly felt like canceling the Fertility Project. But not only that – his mind also started wandering to scenarios where he would be able to work close to his home so that he could come back to his family every day, not just on the weekends. As if reading his mind, Jennie asked.

"So, you ready to start the big project on Monday, Mr. Scientist Man?"

"I guess," he gave her a vague smile. "Hey, maybe Leah can have some pizza?"

"Do you realize how bad that is for her?" Jennie shot Victor a judgmental glare.

"Oh, come on. She'll only eat a few bites. She needs to get used to different kinds of food, anyway.

Jennifer stared at him for a moment, before sighing and relenting. Fifteen minutes later, they were at the kitchen table, Victor and Jennifer sitting across from each other with Leah in Jennie's lap. Victor was eating the still-warm pizza slice, while Jennie fed Leah with tiny pieces that she tore up for her. Leah seemed skeptical at first about trying this new, mysterious food, but once she swallowed the first bite, every subsequent one came faster and easier.

All in all, Victor felt like this was exactly where he belonged – not some scientific mission. An hour later, Jennie put Leah to sleep in her crib and joined Victor on the living room couch. The TV was on and Victor was absent-mindedly watching a show, when Jennifer snapped his thoughts back to reality.

"So, is there anything you wanna do this weekend?"

"Not really, let's just take a break, spend some time together, that kinda thing."

Jennie straightened her back and looked at him with a concerned gleam in her eye. She knew how he felt, and she was about to do something about it.

"What's wrong, baby?" she asked.

He smiled at her and stroked her hair gently, not uttering a word.

"Are you nervous about the project?"

"No, not nervous. Just don't wanna leave you guys for so long. You know? I mean, I'm surprised you're not throwing a fit over me leaving."

"Would you like me to do that?"

Victor hesitated, staring at the TV, before saying.

"Honestly, maybe. It would make the decision to stay easier."

Jennifer sat in a more comfortable position so that she was facing him. She leaned forward and kissed his shoulder.

"I know it's a long time, sweetie. But this is important for your work. If you bail on Professor Richards, he will find someone else to assist him. How will you feel if they successfully achieve something there?"

"We don't know if the project will achieve anything."

"You're right, we don't. The project might fail. But what if it doesn't? You're still young, Victor.

Do you realize how much this breakthrough would help your career?"

Victor sighed, looking down at his lap.

"And what if I spend five months on nothing?" he asked. "I could miss some important moments from Leah, and-"

"Then at least you'll learn something new. And that's gonna help you later in development."

Victor sighed again and scratched his cheek with a grimace. Jennie said.

"Honey, no matter what you decide, I will support you. But I strongly believe that you should do this."

She continued staring at Victor, while he gazed at the TV's moving pictures, not paying attention to the show on the screen.

"Okay, fine," he said. "I'll do it for you and Leah."

Disaster Night, Part 2

"Lights on," Bulldozer commanded.

The team turned on the flashlights attached to their guns. As soon as the doors of the science building burst open, Survivor ran in and covered the right side, moving to the corner where he could better observe the room. Bulldozer and Poseidon moved straight, while Cougar took the left side. Talker stayed at the back, covering the rear. The flashlights of the unit's guns swiveled around the air, brightly illuminating the hallway.

"Clear," Bulldozer called out.

It was much darker in here than outside. They could have simply turned on the hallway lights, but the protocol was not to do that when entering a dark and potentially dangerous building to prevent alerting the hostiles. Bulldozer gave the signal to move forward by raising one hand and outstretching it forward. The team began moving in unison, weapons raised. Since there were classrooms on both sides, they split into teams of two and two (Poseidon and Cougar left, Survivor and Talker right), with Bulldozer in the middle covering the entry point. Once Poseidon and Cougar cleared the first classroom, Survivor and Talker cleared the one on the opposite side.

Clearing rooms was always the trickiest part. You never knew what could jump at you from any corner. And if you didn't know the layout of the room, it was all the more dangerous. Survivor had cleared countless rooms in his life, but the adrenaline that pumped through him whenever he needed to do it never subsided, even after all these years.

"Clear right!" Survivor called out.

"Clear left!" Talker said.

Only when he heard Talker's voice did Survivor allow relief to wash over him momentarily. The two of them stepped back into the hallway to regroup with the rest of the team members. Then, they could move forward and clear the next two classrooms. It was a grueling job, but one necessary to make sure no one got the drop on them.

As they neared the end of the hallway, which then forked left and right into an adjacent corridor, Bulldozer raised his hand to signal to the team to stop. They ceased moving and held their weapons trained ahead of them – two at the left corner, two at the right one, Bulldozer slowly scanning the area from left to right. Survivor understood why Bulldozer stopped. There was a sound coming from somewhere on the right. Survivor didn't register what it was at first, but now that there was complete silence, he heard it again. Something that resembled gnawing or chewing.

As if on cue, the gnawing stopped, leaving only the audible sound of Alpha team members' steady breathing. Bulldozer took a cautious step forward, and then another, keeping his weapon trained on-

Something ran past the corridor from the left side to the right, disappearing behind the corner. It was way too fast for Survivor to register what it was, save for the fact that it was a thin-looking silhouette, but he instinctively flipped the safety of his MP5 off before Bulldozer even managed to say 'weapons hot'. The rest of the team members took their safeties off, too, all of them now visibly on edge. Bulldozer signaled for Poseidon and Cougar to take the right side. The two of them pressed close to the wall on the right side and stopped just at the corner, with Cougar in front and Poseidon behind. Bulldozer, Talker, and Survivor did the same on the left side. From there, each team member would have their own area to cover as soon as Bulldozer gave the signal.

"Squarepants, do you see any movement on the cameras?" Bulldozer asked from the cover.

The team waited in anticipation for Squarepants to respond. They were met with silence.

"Squarepants, come in," Bulldozer tried again.

Since there was no response, they couldn't wait for him before they assessed the situation. Bulldozer raised three fingers. He counted three seconds down by lowering each finger. The moment he lowered the last finger, he stepped around the corner with his weapon raised, pointing it down the left hall. He continued to strafe to the right to give Talker and Survivor the space to observe the area, too. Poseidon and Cougar did the same on their side.

Before Survivor could take up his spot around the corner, he heard something that he knew could only be bad news.

A screech, long and high-pitched, reverberated through the building with such intensity that Cougar recoiled momentarily. Almost simultaneously, Survivor heard Poseidon shouting *'Contact!'* and *'Open fire!'* before he began shooting. Loud gunshots filled the hall, each shot illuminating the dark hallway, and the screech only seemed to intensify and grow louder. Talker, Bulldozer, and Survivor managed to spin around and face the direction of the threat just in time to see Poseidon get picked up into the air like he weighed nothing and being rushed past the other teammates, disappearing on the other side of the hall without a trace.

"Cease fire!" Bulldozer called out, even though he and Poseidon were the only ones shooting in the first place.

In that split second while Poseidon was being carried, Survivor saw something. Some... figure, tall and slender, had picked up Poseidon and carried him away with incomprehensible speed. Even though Survivor had his finger on the trigger, he didn't dare shoot out of fear of hitting his teammate. Not that he would be able to hit him, either, since the figure was so fast that by the time the unit members rotated to face the direction of the heat, the figure was already gone, along with Poseidon. Hell, he didn't even get to see any discernible features on it, save for its height.

"Poseidon!" someone shouted, and Survivor registered it as Cougar's voice.

A few gunshots resounded at the very far end of the hallway before abruptly stopping. The remaining four team members held their guns trained at the hallway, their flashlights unable to reach that far, not even close.

"Alpha, move," Bulldozer commanded as he began moving forward. "We need to-"

A loud crashing sound came from the door on Bulldozer's left, knocking him on the ground. Survivor squeezed the trigger, opening fire on the hostile, along with the other team members, but whatever this thing was, it had already retreated into the darkness. Survivor thought he saw the slim figure of a nude human, although the body proportions seemed... wrong. And why did the bullets not kill it?

Survivor was sure he saw bullets impacting the bony back of the hostile, and it even flinched, but there was no blood. Bulldozer, who had dropped his weapon, held his sidearm withdrawn and pointed at the darkness ahead. With the other members covering him, he stood up and picked up his gun, quickly raising it, while holstering the sidearm.

Another blood-curdling shriek echoed around them, and Survivor felt like a sitting duck for a moment, a prey for something that was toying with them. This feeling intensified even more when he realized that there were actually multiple shrieks and not just one.

"Hide! HIDE!" A crackling voice came over the radio.

Patters of what sounded like bare footsteps echoed in the hall, followed by a savage growl.

"Guys, you have to hide NOW!" The voice over the radio came again, and only then did Survivor register it as Squarepants'.

Bulldozer quickly turned around before shouting.

"Classroom! Go!"

Survivor was the closest one to the classroom, so he ran up to the door and trained his gun in the direction of the threat, covering his team while they ran inside. To his horror, he saw Bulldozer stumbling forward on the ground, something wrapped around his ankle, before he got dragged around the corner. Loud gunshots of Bulldozer's G36 filled the air, but quickly faded before entirely stopping.

"It's coming!" The voice over the radio came again.

"Survivor, get in!" Talker grabbed him by the shoulder.

Survivor jumped inside the classroom and turned around to point the gun at the door. Talker had already slammed the door shut and was holding it firmly with his shoulder while crouching. Cougar and Survivor were pointing their rifles at the door in case of a breach.

"Flashlights off!" Survivor whispered.

Immediately, all three of them flicked their lights off, and for a moment, the classroom was engulfed in complete darkness. Within seconds though, Survivor's eyes began adjusting to the dark, and he was able to make out the silhouettes of his teammates and the surrounding objects. Screams and footsteps reverberated passed the classroom so loudly that Survivor expected one of those... *whatever the fuck they were,* to break inside. But to his surprise, they simply ran by, and soon very quickly, the screams died down until there was only silence, once again.

The three unit members that remained in the classroom waited in silence, ready for a sudden attack. Survivor's trigger finger was at the ready, and he didn't care what came through the door – he was going to take it down. The standard protocol for this situation was to have the team members communicate via radio until they regrouped, so if Poseidon or Bulldozer got back to the classroom, they'd first inform their teammates about it instead of just barging in. The team had excellent trigger discipline, but accidents could still happen easily in adrenaline-pumping situations.

"They're gone. You guys are clear," Squarepants' voice came over the radio again, startlingly breaking the deafening silence.

Talker stood up and breathed a sigh of relief, while Cougar and Survivor lowered their weapons.

"Where the fuck were you, Squarepants?!" Cougar frustratedly asked as he pressed the button on his ear.

"Bad fuckin' signal. I've been trying to contact you this whole fucking time."

"Any sign of Bulldozer and Poseidon?" Survivor asked.

"I can't see them on the cameras."

"What the fuck were those things?" Talker interjected.

"I don't know, man," Squarepants nonchalantly said.

"What do you mean, you don't know?"

"I mean, I don't fuckin' know! The cameras were a little glitchy, and those fuckin' things were fast, alright?!"

Survivor raised one hand and put his forefinger against the earbud.

"Bulldozer, Poseidon, do you copy?" he called out.

No response.

"Shit," Talker scoffed.

"Now what?" Squarepants curiously asked.

"You know what," Survivor calmly replied as he gripped his MP5 tightly. "We go look for them."

Chapter 5
94 days Until Disaster

Saying goodbye to his family was one of the hardest things Victor ever had to do. When he looked into Leah's eyes and saw the confused stare in her shiny eyes, he wanted to drop out of the Fertility Project all over again. He only once saw that stare in her before – when he started working as an assistant professor and had to leave for the week the first time.

"I'll make sure to record everything Leah does. And besides, we can still have video chats every day," Jennie smiled.

That was true. Victor wasn't sure how busy he was going to be, but he already made it up in his mind that he would call Jennie and Leah every day, even if he had to sacrifice sleep for it. He leaned towards Leah and kissed her on the forehead before gently pinching her chubby cheek.

"Bye bye, baby girl," he said.

He kissed Jennie goodbye, got in the car, and drove off, doing his best not to look in the rearview mirror at his wife waving goodbye and his daughter clumsily trying to mimic her.

***

He was surprised at the sight that greeted him when he stopped his car in front of the university gate barrier. Instead of the usual, middle-aged guard (Henry was his name, he believed), a bulkier-looking man in his late thirties dressed all in black stepped out to greet him. Victor noticed that the man had a gun strapped to his holster, and he immediately panicked. Henry never carried a gun. Something was wrong. Victor rolled down his window and kept his hands on the steering wheel, as the guard bent down and put one hand on the side of his car.

"Good morning, sir. Your university ID, please," the guard said.

He sounded polite, but Victor perceived it as an order.

"Right away," Victor said and reached into the pocket of his jeans.

All staff members were required to carry their ID at all times, and in case they lost it, they would need to call the university security right away to have a new ID card issued. Victor handed the ID card to the guard, who promptly took it and examined it with a frown.

"Victor Lukanski, assistant professor, embryology," the guard read the ID aloud, before giving it back to him through the window. "Mr. Lukanski, Professor Richards is waiting for you in the genetics building. You can park anywhere outside the building, and if anyone gives you trouble about it, you can call me."

"Thank you," Victor said, a little taken aback by the politeness of the guard.

"You have a good day," the guard nodded and straightened his back.

"Hey, um..." Victor peeked outside the window. "What happened to the other guard?"

"University hired a private security company. They no longer have their own guards," the guard said with a meager smile.

"Okay. Thank you," Victor returned the smile.

The guard went inside the building and raised the barrier, allowing Victor to drive inside the campus. He scanned the area as he drove through for any irregular activities, but everything seemed normal. Students were flocking in groups in and out of buildings, staff members were hurriedly buzzing here and there with briefcases in their hands...

Finally, he arrived in front of the genetics building, which was located on the West side of the campus. Long before Victor parked, he saw a few cars already parked in front. One young couple was heading towards the entrance. The Fertility Project had already begun.

He parked his Honda Civic behind a white BMW and stepped out of the vehicle. A gust of the heated afternoon air hit Victor in the face, and it took him a moment to acclimatize to the incongruous temperature compared to his car's cool interior. Victor glanced at the entrance of the building and saw the couple from before hugging tightly, the woman entering the building with a sorrowful expression on her face, while the man stayed in front. Victor also noticed another guard standing next to the entrance, staring in front of himself bemusedly with his hands on his belt.

Richards hadn't mentioned anything about guards securing the building. Deciding to ask the professor about it later, he opened the trunk of his car and heaved the three fully-packed backpacks over his shoulders.

"Good afternoon, Professor Lukanski," he heard a feminine voice say from behind him.

When Victor closed the trunk and turned around, he saw a young woman standing in front of him.

"Tara Nugent," Victor smiled. "Have you already talked to the professor?"

"I was about to head in. Say, why is that security guard in front? I thought this experiment was voluntary?"

"It is, it is. It's... probably just a precaution. You know how meticulous Professor Richards is."

"I understand," Tara glanced in the guard's direction.

She didn't seem one bit convinced with what Victor told her, so he decided he would need to prove to her that the guard was no Boogeyman.

"Come on, let's see if the professor is inside," he said and jutted his head in the direction of the building.

The man who was saying goodbye to the woman in front of the building earlier entered the BMW, not even glancing in Victor's direction, and drove off without a word.

Poor guy. Saying goodbye to his wife must not have been easy.

Almost as soon as Victor and Tara approached the building, the security guard took a step forward with his palm raised towards them. Both Victor and Tara stopped entrenched in their spots.

"Your IDs, please," the guard sternly said with a foreign accent that Victor didn't recognize.

He looked much more serious than the guard at the gate. He was in his forties, with a shiny, bald head and a bulky stature. He easily towered over Victor by at least a whole head and must have weighed double his weight. Victor clumsily reached into his pocket while doing his best not to allow the backpacks to fall off his shoulder.

"Janos, it's okay! They're with me!" Professor Richards shouted from inside the building.

The guard, Janos, pivoted his head to the professor, giving him a slight nod of approval, before turning back to Victor. He stepped aside and allowed him and Tara to pass.

"Thank you," Victor nodded out of courtesy.

Tara looked uncomfortable, which heavily contrasted with the usual confidence she had displayed in the interviews.

"See? What did I tell you? No big deal," Victor's mouth contorted into a complacent rictus.

"That guy is scary," Tara said under her breath.

When Victor stepped inside the genetics building, he saw Professor Richards gesturing and explaining something to the five women and two students who stood in front of him in the main hall. Richards must have seen Victor entering with his peripheral vision, because he looked in his direction and, while still explaining, fervently motioned him to come closer.

"-and if there's anything more urgent than that, Professor Lukanski and I will be here," the professor finished and looked at Victor again.

"Victor, good to see you. Let's see now, who are we missing?"

He glanced at Tara and greeted her as well, before turning back to the group in front of him. He pulled out his phone and after tapping on it a few times, he looked up and said.

"Okay, Professor Lukanski is here... I am here... all project participants are here..." he began pointing at the students and calling out each their names. "Tara Nugent, Uriel Mishori, Jackie Strauss, Antonio Brazier, okay... We are missing Nicholson and Coates."

He put his phone in his pocket and clapped his hands together.

"Ladies, let's get you accommodated to your quarters first, shall we?" Richards grinned. "Uriel, Antonio, would you be so kind as to take Victor's things to his quarters while he and I show the ladies around?"

The two male students immediately rushed to Victor's side and helped take the load of the backpacks off him. Victor's shoulder cried out in relief, but he didn't want to show physical weakness in front of the students, especially one as fit as Antonio."

"This way, please," Richards said and began climbing the stairs leading up.

The five young women stuck together, and naturally so. They must have been anxious out of their minds. Not one of them had uttered a single word since Victor arrived. Even Regina, the extremely talkative patient, suddenly seemed to fall eerily silent. As much as Victor wanted to help them feel more at home, he remembered the professor's warning about showing compassion. They climbed up to the second floor and turned left. Almost as soon as they did, Victor's jaw dropped. He didn't see the classroom doors that used to be there. Instead, he was looking at white, sturdy, metallic doors lined up on the left side of the hall.

"Now, if you step over here..." Richards gestured to the first door.

It wasn't just a sturdy door, Victor noticed. On the left side of each door was a small, black panel. Richards fished a plastic card out of his coat pocket and swiped it across the panel. It beeped, and the sound of a door unlocking loudly reverberated. Richards placed the keycard back in his pocket and grabbed the doorknob.

"Welcome, ladies," he said as he pushed the door open.

***

Amanda heard one of the women next to her audibly gasp when they stepped inside. The room in front of them was fit to be used as a hotel suite. There was furniture in the middle of the room – a large couch and a gigantic TV in front of it. A bed was on the right side, with a nightstand next to it. A bookshelf full of books decorated the wall next to the bed, and an enormous wardrobe was next to it. There was even a kitchen on the left side of the room, big enough for Amanda to cook anything without cluttering ingredients and dishes. Right next to the kitchen was a small dining table and a chair.

"Each of you will have your own rooms," Richards said. "You have a fridge that will regularly be restocked with food, and you can use the kitchen as much as you like. You have books, and subscriptions to all popular movie and TV show services. Over there is the bathroom."

He pointed to a cubicle-formed wall with a door in the left corner of the room. The door was open, and Amanda realized that the bathroom was not very big, but at least it had a shower, toilet, and a sink with a mirror above it.

"Wow," one of the women said.

"I know the bathroom is small, but it was all we could do to make it like this in the short time that we had," the professor said.

"Are you kidding? It's perfect!" Isabelle, another woman who Amanda met earlier, said.

"Feel free to look around. Again. Each room is the same, so it doesn't matter which one you get."

Amanda stepped on the carpeted floor, timidly walking between furniture, afraid to touch anything and damage it. Rays of the afternoon sun were gleaming inside, and despite the beauty of the room, she couldn't help but notice the bars placed on the exterior of the two windows. Amanda approached one of the windows and glanced through it.

"Professor, are the bars on the windows necessary? I mean, we're not held as prisoners here, are we?" she asked with a nervous chuckle.

The professor threw his head back and guffawed.

"No, no. Of course you're not prisoners here. This is just for safety precautions. You see, the agent we'll be using for the fertilization can, in very rare cases, cause temporary suicidal tendencies. We'll, of course, be monitoring you to prevent anything like that from happening, but the bars are here to stop you from doing anything... unorthodox," he smiled.

Amanda shuddered. As she stared down at the concrete floor twenty feet below the window, she couldn't imagine throwing herself out to end up like an ugly stain. Starting to suddenly feel a little dizzy from the height, she stepped back from the window. She expected to be put into a bland, white room that smelled like medicine and had only a hospital bed and curtain in it, so this came as a huge surprise. Going through these five months was going to be a little easier than she initially dreaded.

***

Victor wondered when Professor Richards found the time to fix up the building so well *and* hire private security. He must have thought way ahead and decided that some of the details were probably not as important to divulge with his project partner. Victor couldn't help but feel somewhat uninvolved at that thought, but he reminded himself that Professor Richards was the brain of the Fertility Project, even if he chose to have the assistant professor as his equal.

"We wanted to make you feel as comfortable as possible while you're here," Richards said. "You will be spending most of your time in your rooms, with the exception of having medical examinations done in a separate room. My associate and I will be monitoring you via cameras at all times, and we can talk to you via microphones, so don't hesitate to call us if you need anything."

"So, we won't have any privacy?" one of the women asked.

"You will be monitored 24-7 while you're in your quarters, yes. But there are no cameras in the bathroom."

"You didn't mention anything about that during the interview."

Richards shrugged.

"I didn't assume it would be an important factor. However, if you prefer not to undergo the procedure, Ms. Winstone, it's not too late to drop out. The NDA's have not been signed yet," the professor grinned.

Victor never saw him smiling so forcefully and so fakely. The professor must have been really tired from working over the weekend – he probably had no time to take a break at all before the project started today – and now he had to deal with a person concerned with privacy issues. Victor wanted to help take over for him while the professor took a break, but he had no idea where to even start. He assumed that the professor would have enough time to get some rest tonight while the students took the first night shift.

"N-no, it's fine, professor," the woman hung her head down in embarrassment.

"I understand your concern, ladies, but I assure you, this monitoring is for the sake of the project itself, not to breach your privacy. Are all of you okay with that?"

The women timidly nodded, and only Isabelle vocalized a 'Yes'. Richards complacently smiled at this and spread his arms wide to indicate a choice.

"In that case, ladies, feel free to pick your rooms. Again, all the rooms are the same, so it really doesn't matter which one you choose. The students will bring you some clothes after taking your measurements," he motioned for Victor and said. "Victor, and the rest of you, come with me, please."

As soon as the group stepped outside, a perky male voice shouted.

"Professor, sorry we're late!"

Two male students, Douglas Coates and Brian Nicholson, jogged down the hall and stopped in front of Richards.

"You're off to a bad start, Nicholson, and Coates," Richards said. "Nicholson, go to the janitor's office on the first floor and find a soft measuring tape. Coates, go to my office and grab a paper and pen. Take the subjects' measurements for clothes and bring them back to me."

"Yes sir, professor," Brian Nicholson said, and gave the professor a layman military salute.

He and Douglas strode back to the stairs and descended out of view within seconds. The professor shook his head and scoffed.

"Over here," he said and continued walking down the hall, swiping his keycard and unlocking each room along the way.

Past the five subjects' quarters, there was another door on the right, however this one, unlike the subjects' quarters didn't have fancy electronics. Richards pushed the door open and walked inside, flipping on the lights. The room was immediately bathed in a bright, white light, and it became apparent from the architecture of the walls and floor that this used to be one of the classrooms, but was now made into a medical examination room. An array of tools lined the shelves, and above them in the chemical glass cabinet were now medications. Five hospital beds with blue medical curtains around each of them were lined-up – three beds on the right and two on the left.

The desk used by the lecturer was still in place, along with the chair, but the student desks had been removed. Victor noticed that the classroom was pristine, since Richards had taken control of it. The last time Victor came here, visible specks of dust were flying through the air at the slightest movement someone made. Now, it looked sterile enough to eat off the floor.

"Professor, this is amazing. How did you manage to do all of this?" he asked Richards.

"Courtesy of the university's budget. It took some convincing, but the committee agreed to provide more funds than we initially agreed on. That means failure is not an option, Victor."

Victor nodded. The students who entered let out sounds of awe at the sight in front of them. Tara added a comment about thinking she walked into a displaced doctor's office.

"This is where we will be performing checkups for the subjects," Richards turned to face Victor and the students. "We will have checkups every day at 8 am, 1 pm, and 8 pm. I will provide you with the details later about what needs to be performed. All of the students will have the duty of monitoring the patients via cameras at all times. But in addition to that, the students who take up the second shift will be in charge of changing the bedsheets and taking them down into the laundry room for washing and drying – it's on the first floor next to the janitor's office. The ones who take the first shift will have to pick up the sheets and make the beds. Is that understood?"

"Yes, professor," the students unanimously chanted, albeit without synchronicity.

"After each shift, write a report about what happened during your shift. When you write the report, you will need to write anything you noticed about the subjects – what time did they take a nap, did they talk to themselves, what did they eat, how are they feeling both physically and mentally, etcetera. You may ask the subjects some questions or engage in conversations to reduce their cabin fever, but do not get overly friendly with them. Is that understood?"

Another unanimous 'Yes, professor' ensued from the students. Richards continued explaining the students' responsibilities for another few minutes, after which he told the students to wait for him in front of his office. Just then, students Douglas and Brian arrived, erratically running down the hall, one of them carrying a messily folded soft measuring tape, and the other carrying a paper and pen in his hands.

"Professor, we fini-"

"Wait in front of my office. First floor, second door on the right from the entrance," Richards interrupted them, sending them off on their way.

The group of six students walked clustered in a herd down the hall, leaving Victor and Richards alone. The professor turned to Victor and put a hand on his shoulder with a wide grin.

"This is going to be magnificent, Victor. We will tackle this experiment with ease, and by the time the project is over, we will be hailed as the new fathers of reproductive science. Hell, if we do it really well, we may even be able to conclude the project earlier."

That thought appealed to Victor. The thought of being home with his family in three, rather than five months sent a euphoric feeling stirring inside him. But no, he couldn't allow it to take over. He had to focus on the project. If his mind wandered elsewhere, the project might end up being a failure.

"Come, let's give the students their designated tasks, shall we?" Richards asked.

***

Amanda sat on the bed in the room she chose for herself. She picked the third room, which was right in the middle of the five. As she stared at the surroundings that took up a reddish color from the setting sun, she started feeling somewhat melancholic. She already missed Wayne. He was on his way home right now, and would probably arrive within two hours. He'd eat the pot roast that Amanda prepared for him yesterday – hopefully without breaking too many plates.

Whenever she went to visit her friend Kelly for a few days, she'd prepare everything for Wayne and leave specific instructions, but she'd call or text him every now and again to make sure he was okay. Now, she had no means of contacting him – the professor took their phones as soon as they arrived. Wayne would need to fend for himself for five months. Although the sadness was creeping up on her, it couldn't breach past a certain barrier. Her desire to have a baby was so strong that she felt like nothing could stop her. She would make it through this project, and she would come back home to Wayne – and she would not be coming alone.

Footsteps resounded down the hall, mixed with the echoing murmurs. They got louder by the second, and in moments, the student who took her measurements earlier appeared at the door, carrying a neatly folded pile of clothes.

"Just bringing you your clothes, ma'am," he said as he slumped the heap on the bed next to her with a groan.

He wiped the beads of sweat formed on his forehead with a huff and said, "I'll let you arrange them how you like, ma'am. The professor said you can use this wardrobe here," he pointed to the only wardrobe in the room.

"Thank you," Amanda gave him a courteous smile.

"Alright, then," the student said, then started towards the door.

Professor Richards walked inside the room, causing the student to startle and take a step back.

"Brian. Everything okay?" he asked.

"Yes, sir. Everything is just dandy."

"Good. Go downstairs to the office. Your colleagues are already making a schedule, and if you don't hurry, I'm afraid you may end up with night shifts."

"Oh, no problem, professor. I'm a night owl, anyway."

Richards continued staring at Brian with a fascinated smile, which probably caused the young man to feel uncomfortable.

"Right, off I go, then," Brian cleared his throat and made his way around the professor and out of the quarters.

Richards turned to Amanda and gave her a welcoming smile. Amanda couldn't help but notice just now how he had the most perfect, pearly teeth, even though he was around fifty. They were visibly fake – implants or a bridge maybe – but they still made him look handsome.

"Amanda, how are you doing?" he asked.

"I'm... fine, I guess. It's just weird to be in a place like this. But, it's better than I expected," she nervously chuckled.

"Well, if there's anything not to your liking, or if you feel that something is missing, do let me know. We still don't have all the equipment here, but what we will do is take a look at the list of interests you filled out, and we will see if we can fit some of those interests in your room. I personally made sure to bring some calligraphy books with me, and I will bring them to you later."

"You're so kind, professor. Thank you so much." Amanda was touched by his thoughtfulness.

This was another thing that made her stay much easier. She half-expected the project staff to be cold or rude, but the professor was so kind and gentle that it almost made her feel at home.

"Now, I have some things to attend to, but we'll have a checkup a little earlier today, at 6 pm. That's when the project officially starts," Richards said with more formality in his tone.

He excused himself, leaving Amanda alone in the room but feeling a lot less melancholic than she did a few minutes ago.

This was going to be just fine...

Chapter 6
95 days Until Disaster

Victor was starting to feel tired. It was already past 10 pm, but the erratic environment of the project exhausted him. His entire afternoon went by in a blur. He followed Richards around listening to his explanations, he went to his room to unpack his things and text Jennifer that he arrived safely, he followed Richards some more to get the subjects accommodated, and finally, after all that was done, all of the participants – subjects, students, and even Victor – had to sign some legal papers.

That's when the Fertility Project officially began.

At 6 pm they had a checkup with each subject. The women changed out of their personal clothes and into patient gowns. The examination consisted of the basic things, like height and weight measurements, checking the skin for any deformities, irregularities, or otherwise anomalous sightings, drawing blood, etcetera. Afterward, the subjects had a thirty-minute personality test, and finally a fifteen-minute interview, where Victor and Richards asked them how they felt, if there was anything they needed, etc. Once all of that was done, the subjects changed back into their regular clothes and were returned to their quarters and given dinner.

By this time, only one of the six students remained in the building – Tara Nugent. She agreed to take the first night shift from 10 pm until 6 am in the morning. After that, Uriel would replace her, and after that - Victor didn't know. The students were allowed to go home so they could attend their classes or do whatever it is they needed (or wanted) to. They would only need to work for Professor Richards once every two days. Each shift was eight hours, the first shift starting at 6 am, the second one at 2 pm, and the third one at 10 pm.

The professor made it clear that the students were under no circumstances allowed to leave until someone showed up to relieve them of their duties. If someone failed to show up and didn't answer the calls, someone else would need to jump in. The students all wrote their phone numbers on a paper, which was then plastered on the wall of the security room.

The security room was located on the first floor, opposite the professor's office. It was a classroom that needed no tweaking, and the professor simply brought in a computer with a monitor that displayed the live feed of the subjects' quarters. He also connected a microphone to the computer so that the participants could communicate with the subjects at the press of a button. While explaining the security system to Tara, the professor pressed a button at the base of the microphone to demonstrate how it works.

"Hello, Isabelle. This is Professor Richards. Can you hear me?" he said.

Immediately, Victor saw the woman on CAM 1 raising her head in curiosity.

"See? Now you click this here, and you can isolate the sounds and listen to subject one only," the professor said as he clicked with the mouse on a little sound icon in the corner of CAM 1.

"Professor? You called for me?" the woman in the room said, swiveling her head around, not sure where the sound was coming from.

"Yes, Isabelle. Sorry, we're just getting adjusted to the technical parts of the experiment. Can you hear me clearly?" Richards said as he held the button on the microphone pressed down again.

"Yes, professor. I can hear you," Isabelle chirped with a surprisingly perky tone.

"Very well, no need to be alert. We're just performing testing. Now, don't be alarmed if you don't hear anything outside your room. The quarters are soundproofed, intended to help you get the much-needed rest during the experiment, but should you need anything, someone will be at the computer at all times, so all you need to do is call for us."

"Understood, Professor."

Richards clicked the sound icon on CAM 1, and the low sounds of shuffling that occasionally came from Isabelle's room fell mute.

"Now, the microphone will be muted until you press this button. You have to hold it while speaking to the subjects. I suggest you hold it for a second before you actually start speaking, and hold it for another second or so after you're finished. Sometimes it lags a little, and the sound

108

may cut off. Do you understand everything so far, Tara?"

"Yes, professor. All clear," Tara obediently said.

She was sitting on a school chair next to the professor. Victor was on the professor's other side, paying careful attention to what he was demonstrating. As far as he knew, he wouldn't need to use the cameras, but it could always come in handy.

"Alright. Then let me see you using it," the professor said. "Talk to subject three."

"Do we have to call them 'subjects', Professor?" Tara asked with a grimace.

Victor felt the same way as Tara. He found the term 'subject' to be dehumanizing, so he preferred calling the women 'patients'. Richards guffawed at Tara's remark before saying.

"No, we don't have to call them that, Tara. You can call them whatever you like – so long as the names aren't offensive. Now. Go on."

Richards jutted his head towards the screen and stood up from the chair. He motioned Tara to take the seat, and she did so without a word. As she sat down, she pushed her hair to the back of her shoulder and placed her elbows on the desk with spread arms. She hovered the mouse above CAM 3 and clicked the little sound icon in the corner.

Every room looked the same, and the only differences were the numbers and the women in the rooms. CAM 4 had lights out, but night vision was on, so instead of seeing the faded colors of the room, it portrayed black-and-white furniture, a TV with pictures blasting intermittently, and the grey silhouette of the patient. Tara leaned closer to the microphone and pressed the button at the base.

"Good evening, Amanda. My name is Tara. I don't believe we've spoken before."

Patient three, Amanda, was in the kitchen peeling an apple when she heard the voice. It startled her, causing her to jump and glance wildly around, looking for the source of the sound.

"Not so loud, Tara," the professor reprimanded her.

"Sorry," she said as she let go of the button before pressing it again. "I'm sorry, I didn't mean to scare you. I'm a student volunteering for the Fertility Project. I just wanted to check up on you and see how you were doing."

Amanda continued looking around, now scanning the corners of the ceiling for the camera she may have missed.

"I'm... I'm fine, thank you. Um... how are you?" Amanda asked, still searching around, even as she spoke.

She finally located the camera and was looking directly at it now. Comically, she raised one hand in a shy manner and smiled at it.

"I'm good, thank you for asking. I'm going to be taking the night shift tonight, and I'll be here all night. So if you need anything, feel free to let me know. If I don't respond, it's because I went to the bathroom or something, but feel free to try again in a few minutes. I have a very small bladder, and I often need to -"

"Okay, that'll do, Tara," the professor interrupted her.

"Um, anyway. Nice talking to you!" Tara ended the conversation and clicked on the sound icon again.

Amanda waved at the camera once more before tentatively turning around and making her way back to the unfinished apple on the kitchen counter. Tara rotated in her chair and faced the professor, who nodded in approval.

"Now, remember one last thing," he said. "When you click on the sound icon on each camera, you will only hear that camera. And that means you will be speaking directly to that camera only. If you want to speak to all of the subjects at once, you need to click on this option here."

Richards pointed to a small 'Speak to all' text. Right now, it said 'OFF'.

"If it says it's ON, then you're speaking to all subjects, so make sure to keep it off, unless there's an announcement to make. I'll probably be the only one using it, so you don't need to worry about that. And again, make sure to click off the sound icon after speaking to the subject, because otherwise, you won't hear the other subjects. If you want to hear more closely what they're saying, there's a pair of headphones in my office. I will bring them to you later."

Tara nodded without uttering a word.

"Alright. That is all, Tara. If you understand everything, Professor Lukanski and I will leave you for the night. If you need anything, I will be in my office, and the assistant professor will be in his quarters."

"I'm sure it will be okay, Professor," Tara grinned.

"Oh, and don't forget to write the report once you're done!" Richards said as he reached for the drawer on Tara's right side.

He pulled out a notebook and a pen and tossed them on the desk. He opened the first page and clicked the pen before leaning on the desk with one palm. He wrote down the date of the experiment, along with the shift and the name of the student in charge of the camera monitoring.

"This is how you should write it for each shift. Now, if you get bored during the night, you can fill out the blank pages for your coworkers by inserting the dates, or you can leave it to them; it's up to you," Richards neatly placed the pen next to the open notebook.

"I think I'll do it myself, Professor. Uriel has terrible handwriting, and I don't want him tainting this notebook," Tara said as she slid the notebook and pen closer to herself.

"Whatever works best for you," Richards put a hand on her shoulder and moved past her. "Victor, come. Let's discuss tomorrow's agenda."

Victor nodded and followed the professor out of the security room. They went into his office, and as soon as they crossed the threshold, Richards went over to the drinks cabinet. The cabinet was filled with all sorts of dark-colored alcoholic beverages that Victor didn't recognize, and he couldn't help but wonder how the professor managed to bring all that in here. He then remembered that he was Professor Howard Richards, and he probably had a lot of perks at the university, including smuggling alcohol without repercussions.

The professor's office was ostentatious and spacious – in Victor's opinion, it was even better than his actual office in the science building. There was a desk with a laptop atop it at the far end of the room, right in front of a large window. A couch and two chairs placed around a glass coffee table were in the right corner of the room, with the drinks cabinet on their left. A simple hospital-like bed was on the left side of the room, which made Victor wonder why the professor bothered to bring in and arrange his alcohol so meticulously but neglected to bring in a proper bed. He then, yet again, remembered that Professor Richards was a workaholic and probably wouldn't be spending too much time sleeping.

"Would you like a drink, Victor?"

"No, thank you, Professor."

"Right. I forgot you don't drink. Healthy man. Well, you won't mind if I drink one, will you?"

"Not at all. You've earned it after today," Victor shrugged.

"I hardly think I've earned it, my boy, but there will be time for celebration after the experiment."

Richards opened the cabinet and took out a bottle of clay-colored beverage and a glass. He removed the cap from the bottle and poured the liquid into the glass, barely enough for two sips, before returning the cap on the bottle and placing it back in the cabinet and closing it. He turned to make his way to the couch and gestured for Victor to take a seat. Victor slumped into the couch while Richards took a sip of his beverage, slowly walking towards Victor.

"Damn shame that I have no ice cubes here," Richards shook his head with a groan.

"As you said, a proper celebration will have to wait, professor," Victor raised his eyebrows.

Richards sat on the couch next to him and placed the glass on the table. He turned to Victor and said, "Now, we have to discuss our plan for tomorrow. And then we need to get some rest. We'll have to wake up at 7 am every morning to do preparations. Tomorrow, we'll perform the first fertilization attempt. I have the sperms of the fathers-to-be frozen in the vaccine refrigerator, and we just need to combine them with the agents that will induce fertility in the women. You've read the documents I gave you, so you know how the procedure works, I hope?"

"Of course, Professor," Victor confidently nodded.

"Good. Then once we inseminate the five subjects, we will monitor them carefully for any changes. There may be some minor side-effects in their psyches, but nothing noteworthy, hopefully."

"I remember I read it in your document. You said temporary depression is somewhat common in the tested specimens?"

"I wouldn't say common... but more frequent than usually. Again, nothing alarming. Now, we will be following similar routines every day, with

114

minor changes here and there, depending on the phase of the fertility. Let me give you the detailed instructions."

Richards downed his drink in one gulp and strode over to his desk. He unlocked the drawer with a key in his lab coat and pulled out a folder that he then proceeded to give to Victor.

"Now, I know you already have a lot of work to do, Victor. But I want you to at least skim through this in the upcoming few days. Can you do that?"

"Of course, Professor. I'll start tonight."

"No, not tonight. I need you rested in the morning. Start tomorrow."

Victor nodded in agreement. He left Richards' office and went into his quarters. Although his room was significantly smaller – consisting of enough space for a bed, desk with a laptop, TV, and a personal bathroom – Victor didn't mind. He liked small, cozy rooms because they reminded him of his childhood.

Back then, he had a room similar to this one, with the exception of various posters decorating the walls. The room was his escape from reality. He'd read books all day long and avoid coming out unless his parents called for him. He wanted to avoid facing his dad, who was a very angry man. He worked a low-paying job in construction, while Victor's mom worked as a biochemical engineer. The disparity in their pay probably impacted his dad's fragile ego, and he often came home like a ticking bomb.

Both Victor and his mom often felt like they were walking on needles when he was around, especially since the slightest thing could cause him to lash out at them. You want to get something from the kitchen? Better not run in front of the TV. You want to hang out with friends? It's fine, so long as you don't speak louder than a whisper. Victor's mom couldn't give him any chores either because he'd immediately snap at her, telling her that he works hard all day while she sits around playing with potions.

Eventually, it became too much for his parents, and they got divorced. Victor's mom got custody of her son since his dad wasn't too eager to take care of the child, anyway. Victor's mom tried bringing Victor to his dad's place on the weekends so the two of them could reconnect and maintain a somewhat healthy relationship, but it soon became apparent that neither of them had an interest in building a relationship. Then, when they moved to California, the contact with Victor's dad ceased entirely. Victor heard he got remarried and had two kids from that marriage, so he never tried reaching out to him. It was obvious that his dad didn't care enough to do so.

Glancing at the white walls of the room, Victor felt both nostalgic and sad. He often wondered where his dad was and if he ever thought about Victor. That didn't matter anymore. He had a family of his own now. And he vowed he would never be a father like the one he had.

The thought came into his mind how a lot of the family members on his dad's side were a little antisocial. Victor had one cousin who had worked as a realtor, and decided to move to a small town in Oregon. Nobody had heard from him in years.

With those thoughts rolling through his mind, he drifted off into a dreamless sleep.

Chapter 7
94 days Until Disaster

As Victor expected, the morning was hectic. He was woken up by a knock on his door a little after 7 am. It was Professor Richards, wearing a lab coat and looking fresh. Victor took a mental note to research the positive effects of drinking alcoholic beverages before bed, and then he put his own lab coat on and walked out.

He and the professor headed into the examination room, where the professor opened the vaccine refrigerator and showcased the sperm samples from the five men. All of them were carefully labeled with numbers and names underneath so as to avoid inseminating the wrong woman. Victor thought about what a PR scandal that would have been.

Sometime before 8 am, Richards asked Victor to go to the security room and wake up the patients. When the assistant professor arrived, he saw Uriel, the Israeli student sitting in front of the monitor.

"Good morning, Professor," he said, with the distinct mispronunciation of the R letter.

"Good morning, Uriel. How are the patients doing?" he approached the desk and glanced at the monitors.

"They're still sleeping. Tara wrote that subjects three and four were restless, but other than that, nothing new to report."

Victor saw that the patients were, indeed, asleep in their beds.

"I need you to wake them up for their morning exam, Uriel," Victor said as he put his hands behind his back.

Uriel nodded and clicked the 'Speak to all' option. He then leaned closer to the microphone, pressed the button, and said, "Attention, ladies, attention! It is time for your morning exams."

The women stirred. Amanda from CAM 3 got up into a sitting position, displaying her disheveled hair. She tossed her blanket sideways and swung her legs aside to stand up. The patients were wearing two-piece pajamas that the professor provided for them and were supposed to remain in while the examination lasted. Patient two was still sleeping, so Uriel repeated the announcement once more, a little louder this time.

"Tell them to do their morning hygiene and to be ready by 8 am for the professor to come pick them up," Victor said.

Uriel nodded and leaned closer to the microphone again.

"Ladies, do your morning routines if you need to, and be ready for Professor Richards to pick you up for your morning exam at 8 am."

Patient One seemed confused by what Uriel was saying, which was visible from the perplexed grimace she made, so the student repeated one more time what the subjects should do.

"Thanks, Uriel. If you haven't eaten breakfast yet, now's the time. The guard should bring over the food from the courier soon."

"Thank you, Professor. Can I eat it later while I'm working?"

"Of course."

***

It was a little past 8 am, and the five patients were inside the examination room. They were each on a bed, changed into hospital gowns with their legs spread. Professor Richards had already mixed the sperm of the donor with the formula he created and was demonstrating to Victor how to perform intrauterine insemination.

"Now, I want you to do that to subject three, while I take care of subject two," Richards said.

"Will do," Victor said.

He wanted to avoid calling him 'Professor' in front of the patients in order to retain some form of authority, even though it was clear from a helicopter that Professor Richards was the one running the show. Victor prepared the insemination device and approached the bed where Amanda was.

"Good morning. How are we doing today, Amanda?" he asked with a courteous smile.

"I'm doing okay, professor. I actually managed to get enough sleep for the first time in months," Amanda said.

"I envy you. I think I'd need to sleep for three days straight to make up for the lack of sleep I've had."

Victor opened his mouth and then suddenly realized that it was really stupid to have said that. If she asked him why he wasn't sleeping well, he would have to lie and say that it was because of work.

"I understand, having a kid can take a toll on one's rest," Amanda said.

Victor raised his eyebrows, surprised that she knew that he had a child. His confusion must have been visible on his face because Amanda let out a laugh and said.

"One of the students told me a little about you yesterday."

"Oh, yeah? Which one?" Victor felt a stir of anger boiling inside of him.

"Douglas. He thinks you'll do a great job because you're a father. And you don't need to hesitate to talk about kids in front of me. I love hearing about children, Professor."

Victor nodded, feeling relieved.

"Well then, I'm going to begin with the insemination, alright? This may feel a little uncomfortable."

"It's alright, I'm already used to all sorts of uncomfortable down there by now."

As Victor inserted the prepared device into Amanda's uterus, he asked her if she was doing okay. She confirmed she was, and after some silence, she asked Victor about his kid.

"So, do you have a daughter or a son?"

He hesitated. He looked to the right on the other side of the room where Richards was speaking to one of the patients.

"Daughter. Her name's Leah. She's nine months old."

"What a pretty name. Are babies really hyperactive at that age?"

"Oh, yes. Very. You can't look away for a second without them getting into some kind of trouble."

Amanda laughed. It felt weird talking to an infertile woman wanting a baby about a baby. It was like talking to a cripple about running. But at the same time, he didn't feel like he had to be careful with his words around Amanda.

"I always wanted a daughter. My husband Wayne prefers a boy," she said.

"Oh, there's plenty of troubles with girls when they grow up. I dread to think how I'll feel the first time Leah brings home a boyfriend."

"Wayne said exactly the same thing. What is it with dads not wanting their little girls dating anybody ever?"

Victor shrugged. He had finished inserting the sperm and agent mixture, and straightened his back.

"It's like, a father-daughter codex," he said. "The daughter is supposed to stay single for the rest of her life."

They both laughed. Their laugh was interrupted by Richards calling Victor. Victor grinned at Amanda and said, "We're all done here, Amanda. You can get dressed, and we'll tell you what's next in a bit."

"Thank you, professor."

Once Victor finished assisting Richards in preparing one of the malfunctioning devices, they finished up with the rest of the patients. Richards gathered them in front of himself and said.

"Ladies, we are done here for now. You can go back to your rooms, and we will be bringing you breakfast shortly. You may experience some side effects like minor nausea, headache, or dizziness, but don't worry; this is all normal. If you feel the symptoms worsening, let us know."

***

Uriel yawned. He was staring at the cameras, hoping to see something noteworthy, but there was nothing. He flipped open the report notebook, skimming through Tara's notes. She was detailed in her report. She wrote everything, going from Subject 1 waking up to pee at 3:03 am to Subject 4 tossing and turning from midnight until 2:30 am.

Should Uriel take the same kinds of notes? Subjects woken up at 7:30, returned to their rooms at 8:45, had breakfast at 9? Nah, it wouldn't be necessary. Besides, he was only here for the extra score from Professor Richards. For all he knew, he only needed to sit there for eight hours doing nothing, and hope the time passed quickly.

He pulled the phone out of his pocket and browsed the games he had installed. *Alto's Journey*, a game about a sandboarding nomad, caught his eye. He began playing it, making backflips, chasing llamas, and collecting the shiny coins that increased his score (and dopamine). It must have been a while because two piss breaks and one lunch break later, it was already 1 pm.

Brian would be coming to relieve him soon. Every now and again, he glanced up at the cameras just to make sure nothing was out of the ordinary. Subjects one, two, and four were watching TV, subject three was writing at the kitchen table, and subject five was taking a nap.

He continued playing the mobile game. His phone battery was starting to run low, so he closed out of *Alto's Journey*. He made some nice progress in the game, but it never ended with the tasks the game threw at the player. Either way, it was almost 2 pm. As he put his phone in his pocket, he glanced at the cameras once more and saw something that caught his eye.

Subject one was still sitting on the couch and watching a TV show. Nothing unusual there. Subject two, however, was sitting on the couch, huddled in a fetal position. Uriel squinted and saw that she was lightly rocking back and forth, like a drug addict. Subject three was in the kitchen, cooking something in a pan, with various vegetables splayed on the counter.

Subject four was still sitting on the couch in front of the TV, which wasn't' strange in itself that much – except the TV was off. Has it been off this whole time? The subject was sitting with her back straight as if she were staring at something on the screen that Uriel couldn't see. He saw the woman slowly raising a hand to her face and touching her cheek. She stood up and walked up to the TV, rotating her head left and right, inches from the screen.

She was staring at her own reflection. By the looks of it, one would think that she found something strange on her face, but this was different. The woman was curiously touching her face as if she had never seen it in her life. Subject five was nowhere in sight.

Uriel panicked. He leaned in and clicked to isolate the sound for room five. He heard a rustling noise, which he identified as the pitter-patter of a running shower. He breathed a sigh of relief and scanned the other cameras. Subjects one and three were still fine, doing normal everyday activities, as much as their rooms' confinement allowed them to. Subjects two and four were the worrisome ones. Uriel wasn't sure if he should call professors Richards and Lukanski. He decided to try talking to the women first. He clicked on CAM 2 and spoke into the microphone.

"Hello there? Daria?" he said timidly. "Are you okay?"

The woman stayed in her position, not acknowledging that she heard Uriel in any way.

"Excuse me? Can you hear me? Do I need to call the professor?"

"No, everything is fine," Daria looked up at the camera, rocking more vigorously now."

Uriel felt tense and relieved at the same time. He hadn't even realized he was holding his breath until he pressed the button of the microphone again.

"Are... are you sure?"

"Yes, why would you call him? I'm feeling completely okay!" She gave two thumbs-up to the camera.

"Oh... okay then."

Uriel scratched the back of his head. He glanced at CAM 4 and saw the subject now sitting inches in front of the turned-off TV. What the fuck was she doing? He clicked the CAM 4 audio and plugged in the headphones to see if he could hear anything specific. Almost as soon as he put the headphones on, he heard it.

Low whispering coming from camera four. He squinted at the camera. Although the subject's body wasn't moving, her jaw was. She was saying something, but he couldn't tell what. Uriel held his breath as he focused on trying to decipher what the woman was saying. He turned up the audio to the max, but he still couldn't discern any words. The subject put her hands on her face, touching it in various spots. Her chest heaved and then-

A scream pierced through the headphones, causing Uriel to shriek and jump up from his chair. He would have knocked down the entire desktop had there not been a blackboard to hit his back against. He swore in Hebrew and then screamed again when he looked left and saw a figure standing at the door.

It was Brian.

"The fuck's wrong with you, Uriel?" he asked with a chuckle.

"Come check this out! There-there's something wro-wrong with subject four!" Uriel stammered.

126

"Alright, calm down. Let me see."

"Look!" Uriel pointed to camera four.

They both looked at subject four, but she was no longer in front of the TV. She was flipping through the bookshelf, probably looking for a book to read. Brian nodded and said, "She's looking for something to read when she's got Netflix. You're right. Something is really wrong with her."

"No, not that! There's... I don't know, there's something wrong with her! She was sitting in front of the TV, and she screamed!"

"Maybe she was watching a horror movie?"

"No, the TV was off!"

"Huh." Brian's lack of emotional expression at the situation irked Uriel. "Have you told Professor Richards?"

Uriel gulped, now starting to calm down. He started to realize that reporting something like this to Professor Richards might end up getting him in trouble. What if the professor looked at the feed and saw that Uriel missed such a crucial thing for hours while it was right in front of him?

"No, I... actually, maybe you're right. I'm overreacting."

Brian raised an eyebrow in suspicion.

"Well, maybe we should still let the professor know about this," he said.

"No! I mean, there's no need for that," Uriel nervously chuckled. "The professor is really busy, he probably doesn't like being bothered by silly things like these."

"Where's subject five?" Brian asked, squinting at camera five.

"Oh, she's in the shower."

"How long has she been in there?"

"Ten minutes, maybe?" Uriel lied.

Brian nodded, staring at Uriel with a frown. He wasn't buying it, and he was going to tell the professor about it. Uriel would be kicked out of the project, and it was only day two.

"Okay, man. I'm sure you're right, it's probably nothing," Brian finally said as he took off his jacket. "Anyway, you best head on out. I'll take it from here."

"Sure. Thanks. Oh, and let Antonio know that he doesn't need to come for tonight's shift."

"Why?"

"The women had their insemination done today, so Professor Richards wants to monitor them personally tonight for any changes in behavior or side effects."

Brian nodded. Just as Uriel was about to walk out, Professor Victor almost bumped into him.

"Everything alright, Uriel?" he asked.

"Yep, yep. Everything is fine," Uriel smiled convincingly before nodding and saying goodbye to the professor.

He wasn't sure about it, but he figured that he managed to avoid looking suspicious.

***

Victor almost ended up bumping into Uriel. The Israeli looked visibly alarmed. His forehead was sweaty, his eyes were wide, and he seemed to be in a hurry.

"Everything alright, Uriel?" Victor asked.

"Yep, yep. Everything is fine!" Uriel smiled, but it was visible from the lack of cheek muscle contraction that his smile was fake.

"Alright, see you in a couple of days, then." Victor didn't want to press what was wrong.

For all he knew, Uriel had a family emergency or had to run to the bathroom. Victor greeted Brian and asked him if Uriel was alright. Brian seemed hesitant to answer that, so Victor knew that he had to press him. In other situations, he wouldn't bother with such a thing, but this experiment was far too important. He needed everyone to be one hundred percent focused.

"Well, what is it?" Victor raised his eyebrows.

"Uriel thinks subject four is acting weird," Brian spilled the beans.

"Does he, now? Weird, how?"

"I... am honestly not sure."

"Did he write anything in the logbook?"

Brian rotated his chair to the right and flipped a page. It was blank.

"Nothing," he said.

Victor quizzically scratched his chin before approaching the desktop.

"Okay, no problem. Let's just look at the camera feed. See what scared our friend so badly."

"Right," Brian nodded with determination and placed his arms on the desk, ready to jump into the action. "So... how do we do that?"

Victor wasn't sure how to do it, either, but he decided to fish around the program. He told Brian not to click anything that he wasn't sure of, but eventually, they found the recording of the rooms

129

from the past hour. The system saved the videos every hour, so it took some further digging to find the one with the right date and time.

"Okay, here it is," Victor said. "Let's see it."

Brian double-clicked the video, and it opened a video player with the rooms. The timestamp of 1 pm was shown in the lower-right corner. The video only showed camera four, which was better in Victor's opinion, because they could focus only on the patient – it was the talkative one, Regina.

At first, she spent some time watching TV – nothing suspicious. Victor urged Brian to fast forward through the video. At one point, the TV was turned off, but Regina continued watching it. Victor thought that she might have been sleeping, but her back and neck were too straight in rapt attention, which was not a position you'd take while you were sleeping. As the video went on, the patient shifted in her spot, swiveling her head left, but still looking at the TV. She then stood up and got closer to it and began touching her face in a curious manner, pulling her cheeks down, gently clawing at her forehead and lips, stretching her mouth in various grimaces.

"What's she doing, professor?" Brian asked.

Victor hadn't even realized how silent the room fell until Brian spoke up.

"I... don't know," Victor said.

Brian fast-forwarded the video some more, and Regina went from standing in front of it for a solid twenty minutes to sitting in front of it, the screen mere inches from her face. And then her chest began heaving up and down, and she opened her mouth wide. A sound came from somewhere, barely audible.

"What's that?" Victor asked.

"It's coming from the headphones," Brian responded and unplugged them from the computer.

"Play that part again," Victor said.

Brian tapped the left arrow on the keyboard twice, and it took the video back twenty seconds. Regina's chest heaved, and then she screamed at the top of her lungs. Victor felt a cold shiver run down his spine, while Brian looked like he had just seen a ghost.

"What the fuck?" the student asked.

"Language, Brian," Victor chided him.

They continued watching the video, and Regina seemed to go back to normal right after the scream. She went to the bookcase, and then the video ended.

"Let's see the other patients," Victor said as he pulled the wooden chair closer to have a seat.

This was probably going to take a while.

Chapter 8
94 days Until Disaster

"Now, tell me again. What seems to be the problem, Victor?" Richards asked.

He was sitting behind his desk with intertwined fingers and a toothy grin.

"The sub... the patients are acting weird."

"All of them? And in what way are they behaving weirdly?"

"I can't explain it, professor. You would need to see for yourself," Victor said.

He couldn't even begin to think how he would describe to the professor what he saw on the camera feed without it sounding like the ravings of a lunatic.

"I really believe we should perform a checkup, just in case," he said.

The professor nodded.

"Alright, Victor. If you believe that it's necessary, then I trust your judgment," he pushed back his chair and stood up, gesturing to the door. "Shall we, then?"

Richards' lack of counter-arguments surprised Victor, but he wasn't complaining. Besides, there was no time to debate. The patients may have been going through something dangerous. The last time Victor checked the cameras with Brian, the women seemed okay, but that still didn't explain what happened earlier. Richards led the way out of the office and toward the women's quarters. When they arrived, he whipped out the keycard and unlocked rooms one and two.

"You speak to subject one while I check on subject two. And then we'll go on from there," Richards said.

Victor nodded. He entered room one, where he found Isabelle sitting on the couch. Victor greeted her, deciding on the approach to take. He didn't want to sound accusatory or say something that would cause her to misinterpret his words and potentially get worried. He started with a smile.

"Good afternoon, Isabelle. How are you today?"

"Good, good. I have a lot of shows to catch up on, so I'm fine," Isabelle shrugged.

"Good. Are you feeling physically okay?"

"Aha," she nodded.

"Any headaches, nausea, dizziness, vomiting, fever, depression?"

Isabelle shook her head at everything Victor listed.

"Should I be experiencing any of those?" she asked skeptically.

"No, no. This is just a precaution. I'm going to need to perform a small checkup."

He approached her and pulled out a small flashlight pen. He flicked it on and checked her pupils before telling her to open her mouth and say 'Ah'. Then he distanced the pen and told her to follow it with her eyes as he moved it. No problems there.

"Alright, if you happen to feel any of the symptoms I mentioned, or anything you don't feel on a normal day, feel free to holler, okay?"

"Sure," Isabelle nodded.

"I'll see you after dinner, then. Have a good one," Victor nodded and stepped out.

Professor Richards also happened to be finished with the patient in room two, so he unlocked rooms three and four. He told Victor to go inside room three while he checked room four. Victor nodded in agreement and entered Amanda's room. As soon as he entered, the pungent smell of something tasty wafted into his face. It reminded him of Jennie's cooking. Amanda was sitting on the couch when Victor entered.

"Something smells good in here. Maybe we should hire you to cook for the participants, Amanda," he smiled courteously.

"You flatter me, Professor. It's a very simple recipe used in my family for generations."

Victor glanced towards the kitchen counter where the savory-looking grilled sandwich rested. He sniffed, feeling his mouth salivating at the sight of the food.

"Pulled pork, I assume?" he asked. "And what's that brown stuff?"

"Caramelized onions. I like adding them to everything and anything. Do you want to try it?"

Victor grinned at the nice gesture. He wanted to, but he wasn't sure if Amanda was only offering it out of courtesy, so he said.

"No, no, I couldn't. Thank you, though."

"It's fine, professor. I won't be able to eat the whole thing, anyway. Let's split it," Amanda insisted.

She clambered up to her feet and loped to the kitchen, where she grabbed a big knife. She carefully and aesthetically cut the sandwich into two triangular pieces, sliding one half toward Victor.

"Alright, alright," Victor said, grabbing the still-warm piece.

He saw the melted cheese around the edges, the thinly pulled pork, the caramelized onions, and something green he assumed were pickles. Amanda stared in anticipation with a hopeful look in her eye. Victor took a big bite – to ensure he grabbed all the contents of the sandwich. The savory mixture of the meat, vegetables, cheese, and bread filled his mouth, and for a moment, he thought he was in heaven. His sense of taste seemed to intensify more with each passing second.

"Yum!" he exclaimed theatrically.

"I know, right? The recipe is secret, but I can share it with you if you like," Amanda winked.

"That would be amazing. I gotta tell my wife to make this. Every night."

Amanda laughed. As much as Victor wanted to wolf down the entire sandwich immediately, he placed it on the counter and wiped his hands to get the crumbs off.

"Well, Amanda. I'm here to perform a checkup, so don't try to distract me," he said.

"Oh, no. I would never do that, Professor. By the way, I also know how to make raw cakes, and it only takes five minutes."

"Nice try. I'm tempted, but it will have to wait," he gestured to the couch.

Once Amanda was seated, Victor proceeded to perform the same test on her with the flashlight pen. He asked her if she experienced any of the symptoms.

"Well, now that you mention it, I do feel a slight stomachache today. But, it could be a placebo."

"Let's check it out. Would you lie on your back and lift your shirt, please?"

Amanda nodded and swung her legs up on the couch. She rolled up her t-shirt, revealing the flat abdomen. Victor knelt next to her and began touching her abdomen from the epigastric region. Although he wasn't a doctor, he learned the basic checkups that doctors usually perform – in case Jennifer ever needed it.

"Do you feel any pain here?"

Amanda shook her head.

Victor continued gently touching lower towards the umbilical region until he reached the hypogastrium.

"Any pain?" he asked.

"There's... a little bit over there," Amanda moaned slightly.

Victor massaged the area to determine if there were any anomalies over there. Everything seemed okay, but he wanted to double-check before he-

He felt resistance against his finger for a second. No, he didn't just feel it. He *saw* it. Where his forefinger and middle finger were, a small bulge hit against his fingers and disappeared instantly.

"Whoa," he said.

"Is everything okay, professor?" Amanda asked apprehensively.

"Yeah. Yes, everything is fine," Victor responded frantically as he continued massaging the area where he felt the bump just now. "Do you feel any pain here?"

"No. Actually, I don't feel any pain anymore all of a sudden. It really must have been a placebo," she nervously chuckled.

Baffled and unconvinced, Victor told Amanda she was free for now, but that she should let him know if she felt the pain again. She thanked him, and as he was about to turn around to leave, she jumped to her feet and called out to him.

"Professor, wait!" she strolled to the kitchen and opened a cupboard.

She pulled out some napkins and packed both halves of the sandwich before hurriedly returning to Victor. Victor raised a palm towards her and opened his mouth to protest, but she interrupted him.

"Please. As a token of gratitude."

"Oh, you really don't need to, I'm only doing my job."

"Then take it as a gift."

She flashed her pearly grin, and Victor knew that it would be no use arguing – and he had no patience to argue. Plus, it was a damn good sandwich. He took the packed sandwiches from her and put them in the pocket of his lab coat.

"Thank you, Professor Lukanski."

"Victor. You can call me Victor," he said.

"Victor," she repeated.

He knew that Professor Richards wouldn't be happy to see him making small talk with the patients and exchanging favors for pulled pork and caramelized onion sandwiches, but to hell with that. If he could make the women's stay less unpleasant simply by talking to them for five minutes a day, then he would do so.

Victor exited Amanda's room and saw room four locked and room five open. Richards must have already finished up with patient four and was examining patient five. Victor approached the widely ajar room five and immediately heard a feminine voice coming from it. He stopped in front of the door because of the tone of the voice. It sounded like the woman was saying something through sobs. Her sentences were incoherent, strung together, and fast. Victor perked up his ears in hopes of discerning something, but the patient spoke too fast. At the same time, she spoke in a hushed manner, as if she wanted to avoid being heard. Among the words, Victor recognized the phrase 'Please, Professor'.

Victor knocked on the door and tentatively peeked inside. He saw the patient sitting on the couch, tear-stricken. In front of her was Professor Richards, kneeling inches from her and holding his hand over hers. When Victor knocked, both the professor and the patient looked towards the door.

"Professor, do you need assistance?"

"No, no. Everything is okay, Victor. I will be there in a minute," Richards said.

Victor took that as a sign that he was intruding, so he stepped into the hallway and crossed his arms. He didn't hear the patient's voice anymore, just Richards murmuring something quietly. A minute or so later, his voice boomed clearly from the room.

"Well, then. I will see you tonight after dinner, Marie."

The woman thanked him, and Richards left her room, closing the door behind her. The lock clicked, and Richards gave Victor a nod of approval before heading down the hall. Victor followed him, a little irked by the fact that the professor didn't tell him what had just happened with the patient.

"Professor, is the patient okay?" he dared ask.

"Subject five just has some trouble sleeping. She says that she couldn't sleep last night and that she experienced some nightmares when trying to take a nap today. This transition seems to be shocking for her, so I told her I'd give her some pills."

"I see," Victor frowned. "She sounded really distressed, though."

"Yes. It would seem that the nightmare she had was extremely vivid."

They began going down the stairs, their footsteps echoing on the stairwell.

"Is this a common side effect of the formula used to inseminate them?"

"Not so common. When I tested it in mice, some would have disturbed sleep, but unfortunately, brains of mice and brains of humans work in different ways, so there's no way to tell what exactly was going on, save for the brainwave activity."

They made it down to the first floor, and Richards put a hand on Victor's shoulder as they walked side by side.

"Tell me. What did you find out from subjects one and three?" the professor asked.

"Subject one seems to be okay. No visible behavioral changes and she reported no symptoms that you listed. But as for subject three, Amanda..."

"Yes?"

Victor hesitated. He wasn't sure how to explain what he felt on his fingers, or if it even had any significance. The image of the bulge sticking out of Amanda's stomach popped into his mind, a lump that bounced on the inside of her abdomen like a tennis ball before returning to the hypogastrium.

"Well?" Richards insisted.

They had stopped in front of Richards' office and were facing each other.

"Subject three complained about a stomachache. And when I examined her stomach, I felt something on the hypogastrium."

"Was it an anomalous mass?"

"No... I mean, I think not. There was nothing there, but for a moment, I felt something giving resistance to my fingers for a split second, and it looked like a bulge."

"A bulge?" the professor raised an eyebrow.

Suddenly, Victor felt like a layman – no, like a patient – explaining something to an educated professional. And still, he couldn't stop speaking. He had to tell the professor what he saw.

"Yes. That's at least what it felt like for the moment it appeared."

Richards nodded. He scratched his clean-shaven chin and turned to open the door of his office.

"Involuntary contraction of the abdominal muscle," he said as he swung the door open and entered.

"Come again, professor?"

"Spasm. What you saw must have been just a spasm of the abdomen, Victor," the professor said.

Victor replayed the event in his head. A millisecond resistance on his fingers before retreating. And the bulge he saw... was it really a bulge? Maybe his mind was playing tricks on him because it happened so fast. What if it really was just a contraction? Yeah, that's probably what it was. It couldn't have been anything else. Now that he thought about it, it sounded ridiculous. What did he expect to see? A little alien-like creature formed in the uterus in less than half a day, bursting out of the mother's abdomen? He laughed out loud at his own ridiculousness.

"I appreciate your astuteness when examining the subjects, Victor. Did you notice anything else during the examination?"

"No, Professor. Everything else seems okay."

Richards nodded and sat behind his desk.

"And how about on your end, Professor?" Victor asked.

Richards looked taken aback by this question for a moment, and Victor almost thought that he crossed the line. But he had the right to know. After all, Richards chose him as his equal, not an apprentice.

"Nothing with subjects two and four," the professor said. "Subject five has trouble sleeping. Nothing else is out of the ordinary."

"You haven't noticed anything strange with subjects two and four, professor?"

Richards shook his head with downturned lips.

"There have been no changes in their cognitive or behavioral abilities that would indicate anything serious."

Victor darted his eyes down, reflecting on what he saw on the camera feed. He wasn't exaggerating, he was sure of it. At least not for subject four. She screamed at a blank TV. Maybe there were some minor side effects that the professor wasn't aware of, which posed no threat to the women's health. He figured that if anything weird were to happen, Richards would have a chance to see it for himself during his shift tonight.

Knowing that there is nothing else he could do right now, and given the fact that he had enough time until the dinner checkup, he left the professor's office in an attempt to go to his quarters and call Jennifer and Leah.

But first, he would eat the sandwich Amanda gave him.

Chapter 9
93 days until disaster

When Uriel walked into the security room that morning, it was empty. The security cameras were still operational, but no one was monitoring them. Uriel knew that this wasn't really a big deal. After all, it was Professor Richards' shift last night. If he fell asleep during the night, no one would be getting in trouble.

"Hello?" Uriel called out, just to make sure he was really alone. "Hm. Nobody here." he said aloud a moment later with a shrug. He swung his backpack on the desk next to the monitor and sat down. An hour ago, he grumbled and complained about having to wake up so early to take Douglas' shift. The fucker apparently wasn't feeling well, but at least he would cover for one of Uriel's shifts, so he could take an extra day off. Maybe they should arrange the shifts that way, for three people to work two or three days in a row, and then the other three, while the first batch takes a break.

No, they wouldn't agree to that. Tara and Antonio worked night shifts, and working too many nights in a row would probably be difficult for them. But maybe Uriel could bite the bullet and take the night shifts instead of them.

As he brainstormed in his head, he noticed that the subjects on cameras two and four were gone.

The other three were in their beds, peacefully sleeping, but the first two were nowhere in sight. Uriel decided to wait. Maybe they were using the bathroom. He suddenly remembered hearing subject four screaming yesterday. He shuddered at the thought of it and hoped he wouldn't need to interact with the women too much today.

Just to be on the safe side, he decided he would pay more attention to the camera today. He would play *Alto's Journey*, but he would glance at the cameras more often. As he glanced to the right, he remembered in horror that he forgot to write a report in the notebook yesterday. He slid the logbook closer to himself and flipped the pages. There were meager notes taken by Brian yesterday, with a 'sooo boooring' written underneath, and a drawing of a stick figure pointing a gun to its head.

Maybe they didn't notice Uriel's missing notes? He quickly wrote down something on the page for his shift yesterday and flipped to a blank one for today's shift.

Nobody saw nothing, nobody heard nothing, he thought to himself cleverly.

He began his boring shift of staring at the cameras, but he couldn't help but be bothered by the fact that subjects two and four were still missing. What if they had another fit and hurt themselves somehow? If it did happen, it would have happened in the professor's shift. But why didn't Uriel report their absence? He wasn't the professor, and he could get in trouble. And what if he not only got kicked out of the project, but got into legal troubles as well?

Just like that, he began panicking again. Should he tell the professors? No, he could try by speaking to the subjects, first. Since there was no option to speak to multiple selected rooms at once, Uriel started by clicking on room two.

"Hello, can you hear me? Ma'am, are you there?"

He waited with bated breath, hoping against hope that the subject would say something, anything, and make his shift easier. Five seconds passed, then ten, agonizingly slow. He clicked on camera four and tried speaking again.

"Lady, are you in there?" He didn't care right now about manners.

Just like with room two, there was no response. Dammit, why did his shifts have to be so damn complicated all the time? Once he was done with today's shift, he would find someone to switch mornings with. Uriel switched back to camera two and spoke again.

Nothing.

Back and forth and back and forth again he spoke, rationalizing that the subjects would say something any second now. But nothing ever came from it. There wasn't even a shuffling noise which would prove that the subjects were even present inside their rooms. Left with no other choice, he had to tell someone. But it would have to be professor Lukanski; he would be more understanding. He could tell Lukanski, and then the assistant professor could tell Richards. That way, Uriel would be off the radar for Richards. Yeah, that was a good way to go.

He stood up and rushed out of the security room, making his way downstairs and towards Professor Lukanski's quarters. Before he even approached his room, he saw the professor walking in his direction. He was wearing a lab coat, and he held his hands in his pockets. When he saw Uriel, he raised both hands in a comical surrendering pose and said.

"Whoa, whoa. Where's the fire, Uriel?" his voice was a little raspy, a testament to him recently waking up.

"Professor, there's something wrong with the subjects!" Uriel exclaimed breathlessly.

***

"Calm down, Uriel. Tell me what's wrong," Victor said.

He had just woken up ten minutes ago and wasn't ready to start his day with trouble. Uriel was panting, and he had wide eyes, just like he did yesterday.

"Subject two and subject four... I don't see them on the cameras! They've been gone since I arrived, and the professor wasn't in the security room!"

Victor didn't want to raise an alarm, so he calmly nodded and said, "Okay, it's probably nothing. Let's check the cameras."

Uriel nodded fervently and then turned around on his heel and loped towards the security room. Victor followed him with striding steps in order to catch up. When they arrived in the security room, it immediately became apparent that cameras two and four had no figures in the displayed beds. Just to make sure, Victor scanned the cameras with his own eyes to see if they were sitting still, somewhere else in the room. It was still dark, and the camera's night vision was turned on, so it would be easy mistaking a piece of furniture with a dormant person.

"Hm," he said when he finally deduced that Uriel was right.

By this time, the Israeli had somewhat calmed down, but was staring up at Victor from the computer chair with rapt apprehension.

"Have you tried speaking to them?" Victor asked.

"Yes. They didn't respond."

Victor scratched his cheek, still feeling somewhat unfocused from the sleepiness, but his brain comprehended the severity of the situation. If the patients in rooms two and four had psychotic side effects, they might have done something self-harmful in the bathroom. He had to tell Richards.

"Keep looking at the cameras, I'll go tell the professor," Victor put a hand on Uriel's shoulder, a gesture he suddenly realized Richards often made.

He exited the security room and went down to the professor's office. Through the crack under the door, he could see that his office was still dark. Victor knocked on the door three times rapidly and loudly, to convey the urgency of the situation with the knocks.

"Professor?" he called out but got no response.

He knocked again, and again - no one answered. Victor turned the knob and pushed the door inward. It opened smoothly without a creak, revealing the darkened interior of Richards' office. Immediately, the soft, steady snoring of a sleeping person filled the air from the left side of the room. Victor tip-toed to the bed, where Richards' figure lay splayed on his back, mouth agape, still wearing his lab coat, one arm dangling off the side of the bed. His chest steadily rose and fell with each breath, letting out raspy snores.

"Professor!" Victor shook the professor by the shoulder.

A louder snort came from the professor, and he immediately jerked his head up, closing his open mouth. He looked around in confusion with unfocused eyes before realizing that Victor stood in front of him.

"Victor?" he said groggily. "What time is it?"

"Almost seven. Professor, we have an urgent problem with the patients."

Richards stared around the room as if seeing it for the first time. He cleared his throat a moment later and rubbed his eyes with one hand while propping himself up with the other and getting up into a sitting position.

"Okay... tell me what's going on, Victor," he said, now a little more awake, staring up at Victor with bleary eyes.

"Patients two and four are not in their rooms. I think they're in the bathroom, but Uriel says they've been gone a while. I fear that may have injured themselves."

Professor Richards looked away mid-sentence, causing Victor to wonder if he was even listening to him. He stood up from his bed with a groan. The bed creaked slightly in response.

"Oh, you don't need to worry about subjects two and four, Victor," he said.

"Why?"

Richards put his hands in the pockets of his lab coat and said, "Because they're no longer participating in the experiment."

***

Marie woke up from her sleep in a jolt. As she lay in her bed with her eyes wide open, she felt cold sweat enveloping her. Her heart was pounding, but she didn't understand why. Did she have a bad dream? No, it must have been the stomachache. Ever since yesterday's morning exam – when the professor injected her with the sperm mixture that was supposed to help her conceive – she'd been having pain in her stomach.

It started off mildly during the noon hour, but then it intensified later on, so badly that she could hardly get any sleep. She called the professor – or whoever was working the night shift – multiple times, asking for painkillers, but no one responded. In the end, she spent most of her night tossing and turning. At moments, the pain intensified in waves, causing Marie to assume a fetal position and breathe labored breaths in hopes that the pain would go away soon. At other moments, it felt like kicking, similar to what she felt when she had put her hand on her friend Arianna's stomach and felt her baby, but Marie had gotten the insemination done less than a day ago, so that couldn't have been it.

She told Professor Richards about it earlier yesterday, but he assured her that it was normal. He gave her a pill for the pain, and when she took it, it worked at first. But then the kicking and the pain came back even worse, later on, and she knew that something must be wrong, something that the professor wasn't aware of. That's at least what she thought up until an hour ago. Now, the pain was almost completely gone. Either way, it was almost time for them to wake up. She would tell the professor about the stomachache, just to be on the safe side.

***

"What do you mean, they're no longer participating?" Victor frowned.

Richards scratched his temple and sighed. As he turned away from Victor, he spread his arms and let them fall limply against his sides before saying, "They left last night. Subject two, Daria Conley, said she changed her mind. Wanted to go back to her husband. She got hysterical when I tried convincing her to stay, so I had no choice but to let her go."

"And subject four? Regina Sniff?"

"She felt unwell. Began doubting the entire experiment. Frankly, I think she got cold feet. I understand her. A lot of women dropped out in the initial interview exactly because of that. They couldn't bear the thought of being inseminated by an artificially created formula." The professor turned to face Victor and shrugged forlornly. "I thought that these two candidates would be ideal, but... I can't hold them here against their wills."

"So you let them go, Professor? Just like that?"

Victor didn't see the professor letting the patients go without a proper fight. He probably tried convincing them to stay, maybe even promised that they'd have a healthy baby by the time they're done. Perhaps even threatened them with the NDA they signed.

"No, of course not, Victor," Richards frowned. He looked like he was offended. "I tried convincing them, but they refused to stay I suspect they may have spoken to each other during the day, maybe stressed each other out until they were both freaked out. Subject five's behavior may have scared them, too. Either way, I terminated their NDAs and released them."

He turned around and headed for the desk.

"What about the insemination?" Victor asked.

Richards froze in his steps before slowly turning around and saying, "Right, that would be a big problem, wouldn't it? As unfortunate as it is, I had no choice but to have the subjects take a morning-after pill in front of me. That way, you, I, or the university, wouldn't have to deal with any legal repercussions in case of any complications."

Victor nodded wordlessly. He brainstormed in his head what they could have done to have the women keep the potential conceived baby, but he knew that there was no way around it. As much as he wanted these women to have a happy life full of children, he knew that the university valued its reputation.

"I'm just surprised I didn't hear you escorting them out," Victor smiled. "I mean, you could have woken me up to assist you, professor."

"Oh, it's was no trouble, Victor. Besides, as I told you before, I need you fully rested. I am an older man, and I don't need as much sleep, but you're young." He approached Victor, put a hand on his shoulder, and smiled. "Now, let's get ready and begin the examination, shall we?"

***

Richards and Victor carefully monitored the remaining three patients over the next few days. Victor made sure to pay careful attention to any abdominal pain or behavioral changes that the women might have been experiencing. Victor's job was to monitor Amanda, and sometimes Isabelle, while Richards took care of Marie. Isabelle and Amanda seemed perfectly fine, no pain, no complaints, and when he examined their abdomens, no spasms or kicks – much to his relief.

Patient five, Marie, was a different story. She always looked like she had spent a sleepless night, with disheveled hair and bleary and unfocused eyes, responding to questions slowly and without any details. Oftentimes, she looked like she didn't understand the questions Richards asked her. Although Victor never examined her, he cast furtive glances in her direction in the examination room.

Three days after patients two and four left, Richards and Victor prepared to examine the remaining patients in the exam room. Richards

153

had explained to them that they would carefully monitor the women's conditions and find out in a few days if they were pregnant or not.

Victor had finished examining Amanda, who was in a particularly good mood that day. In fact, she had been in a good mood in the past few days. Victor assumed that she had become adapted to the conditions of the 'facility', despite the fact that there were still more than four months remaining.

"So, how was the sandwich? It didn't end up in a trash can, I hope?" she asked.

Victor guffawed.

"Amanda, I unwillingly admit this, but I have never tasted a better sandwich than yours. In fact, they're better than my wife's famous 'hot sandwiches', and I don't say this lightly."

Amanda laughed.

"Well, if you like, I can make more for you. I understand that you don't have time to cook, and I have way too much time on my hands."

"I wouldn't like to bother you with it, but I'll let you in on one secret." He leaned closer to her and said in a hushed tone, "I think about that sandwich of yours quite a lot."

"Tell you what, I'll do that for you if you can do one thing for me."

"Name it."

"Can you try and get me some erythritol?"

Victor frowned and pulled his head back in confusion.

"Some what, now?" he asked.

Amanda chuckled.

"It's a substitute for sugar. Can be used to make sugar-free desserts."

"Oh, so you're a healthy recipe guru, too?"

"A little bit. I used to make these ketogenic muffins for Wayne, and I kinda crave them these days. The food I get in my room is great, but I need more... unconventional ingredients. And I really love those muffins."

"How about erythritol for two of those muffins and one sandwich?" Victor asked.

"A muffin and one sandwich."

"Two sandwiches and a muffin."

"How about a muffin, a sandwich, and I don't tell your wife you said my food is better?"

"Deal. I'll ask the guard outside to buy one."

"Take as long as you need. I'm not going anywhere."

Amanda was finished with her examination, so Victor told her to get dressed.

Richards called Victor and said, "Victor, I need to fetch my notes from my office. Can you finish examining Marie? We still need to measure her pressure and draw blood."

"I'm on it, Professor Richards."

Richards left the room in a hurry while Victor approached Marie to finish the examination. He stopped next to her bed and gave her a smile before turning to grab the sphygmomanometer splayed on the desk next to her bed.

"Alright, Marie, we're just going to-" Victor started, but abruptly stopped when he felt a strong grip on his forearm.

He immediately jerked his head in Marie's direction, stifling a gasp. Marie was gripping him by the forearm with a feverish grip, causing Victor's sleeve to wrinkle and Marie's fingertips to turn white. Her eyes were wide, and her eyebrows upturned in a pleading manner, while her lips quivered.

"Professor Lukanski..." she spoke his name and said something else, but it was so quiet that he couldn't discern it.

"What is it, Marie?" he asked.

He wanted to lean closer, but he suddenly found himself feeling afraid. What if she did something unpredictable, like bite a chunk of his face off? The chances of that happening were low, of course, but still not non-existent.

"Please... help me!" she said in an equally quiet tone.

Victor subtly tried pulling his arm away, but Marie's grip remained vice-like. He looked around and saw Amanda and Isabelle talking to each other on the other side of the room, oblivious to what Marie was doing.

"Please!" Marie's voice came again, still hushed, but much louder this time.

Victor jerked his head back towards her and slightly bent down, careful not to get too close.

"Tell me what's wrong."

Marie subverted her gaze over Victor's shoulder, towards the entrance, before looking back at him. She was pulling him closer by the forearm, but he resisted. He noticed Marie darting her eyes towards the door every few seconds. Was she looking out for Richards? Deciding to take the risk – but ready to react in case she tried something violent – Victor leaned down so that Marie's mouth was right against his ear. He felt her hot, quivering breath, and then-

"I apologize about that," Professor Richards' voice came from the entrance, followed by the patter of footsteps approaching Marie's bed.

Victor jerked back, Marie's pleading eyes locked with his. She let go of his forearm and glanced towards Professor Richards before smiling. She did it convincingly, too. A relaxed facial expression replaced her quivering lips, upturned eyebrows and wide eyes.

"Everything okay here, Victor?" Richards asked.

"Um..." Victor started, still staring at Marie.

She looked back at him, still smiling widely with her mouth closed, but the smile seemed anything but genuine now.

"I'm sorry, professor. I didn't have the time to take her pressure," he said.

"Not a problem. I'll finish up here. Can you send the student to bring in breakfast?"

Victor nodded. He turned to leave the room, but before he did, he gave Marie another furtive glance. She briefly looked at him before turning to the professor and answering a question he asked. As Victor strode down the hall, he stared at his feet, reflecting on what just happened.

At the moment when he leaned in, and she had her mouth against his ear, she whispered something. Did Victor really hear her correctly?

And what did she mean by it? Maybe the lack of sleep was starting to get to her psyche.

She said, 'It's inside me'.

Disaster Night, Part 3

"We'll have to ignore standard procedure of breaching and clearing every room," Survivor said. "What we're facing here is way too dangerous."

HQ had contacted them earlier and said that Delta Team would be taking up sniper positions around the campus. The Fat Guys would be arriving within an hour, but Professor Richards was still in danger, so the rest of the teams were to locate him and evacuate him out of the hot zone.

"Squarepants, keep a lookout on those cameras," Survivor said with slight frustration in his voice.

Now that the adrenaline had subsided, he started to get angry with Squarepants for not informing the team of the danger they were facing. He then told himself that it wasn't his teammate's fault. It wasn't like Squarepants deliberately ignored their radio calls. He just hoped it wouldn't happen again.

"Alright, let's move," Cougar impatiently said.

He opened the door, and Talker was the first one through with his weapon raised. He turned right, and Survivor went through and turned left. His eyes were entirely adjusted to the low dark now, and he could tell with certainty that the hallway was clear without utilizing the NVG. Cougar was the last one out and was supposed to cover Talker's side, but he instead improvised and covered Survivor's side since that was the direction of the danger.

"Clear," Cougar called out quietly.

Talker turned around, and the three team members quietly went down the hall. They turned left where Poseidon and Bulldozer had gone missing and scrutinized the hall before determining it was safe enough to proceed forward. Any moment now, Survivor expected something tall and inhuman to jump out in front of him, so he had his finger just above the trigger.

It wasn't long before they saw blood on the floor, thick and fresh, leading away from them in a straight, broad trail. The team significantly slowed down and tip-toed from there. Both Cougar and Talker got more apprehensive, which Survivor could sense from their breathing and movement. Intermittently, Survivor glanced down at the blood trail and up through his red dot sight.

Suddenly, he saw something coming into view on the floor. He raised one hand for his teammates to stop as he observed the object. He took a step closer and realized it was a boot – the response unit members' boot. As he got closer, he realized that he was wrong. It wasn't just a boot. It was an entire fucking foot inside the boot, lying forlornly on the floor, surrounded by a pool of blood. Beyond the pool of blood, the red trail extended, and Survivor saw a distinct footprint in the blood. It was from a bare foot, elongated and thin, with four toes of uneven shapes and width between each other. Between the second and third toes was a larger width, as if to indicate that one toe was missing.

One thing was for sure, though. Whatever the fuck this thing was, it was not human.

The team tiptoed forward, stepping around the blood and the foot in the boot to avoid slipping or causing noise. Suddenly, the trail ended a dozen feet in front of the foot, at the base of something on the floor, and Survivor realized what they had stumbled into.

On the floor, splayed in front of the three team members, on its back, was Poseidon's body – or what was left of it. His left foot was missing, and it became evident that the blood trail was coming from the stump in his leg. His torso, however... He was literally split open from the chest all the way down to his crotch, making his legs jut out in a stretched position to opposite sides, revealing bones, cartilage, torn muscles, and other tissue, covered in copious amounts of blood. A large pool of blood surrounded his body. When he looked at his face, Survivor saw his team member's eyes staring vacantly at the ceiling, his mouth slightly ajar. Poseidon was a tough and fearless son of a bitch who Survivor had known somewhat well from the three missions they'd been on together, but his face still expressed pure terror in death.

"Fuck," Talker muttered under his breath.

"Hostiles could still be around. Eyes open," Survivor said.

He knew that the morally right thing to do would be to transport Poseidon's body out of the hot zone for proper burial, but the mission always came first. Survivor was so used to these occurrences that it became as normal as saying 'Good morning'. The first time he saw a teammate die, he wondered if he had a family that would mourn his death. Now, that thought didn't come to him, even after the mission. Lingering on those thoughts could destroy a man in this profession. That's why a lot of the guys from the Intervention Unit ended up blowing their brains out.

"There's movement around the corner to your right," Squarepants said over the radio. "They just entered one of the classrooms."

"One of ours?" Talker asked.

"Don't know. He looked human, so..."

"We'd better check it out," Survivor said.

He briefly glanced towards Talker and Cougar, who nodded in approval. Without a word (or glance), they stepped around Poseidon's body and continued down the hall, a little faster this time. The building hall was O-shaped, and would eventually end up in the same spot where the entrance corridor forked left and right.

"That classroom, to your right. I can see you on the cameras," Squarepants said.

Survivor stopped next to the door. Cougar took up a position opposite of him, and Talker faced the door. Survivor grabbed the doorknob and pushed open the door. Talker rushed inside, with Cougar following closely behind.

"Hold your fire!" a voice boomed from the classroom on the left side.

All guns were pointed at the person, and it took only a second to realize it was Bulldozer. He was standing with his gun raised, but he lowered it a moment later, assuming a more relaxed stance.

"Jesus Christ, Bulldozer. What the fuck, man?" Talker asked.

"Why didn't you use your fucking radio?" Cougar asked.

"One of those fucking things yanked it off me. I'm lucky I'm still in one piece," he scoffed.

"What the hell is going on here?" Talker asked.

"Don't know, don't care. We gotta find the professor and get the fuck outta here before more of us get killed."

"Where is the prof, anyway?"

Squarepants' voice came over the radio.

"Guys, I see some movement on the second floor. Front of Richards' office."

"Might be the professor," Talker said.

"Roger that, Squarepants. We're on our way there," Survivor said before turning to Bulldozer, who had a look of anticipation on his face. "Squarepants saw someone on the second floor."

"Alright, let's move," Bulldozer nodded.

***

The trek from the classroom to the stairwell was slow but uneventful – if running into the dead bodies of Charlie Team could be called uneventful. The entire hallway from the South entrance was littered with the six bodies of the unit – and not in one piece. There was blood everywhere, and limbs were scattered around the place like broken off toy pieces. The sinew and the cartilage and bones that were jutting out of each stump made it clear that

163

the limbs were ripped off, rather than severed cleanly.

The one body of the Charlie member that had all its limbs still attached looked badly bashed-in at the chest, as if something extremely heavy had fallen on top of it, crushing the ribcage and splaying the bones and internal organs for everyone to see. The smell of death was in the air; a smell Survivor had become so accustomed to that it felt weird when it wasn't around. That smell would stick around for days the first few times you encountered it, and you would wake up at night thinking you were still surrounded by the dead bodies. You'd even hear screams and gunshots from time to time, only to find yourself in the safety of your bed. That excruciating feeling would either linger until it devoured you or until you got entirely desensitized to it.

Those who didn't get used to it were either dead or in an insane asylum.

The team slowly climbed the stairs. The stairwell was too dark, so they flicked the flashlights back on when Bulldozer commanded them to. Thankfully, the second floor had no bodies, which meant that it was most likely clear of the creatures inside. Still, the team kept their guard up, as they were always supposed to. Squarepants guided them to Richards' office, and once they were in front of the door, he told them that he saw them on the camera.

Bulldozer tried the door, but it was locked. The team immediately took up positions for breaching and turned their flashlights on. Cougar kicked the door in, and this time, it was Survivor who ran inside first. The office was small, and he had a clear view of the entire room, but there could still be some corners where danger lurked. Sure enough, he immediately saw a figure crouching behind the desk on the other side of the office, even in the dark. Years of training for these exact kind of situations helped his eye coordination, especially seeing things that would stick out in ordinary rooms.

"Hands up!" he shouted at the person, keeping the red dot pointed at him. "Lemme see your hands now!"

"Don't shoot! Fuck!" a timid voice came from behind the desk.

The figure shot up with hands high in the air. The flashlights of the unit momentarily blinded the young security guard who stood before them. Survivor noticed that he had a red-soaked bandage wrapped around his forearm.

"Hey, I'm not one of those things, okay?! I work for The Company!" the guard pleaded.

He started lowering his hands, and immediately the room was filled with the bellowing of the Intervention Unit members ordering him to keep his hands up. The Company dealt with all sorts of crazy shit, and just because a person identified himself as a guard and even looked like one, didn't mean he wasn't a threat.

"What's the passcode?" Bulldozer asked him.

"Screaming weasel," the guard recited immediately.

The guards used daily passcodes that were issued by HQ. Each outpost had a different code, and the Intervention Unit was always told what the passcode was, so they could make sure that everything was okay. Ever since that Skinwalker incident where one unit member got killed the moment they lowered their guard, The Company had changed its policies.

"Alright, he's good," Bulldozer said, lowering his gun.

The rest of the members did the same, but the guard kept his hands up.

"Put your hands down," Bulldozer commanded.

The guard did so and sighed in relief.

"Oh, shit. Am I glad to see you, guys," the guard said.

"Report," Bulldozer coldly said.

"Armed Security Guard Lopez, sir. I was stationed in the guardhouse at the entrance." The guard suddenly became more formal. "When I heard on the radio that we had a code red level three, and then the screams, I went outside the guardhouse to see what was going on."

"You weren't supposed to leave your post," Bulldozer interjected.

"I didn't leave my post, bro."

"I'm not your fucking bro. What happened here?"

"I exited the guardhouse and stayed there for a few minutes. I tried contacting the other guard at the Genetics Center, but he didn't respond. And then, this... this fucking thing came out of nowhere. I shot it, but nothing happened. I ran inside the guardhouse, but it followed me there. I somehow managed to duck under it and started running, and I don't even know how I got out alive. It cut my arm somehow, and I ran to the science building for some cover."

"Where's your radio?"

"Dropped it somewhere in the building."

"And your gun?"

"Dropped it when that thing slashed me."

Survivor understood the guard's reaction and didn't expect him to be as brave and versatile as the Intervention Unit. These were regular Armed Security Guards, who only had the basic training in using a handgun and following the rules based on the outpost. If anything went wrong, it was their job to call the Intervention Unit to take care of the dirty work; the guys who were truly trained for these situations.

"You said the other guard was in the Genetics Center?" Bulldozer asked.

"Yeah. But I doubt he's still alive. Did you see those monsters?"

"What about Professor Richards?"

"Yeah, he was last seen inside the Genetics Center. That's where they conducted their research. That's where this whole fucking thing started."

"It's not safe here. But you can't go outside right now, either. Stay here until the Fat Guys arrive. Got it?"

"Yeah, I got it. Trust me, bro, I have no intentions of going anywhere until it's clear."

"I'm not your fucking bro. You're the one who spoke over the radio earlier, right?"

The guard nodded.

"You said, 'Kill the children'. What did you mean by that?" Bulldozer asked.

"Right. About tha-"

The sound of glass shattering pierced the air. A hand clawed its way through the broken window behind the guard and grabbed him by the arm. The guard screamed, then wriggled his way out of the bony, child-like hand that held him and scrambled behind the unit, and immediately, gunshots filled the air, along with the smell of gunpowder. The tip of a small, bald head popped up at the bottom of the windowsill, but Survivor's precise shot knocked it back out of sight. Whatever the fuck that thing was, it wasn't friendly. A scream pierced the air, followed by the familiar patter of heavy footsteps that reverberated through the building. The unit members turned around to face the door, just in time for the footsteps to reach them.

What Survivor stared at made him feel, for the first time tonight, palpable fear.

Chapter 10
91 days until disaster

It's inside me.

The words repeatedly returned to Victor in the quiet moments, like a moth drawn to a lamp. He told himself that the words bore no significance and that Marie was simply distressed. He couldn't help but wonder how Richards hadn't noticed it. Or maybe he did and chose to ignore it – because it wasn't important? Victor didn't tell Richards what Marie told him. It was between the two of them, and he felt that telling Richards would be a breach of trust.

What Victor decided to do instead, however, was to keep a closer eye on Marie. He went over to the security room. It was the afternoon, and upon entering, Victor saw Brian sitting in front of the monitor with his arms crossed. The student glanced in his direction and greeted him, swiveling his chair to face Victor.

"Brian, how's everything going today?" Victor asked.

"Good. Nothing special to report for now," Brian shrugged.

"Good, good. Keep at it. Would you mind if I take a look at the logbook?"

"You're the professor, Professor," Brian turned to the right and grabbed the notebook before handing it to Victor.

Victor thanked him and started from the first page. Tara's shift was first. A detailed summary of the patients' activities, but nothing suspicious. He flipped through the pages at the other recaps. No one was as detailed as Tara – her report took up the whole page and the footers, while the others wrote barely three sentences. As he flipped through, he saw one particular thing written in Douglas' shift.

Douglas noted that patient five seemed restless throughout the day. She spent a lot of her time in the bathroom, even up to one hour during his shift. Then in Tara's nightshift, patient five stirred a lot in her sleep. She got up to go to the bathroom three times and stayed there for at least twenty minutes each time. When she returned, she kept touching and grabbing at her stomach. Tara tried talking to her, according to her report, but Marie confirmed she was okay.

There was nothing in Uriel's morning shifts, but then in Brian's shift, he noted the same thing as Tara – patient five was restless. Something was definitely wrong with her, no matter what the professor said. Victor would need to talk to her. But he couldn't enter her room, since he had no keycard. He had to find another way to speak to her, see what she had to say about whatever bothered her.

***

Marie splashed some water on her face. She looked in the mirror above the sink, staring at her troubled reflection. She was looking at a different person now, compared to when she first arrived at this facility. Her hair was messy and unkempt, jutting in various directions. As if she slept in a haystack, her mother always used to say.

The creases on her forehead were more visible now than before, and the heavy bags under her eyes clearly blue. She couldn't be sure, but she also thought that she had lost some weight. When she first put her pajamas on upon arrival, they had fit perfectly. Now they were slightly baggier. Was all of it simply her imagination? Was she stressing too much?

She wanted to quit the Fertility Project, but she couldn't. There was too much at stake here. She would be getting a new baby; that's all that mattered. She just had to tough out these five months. A kick in her gut sent her bending over with a gasp. She instinctively put her hand on her stomach, but this time felt something different. Not spasms or pulsating, but rather movement. Marie yanked her shirt up and stared at her stomach. She saw nothing on her smooth stomach, but upon putting one hand below the bellybutton, she felt it again—steady movement in a two-inch area, like waves going from left to right, over and over.

Marie began hyperventilating. She pressed her palm against her stomach where the movement was, hoping that the pressure would make it stop. She only felt it harder against her hand now, and panicked even more.

"Stop it! Stop it! Stop it!" she screamed as she smacked her belly button with the palm of her hand.

As if hearing her words, the movement stopped, just like that. Marie looked up at her reflection in the mirror again, panting. She saw her own eyes, as wide as saucers in palpable fear. As she pressed her hand against the stomach again, she felt no movement under the skin. She sucked in her stomach as much as she could, so that she saw her ribcage against her skin in the mirror. She ran her hand down the lower part of her stomach once more. When she felt nothing, she pressed with the tips of her fingers until she began feeling pain.

Pain, but no movement. She was okay.

***

Professor Richards was extremely busy over the past few days, always buzzing around and attending to matters. He barely had time to speak to Victor, even in between the examinations. Victor was tempted to talk to him about Marie, tell him what she said, but he suddenly found himself conflicted. He didn't realize why until then, but the more he thought about it, the more it made sense.

He didn't trust Richards anymore.

The paranoid feeling of the professor hiding something from Victor only exacerbated since the other two patients had left. They left in such secretive and mysterious circumstances. Victor thought about asking the professor to see the patients' files, but for some reason, he thought that it might offend Richards, give him the idea that he suspected something. He didn't want to risk falling out of the professor's grace in case he happened to be wrong.

Afternoon, after the midday examination, Victor strode down to the entrance of the building where the guard was. Instead of the scary-looking foreign guy, an average-looking uniformed man around Victor's age was standing at the front. When he saw Victor approaching the entrance, he turned to face him with a courteous smile – but also blocked his path.

"Hello, sir. I assume you're Professor Lukanski?" the guard asked.

"That's right. But you can call me Victor."

Victor outstretched a hand to shake, and the guard shook it, but didn't introduce himself. Maybe they had a no-real-names policy in their company. Victor noticed that there were no logos of the company anywhere on the guard's uniform. Usually, there'd be something either on the badge or on the shoulder, but this uniform was plain black, with the letters *SECURITY* printed on the back.

"So, how can I help you, Victor?" the guard asked.

He still wasn't moving from the spot. Victor suddenly felt like a prisoner. Were the guards ill-informed, or did Richards really order them not to let him out?

"I actually wanted to ask you for a favor," the assistant professor said.

"Sure, name it."

"When is your next shift here?"

"Tomorrow."

"Can I ask you to go to a store closest to your place and look for some erythritol?"

The guard frowned in confusion. Seeing this, Victor laughed it off and said.

"Erythritol. It's a substitute for sugar. One of the patients here can't really have sugar, and she wanted to bake something for herself."

The guard scratched his chin quizzically before nodding and saying.

"Okay. No problem. I can do that. Just... how much does that cost?"

"I'll give you the money, no problem."

Victor swung the lab coat back and reached into the pocket of his jeans. He pulled out his wallet (he was paranoid about leaving it back in his quarters) and whipped out a twenty, which he promptly handed to the guard.

"You can keep the change. For your troubles."

The guard scrutinized the twenty-dollar bill as if to determine if it was forged or not. A moment later, he raised the bill before folding it and putting it in the pocket on the back of his jeans.

"Okay, you got it. I'll be here tomorrow after three."

"Thank you. I really appreciate it," Victor outstretched his hand again, and they shook hands in a friendly manner.

As Victor turned back towards the building, he suddenly remembered something. He shot around towards the guard, who was already facing away from the building.

"Hey, I wanna ask you something," Victor said.

The guard didn't register that Victor was talking to him until a moment later. He spun around with raised eyebrows and thumbs tucked under his belt.

"I have a question about the two patients who left the building a few nights ago."

The guard cocked his head slightly, portraying visible confusion. As soon as Victor saw that, the only thought that came to his mind was, *'Oh, this is bad.'*

"Two of the five women left the building. You know about that, right?"

The guard shook his head slowly, not taking his eyes off Victor.

"Nobody left the building except the students who come and go," he said.

"Well, this was during the night. It probably happened during the other guard's shift, right?"

"Not that he told me. And we report anything out of the ordinary to each other."

Victor opened his mouth but found himself not knowing what to say. He looked to the right, nowhere in particular, before averting his gaze back at the guard.

"But it's possible that your coworker just didn't tell you anything, right?"

"Sure, it is. If he wants to get fired. As I said, we have to report everything and anything that isn't an everyday occurrence. Company policy due to... well, some strange clients we deal with."

Victor was baffled. The guard obviously didn't know anything about the patients leaving, which left only two options – either his partner didn't tell him about it, or Richards lied to Victor.

Victor hoped to god that it was the first one.

***

The rest of the day passed in a breeze. They had the evening examination – and Victor kept sneaking glances at Marie the entire time. He saw her looking towards him, too, but since Richards was examining her, she seemed careful about it. What the hell was she hiding from Richards? Amanda seemed to notice Victor's absent-mindedness, but he shrugged it off as being tired from too much work during the day. She hopefully bought it.

While Victor was having his dinner of university-made steak and fries in his dorm room, a knock resounded at his door. He stuffed two extra fries in his mouth and wiped the oil onto his jeans, not even caring about making them dirty. He had the privilege of free laundry services while he was in the experiment. He quickly chewed his food, swallowing it before swinging his door open. Professor Richards stood there, still wearing his lab coat, his hands tucked in his navy suit vest.

"Victor, I apologize for interrupting your dinner," he said.

"Not a problem, Professor. Is everything okay?"

"Yes, and no. We need to discuss the results so far, the agenda for the next two weeks, and see if there are any potential... issues we've run into so far."

He emphasized the word 'issue' in a way that sounded serious. It made Victor suddenly lose his appetite, despite starving beforehand.

"Once you finish your dinner, please meet me in my office." Richards flashed him a pearly smile.

"I'll come with you right away, professor, because this sounds urgent."

He was hoping that the professor would correct his final statement, which he did almost immediately.

"No, no. Nothing serious, my boy. But we do need to cover everything. This shouldn't take longer than ten minutes, I assure you."

***

Richards poured the same clay-colored drink into his glass. Victor noticed that he had a mini fridge right next to the drinks cabinet, plugged into the wall. He opened the fridge and pulled out the ice compartment. He took out a tray of ice, the vapor billowing up in the air momentarily before dispersing. Victor couldn't help but notice how the fridge was empty and that Richards only used it for the ice.

The professor raised the ice tray above the glass, which rested atop the fridge, and turned it upside down. He pressed the silicone mold, which caused the ice cube to drop with a crack and clink into the glass. He dropped two more cubes into it before throwing the tray into the ice compartment and promptly closing it, along with the fridge. The entire time, Victor sat on the couch in the corner of the room, impatiently waiting for Richards to talk about whatever serious matters he had in mind. The professor took a sip of his drink and let out an 'ahh' sound before turning and making his way towards Victor.

"So, Victor," he said, as he sat on the couch and placed his glass on the table. "How are you getting used to this lifestyle?"

"It's fine so far, Professor," Victor said reticently. "It's obviously a little difficult being away from my family, but I'm enjoying this work. I feel like we're actually contributing to something big."

"And we are. This is big. No, huge. We are creating new laws of reproductive medicine as we speak! In a matter of days, we will find out if the inseminating procedure was successful in any of the subjects. If we can get even just *one* to be successful, Victor..." he leaned forward and patted Victor on the knee.

"But we'll try to help all three of them, right? I mean, that's why they joined in the first place."

Richards pulled back and nodded with his eyes closed.

"Of course. We will do our best to get all three of them pregnant. But you have to remember that our primary goal here is to create a groundbreaking discovery that can help future generations of women. Right now, this is still just in the experimental phase, but imagine where it will be in ten or twenty or fifty years if we manage to convince the world of its value! They could continue perfecting it long after you and I are gone, but our names will always be revered as the fathers of reproductive science who solved infertility."

It sounded appealing. No, much more than appealing. Victor imagined a university professor teaching reproductive medicine some fifty years from today and casually telling the students to flip onto a page where Victor's name along with his picture would be.

The fertility problem was first solved by Victor Lukanski and Howard Richards...

"And, if the procedure isn't successful, we simply try again in a week, correct?" he asked.

"Yes. That's why we are here. The odds of succeeding are already high, but a few tries are required sometimes," Richards nodded.

Victor shifted in his seat before running a hand through his hair.

"Now, you wanted to go through some 'issues' that you mentioned earlier, Professor?"

Richards' facial expression turned grievous. He reached for his drink and took another sip, the already half-melted ice clinking against the glass walls, along with the swaying liquid. He placed the glass back on the table with a loud thud, now with only a thin line of the dark liquid remaining below the ice.

"We need to talk about subject five," he said.

Victor nodded, but said nothing. He wanted to remain as neutral as possible without revealing what Marie had whispered to him during the checkup. Richards stood up and began pacing around the room, facing away from Victor.

"You've noticed her mental state as of late, I assume?" he asked.

"I have seen that she looks somewhat unwell, yes," Victor prudently agreed.

"I'm afraid that this entire experiment is not impacting her well. Of all the patients, she seems to be handling it the worst. Now, she is probably stressed a lot due to being away from home, but I won't deny that the formula we injected her with may or may not have some detrimental consequences, as well."

"Professor, those are some serious consequences. I thought you said that the procedure shouldn't impact the patients all that much."

"It shouldn't. It shouldn't," Richards shrugged as he faced Victor. "In some rare cases, this has been observed in phase one, but... I'm afraid that these circumstances... being locked up in a room most of the day, and the minor side effects of the formula... as a combination, may have triggered something in the subject. She's even been experiencing certain hallucinations, confusion, etcetera. Now, this is all still within the borders of normal, so there's no reason to panic."

Victor leaned back, staring at the glass on the table.

"So, what do you propose?" he asked.

"I'm not proposing anything... yet," Richards made his way back to the couch and sat down. "We can continue monitoring her and see how she reacts further in the experiment. If her health deteriorates past the allowed threshold, we will have to terminate her NDA. If her health improves, however…"

Victor listened with undivided attentiveness, nodding the entire time. This conversation was somewhat shocking to him. Richards showed that he cared for the wellbeing of patient five, and that put the assistant professor's mind at ease. This whole time, he kept the thought at the back of his mind that Richards would push Marie to the boundaries of her mental capabilities, but that was silly, of course, now that he thought more about it. He was Professor Howard Richards, the most renowned embryologist in the country. He wouldn't sacrifice an innocent woman for the sake of an experiment.

And the two women that left, but no one saw? It was probably just miscommunication between the guards. Victor suddenly felt overwhelmingly relieved.

"I've also told the students to specifically pay more attention to subject five, in case they notice anything alarming," Richards said.

"It's probably a good idea, professor. What do you think is the worst that can happen to her?"

Richards shook his head.

"Nothing severe, as long as we monitor it. Sleep deprivation, anxiety, and paranoia are common in some cases, but even if we allowed the symptoms to slip further, there would be no lasting effects unless we allowed them to go on for months. As I said, this is all still normal and has been observed before. A famous young man who was sleep-deprived for ten days recovered with no long-lasting side effects. Another patient subjected to visual and auditory hallucinations also recovered and continued to live a normal life. And those people were subjected to *extreme* exposure under those circumstances. Subject five is nowhere close to that spectrum."

"Understood, professor. When will we know if the patient has reached her limit? I mean, I suppose we need to let her go long before that, right?"

"We'll know it when we see it. We're conducting careful checkups every day, three times a day, so there's no way it will slip past us. I mean, you can imagine the repercussions such an incident could have on both the university and us. I'm not willing to risk our careers and reputation for the sake of testing human boundaries."

Victor grinned. The immense relief washed over him like a cold shower after a hot day. He let out a light peal of laughter before saying.

"I'm relieved to hear you say that, professor. Honestly, I was worried that we might be pushing the patient too hard. If she gets pregnant, we have to ensure that she's as comfortable as she can be."

"Absolutely. I have already spoken to her about what she'd like added to her room. She apparently likes listening to podcasts, so I've arranged to have over one thousand hours of her favorite podcasts uploaded to a device, so she can listen to them while she's in the room. I will also upload some relaxing nature sounds to soothe her and give her a sense of normalcy."

"That's great, professor. I'm sure it will make her feel better."

"I sure hope so. And if it doesn't, we still have one last option, which is to call her husband and have him come for a visit."

Victor frowned.

"Wouldn't that aggravate the situation further, professor?" he asked.

"Not necessarily. If a visit from the loved ones doesn't help alleviate the stress, then the patient will have to be released from the project anyway. Again, this is the final solution we will resort to in case subject five doesn't get better."

Victor nodded.

"Anything else we need to discuss, professor?"

"No. That is all for tonight, Victor. Get some rest, since we have a lot of work to do tomorrow."

Chapter 11
82 days until disaster

It was 2 am, and Tara's eyelids were already getting heavy. She had taken a nap prior to coming to work, but her body still refused to adapt to being awake at night. Cameras two and four were off, displaying black screens, while cameras one, three, and five showed the patients sleeping. Patient five, Marie, was tossing and turning. She never stayed in one position longer than ten minutes, and Tara made sure to pay special attention to her.

The night rolled by slowly, but Tara refused to pass her time with something else. She brought her cellphone and had her own internet, but she didn't give it more attention than to answer social media messages or comments. She thought about not bringing her phone to the shift to avoid the temptation of scrolling through Instagram and Tiktok but ultimately decided against it. So far, she had managed to avoid falling into the trap of endless social media scrolling.

Her first night shift in the Fertility Project was effortless, and she had even felt good enough to attend some morning classes after, but now it was starting to get to her – accumulated exhaustion, she was sure of it. She whipped out her phone and opened Youtube. She looked through her notifications for any recent updates from her list of subscribed talk show hosts. There were a bunch, since she hadn't had the time to catch up, so now she could listen to some while she worked.

Tara looked up at the monitor and realized that patient five was no longer in her bed. The bedsheets were swung messily over the side, the bed empty, with the woman nowhere in sight. Tara placed her phone on the desk and straightened her back. She darted her eyes around the camera but found the room to be empty. She double-clicked CAM 5 to enter full-screen mode, but still nothing was visible. She must have been in the bathroom, nothing alarming, but Tara would need to pay careful attention to how long Marie would be in there.

She had just double-clicked to exit full-screen mode again when she saw Marie stumbling out of the bathroom. She was holding both hands on her stomach and was slightly hunched over, but from what Tara could see, Marie's facial expression was contorted into a painful grimace. She made her way to the kitchen on what looked like wobbly legs, propping herself on the counter with one palm. Tara felt a cold sweat enveloping her. An inexplicable shiver ran down her spine as she stared at CAM 5.

She clicked the audio button and leaned closer to the microphone. As she pressed the button on it and spoke up, she heard herself stammering, "M-Marie? A-Are you okay?"

Marie gave no indication that she heard her. Tara heard labored breathing coming from Marie. There was mumbling, erratic and incoherent, as

Marie held her stomach with one hand and held the other on the counter.

"Marie? Marie, do you feel unwell? Should I call the professors?"

Marie screamed in pain and bent down further before continuing to breathe shallow, labored breaths. She looked left and then right, and her eyes fell on something. She slid the hand that was on the counter forward, towards the wooden kitchen knife holder.

"Marie, what are you doing?" Tara cried out, now in a full-blown panic.

Marie's fingertips grasped the knife handle. The knife slid out of her grasp at first, but then she managed to grip it firmly and draw it out of the holder. She straightened her back and used the hand on her stomach to pull her shirt up. She grasped the knife handle so that the blade was pointed at herself. Her chest heaved violently up and down in whimpers.

"Marie! Stop!" Tara screamed, tears filling her eyes.

Marie plunged the blade into her stomach.

Tara screamed.

***

Marie couldn't sleep again. She had tried all sorts of meditation methods, mind-blanking methods, etcetera, but none of them seemed to help her fall asleep. The stomachache came in bouts, sometimes potent enough to immobilize her entirely for a whole minute, other times as slight pangs. She spent a lot of time in the bathroom, checking her stomach for any irregularities. She thought she noticed stretch marks appearing below her belly button, but for all she knew, it could have been from her scratching, clawing, and pressing.

The pain progressively became stronger. As she lay in her bed, curled in a fetal position, she felt something churning inside her stomach. She pressed her palm against it, and then she felt it – movement. The same kind of movement that she'd felt in the past few days, only this time, it was much stronger, enough not to be confused with a mind trick. Marie swung the bedsheets off her and pulled her shirt up.

There it was – a small, sharp bulge at the bottom of her stomach, sticking outward. The bulge protruded, causing Marie's abdominal skin to stretch, sending searing pain throughout her stomach. Marie screamed and pressed her hand against her belly. She felt something hard and lumpy being pushed back into her stomach.

What the hell is happening to me?!

She stood up from the bed, bracing herself against the pain, and felt the burning in her stomach getting stronger. It was so intense that she felt the strength in her legs waning. She stumbled towards the bathroom, gasping and trying not to breathe too deeply, as each breath sent daggers into her stomach. By the time she made it to the bathroom, she was drenched in sweat from the pain. She stopped in front of the mirror and raised her shirt. The bulge was still there, prominent and intermittently appearing and disappearing, in and out, like a cancerous lump that came to life.

Marie let out a scream, this time more in terror than in pain. She couldn't take it any longer. She had to call the professor and get him to remove this thing from her body. She walked out of the bathroom and felt another sharp pang of pain. She keeled over, barely stopping herself from falling. As if on stilted legs, she made her way towards the kitchen, where she would have at least some support to help hold herself up.

"He... help... Agh!" she tried calling out, but felt another sting of unimaginable pain.

She heard someone's voice coming from the speaker, but it was as if she heard it from a tunnel. Marie made it to the kitchen, just in time to place one hand on the counter and stop herself from falling. The voice from the speaker resounded over and over, but she couldn't respond. She couldn't even focus on what it was saying due to the sheer pain she felt.

As she held her hand against her stomach, she felt the protrusion jabbing at her fingers over and over, each jab sending wrenching pain throughout her belly. Marie scanned the counter and saw a wooden knife holder on her right-hand side. As if through a fog, she saw the outline of the knife handle. She tried moving her hand towards it, but it proved to be too painful for her. She groaned and moaned, slowly sliding her hand down the counter towards the knife holder. It was at her fingertips now.

She almost managed to grasp it, but it slipped past her fingers. The pain was so intense now, like someone was cooking her stomach from the inside. With her final atom of strength, Marie reached forward. She felt her fingers wrapping around the handle of the knife, and she feverishly grasped it.

With extreme effort, she pulled the knife out of the wooden holder. It came loose easily, and all of a sudden, the pain in her stomach subsided momentarily. Marie straightened her back, expecting to feel more stabs and jabs, but none came. She pointed the knife at herself and looked down at her stomach. Even through the pajamas, she could see the protrusion in her belly. She pulled her shirt up and stared at the abomination that swirled and twisted inside her.

Before she could give herself the time to chicken out, she plunged the knife into her stomach. She felt no pain as she did so. She saw red liquid oozing out of her belly and sliding down her pajamas, and dripping on the floor, like a fountain. Marie heard a scream, but it wasn't her own. Despite the stab, the protrusions kept appearing. She slid the knife to make a larger slit and then dropped it. It clattered loudly to the floor, covered in fresh blood.

Marie dug her fingers into the stab wound, searching for what was moving inside her. She felt how warm her fingers were against the blood oozing out, and something wiggling, but she couldn't grab it since it was all slippery inside her. Marie dug her fingers deeper, all the way to the knuckles, but the slithering mass inside her slipped deeper. She stuck her hand inside, all the way to the wrist, more and more blood spurting out like a fountain. She knew she didn't have much time left before she lost consciousness or died from blood loss.

She felt something on the tips of her fingers. It was there, just a little... there! She managed to pinch it between her forefinger and thumb, a soft, squishy, wet, and warm mass. Marie wiggled her hand inside deeper to grip the mass more firmly, and once she had a strong grasp, she yanked her hand out, triumphantly staring at the successful extraction.

But she wasn't staring at the mass that wiggled inside her. She was staring at her intestines.

Another scream ensued, but this time, it was her own.

**

Leah made a 'goo' sound as she swung her tiny arm at the cellphone. Jennie reprimanded her (gently) while Victor laughed. As he stared at the live video of his wife and daughter, he began to realize how much he missed them. They seemed to be doing well without him so far though, and as much as that pained him, it also gave him some solace. Victor couldn't sleep prior to the call and was browsing social media when he saw Jennifer online on messenger. Although they talked a few hours earlier when Leah was asleep, she was now awake, and Jennifer had trouble getting her to fall back asleep.

"How's the experiment going, babe?" she asked.

"Good for now," Victor was surprised at how smoothly he was able to lie to her. "We have one problematic patient, but nothing serious."

"Oh. Well, just don't work too hard over there, yeah?"

She didn't seem to register the problematic patient part because Leah was restless, and Jennifer focused on rocking her to calm down. The cute thing, Victor thought, was the fact that Leah seemed to recognize her dad on the video chat. One moment, her attention was diverted everywhere around the place, and then Jennifer pointed to the screen and said, 'Look, it's Daddy!', and Leah's eyes widened in amazement and confusion. It filled Victor's heart with an immensely warm feeling.

"How are things at home?" he asked.

"Never quiet. I think Leah can sense that you won't be coming home soon, and she's a little agitated," Jennifer said, as she continued rocking Leah.

The baby produced various sounds of comfort, staring at her mother's face.

"Are you getting enough sleep?" Victor asked.

"Of course not. But I sneak in some power naps here and there," Jennie said.

"Well, as soon as I'm back, I'll take over for you. We'll be famous and rich, and we'll finally be able to take it easy and spend more time together."

"I hope so. I don't want you being away for too long if you don't have to. And I don't want Leah having to move around a lot when she gets a little older. That can be tough on a kid."

Victor nodded. He knew Jennifer was right. Her parents moved a lot when she was a kid due to her dad's business, and she never had a chance to make friends or adapt to the environment she was in. Victor wouldn't want Leah to go through the same thing, no matter what his work required from him.

"Hey, we can always do that one thing we always talked about," he said.

"You mean move out to the countryside?" Jennie asked.

"I mean, if you're still up for it."

"Of course I am. And I'm sure Leah would love it there, too. Isn't that right, cupcake?" Jennie asked that last sentence in a baby tone.

Leah's energy suddenly seemed to drop drastically. Her eyes were less wide than usual and she was no longer flailing her arms around or looking anywhere in a focused manner.

"Guess she's getting sleepy," Victor grinned.

"About time. You got exhausted from today's playing, huh?" Jennifer spoke in a baby tone again, before giving Leah a kiss on the head.

Victor shifted in bed and leaned on his elbow. He said, "Anyway, we'll figure something out on the way. Right now, I need to focus on the experiment, but as soon as it's done, if it's successful, things may change for the better. Oh, and the good thing is that the professor said if we succeed earlier, we can-"

An blood-curdling scream pierced the air, long and loud. It wasn't an innocent scream, like playfully getting pranked or seeing a mouse. No, this scream carried the unmistakable tune of terror with it. Victor jerked his head to the door, abruptly stopping mid-sentence.

"Victor? What was that?" Jennifer asked.

Victor heard the loud patter of footsteps resounding in the hallway and a door opening.

"Professors! Come quick!" Tara screeched in the hallway.

A muffled, erratic voice came from Professor Richards, followed by a distinct 'Oh my god'. Victor looked at his phone's screen and saw Jennifer's confused and somewhat terrified face. He stood up from the bed and said.

"Jennie, I have to go. I'll call you tomorrow, okay?"

"Victor wai-"

Victor pressed the end call button. A second later, he heard loud banging on his door, followed by Richards' panicked voice.

"Victor! Victor, wake up!"

Victor rushed to the door and swung it open. Richards stood in front of the door, his shoulders tense and his knees slightly bent, as if ready to run. He had his lab coat over his t-shirt and underneath, sweatpants and slippers, a very unusual way for the professor to dress.

"Victor, put on your lab coat, we have an emergency!" he recited quickly, in one breath.

"What's going on, professor?"

"Hurry!" Richards had already made his way down the hall, headed toward the staircase.

Victor ran to the coat hanger and grabbed his lab coat. He slipped his arms into it, pushed a pair of slippers smoothly onto his feet, and then rushed out of the room, not even bothering to close the door. He was only wearing pajama bottoms and a t-shirt, and didn't bother putting anything else on under the lab coat.

He raced to the stairs where he saw Richards hopping up as fast as his age allowed him to. They climbed up on the second floor, and Richards pulled out his keycard.

"Professor, what's going on?!" Victor demanded more sternly this time.

"Subject five... something's wrong with her!"

"What?!"

Richards didn't respond. He loped to room five and swiped the card across the reader. He did it too quickly, and the door didn't unlock. He did it again, and this time, the reader beeped. The lock clicked, and Richards put the card in his lab coat pocket before barging inside room five. Victor stepped inside the room and then froze in his steps at the sight before him.

Blood. Everywhere.

There was blood on the kitchen counter and floor, on the walls, on the couch, the bed, the TV... A large puddle of blood covered the kitchen floor, with a trail leading towards the entrance. Just four feet away from Victor, Marie was laying on her back, on the floor. She had her head up and was holding one arm outstretched towards Victor. The other hand was on her stomach – and her intestines were protruding between her fingers and out of a horizontal slit. Her entire lower part of the pajamas was drenched in blood, along with her arms, all the way to the elbows.

"Help... me..." she weakly uttered before her head hit the floor and her arm limply fell next to her.

"Oh, my god!" Victor barely managed to utter through the sudden suffocation he was feeling.

He felt like he was watching an incredibly realistic gory movie. This couldn't be happening. No way. Richards was already running up to Marie and knelt next to her. He wasted no time using both his hands to press against the stomach. He turned his head to Victor and shouted something, but Victor didn't register it.

"Victor!" Richards' voice snapped him back to attention. "Get a towel! Now!"

Suddenly, Victor's fight or flight instincts kicked in, and he immediately rushed into the bathroom. He slipped and almost whacked his head on the edge of the kitchen counter on the way, but somehow managed to maintain his balance. He grabbed a white towel from the pile next to the sink and sprinted back out.

The professor's hands were already covered in blood up to the wrists, along with the sleeves of his lab coat. Victor rushed over to the professor, and Richards grabbed the towel with one hand, pressing it against Marie's wound. Marie's eyes were fluttering at an incredible speed, as if she were fighting not to lose consciousness.

"Victor, there's a stretcher in the examination room. Bring it here. Go!" Richards commanded vigorously.

Victor didn't argue. He shot up, sprinted out of the room, across the hall and into the examination room. He practically burst inside with his shoulder, causing the door to slam against the wall. In the corner next to one of the beds was a stretcher with wheels. He pushed it back to room five, hitting it against the doorframes along the way. Once he managed to get the stretcher inside, Richards said, "We need to put her on the stretcher and get her downstairs! The ambulance will be here any minute now!"

Victor nodded and muttered a feeble 'Okay',

"Grab her legs!" the professor said as he left the now red-soaked towel on Marie's belly and got behind her head.

Her eyes were closed, indicating that she was (hopefully) unconscious. Victor grabbed Marie by the ankles, while Richards took her under her arms. The professor counted to three, and they lifted her limp body with groans and slumped it onto the stretcher.

"Good. Now hold the towel on her belly while we get her down!" Richards commanded.

Victor pressed the soaked towel, but not too firmly, as he was afraid he might do more damage to the intestines. Richards began pushing the stretcher. They made it effortlessly through the hall, but going down the stairs was the problem. They had to slow down and hold Marie tightly, so she didn't fall off. One of her arms dangled limply off the side of the stretcher, but they managed to get her to the first floor in one piece.

Tara stood in the hall near the entrance, with tears streaking her face. One of the guards was there, too, with a grievous expression. When he saw Richards and Victor approaching, he rushed to assist them. Sirens resounded in the distance and they progressively got closer until they filled the air with ear-piercing intensity.

Bright red and blue lights filled the entire front area and illuminated the figures pushing the stretcher intermittently with the rays of the ambulance vehicle. Two paramedics stepped out, and Victor took it as a sign that his part here was done. The guard stayed behind as well, while the professor continued pushing the stretcher with the paramedics to the back of the vehicle.

Within seconds, the stretcher with Marie was inside, along with Richards and the paramedic, while the other paramedic jumped behind the wheel and drove off with the sirens still blaring. Victor wiped his sweaty forehead with the trembling hand and felt something sticky. He moved the hand away and saw blood up to his sleeves.

His hands began shaking even more, and now that the ambulance had driven off, he felt like he was standing on stilted legs. He wanted to puke, but instead felt just acidic bile climbing into his throat. He swallowed with a gag and turned towards the building. He saw Tara standing in front of him, tear-stricken and shaken to the core. In that instant, he forgot all about his own trauma.

"Tara, it's okay, Tara," he said. "I'll call you an Uber. You can go home tonight, alright?"

Tara didn't respond.

"What the fuck happened in there?" the guard asked after a long moment of unnerving silence.

"Wish I could tell you," Victor retorted.

He wiped his hands on his lab coat to get at least the wet blood off his hands. The dried parts wouldn't come off. He pulled out his cellphone and saw a bunch of messages and missed calls from Jennie. He clicked on the text and began typing 'Everything is okay, don't worry', but since he tried typing it too quickly, the message came out with a bunch of typos, and he had to delete and retype it multiple times. He then got an Uber to come to the university. The app said the driver would be in front of the university in fifteen minutes.

"Tara, let's go inside until your Uber arrives, okay?"

Tara didn't nod, but she followed Victor's instructions without complaints, albeit lethargically. On the way back into the building, Victor heard her sniffling and gasping from sobs. They entered the break room that the staff used for coffee and meal breaks, and he pulled out a chair for Tara to sit down. He raised a hand to pat her on the shoulder before realizing his hand was bloody.

"Hold on, I'll be right back," he said.

He went to the bathroom to wash up. There was a bloody smear on his forehead, and he had to scrub hard to get all the blood off his face and hands. He took the bloodstained lab coat to the laundry room, grateful that he only wore a t-shirt under it. He then grabbed his wallet from his room and returned to the break room, where he found Tara still sitting catatonically. He went over to the vending machine and inserted a quarter. He placed a cup in the dispenser and pressed the 'hot chocolate' button. The machine beeped, and within seconds, the sound of the cup being filled with the warm, aromatic liquid filled the air.

It was a shitty, watered-down version of hot chocolate, but right now, Tara needed it. Victor grabbed the paper cup from the dispenser, careful not to burn himself, and took it over to the table where Tara sat. She still had a blank, unfocused stare in her eye.

"Here," Victor carefully slid the cup closer to her, watching the steam rising from the warm drink.

Tara bemusedly glanced at it before cupping it with her hands. Victor pulled out a chair next to her and took a seat. He suddenly felt tired – really tired. He felt a buzz in his phone, and upon pulling it out, he saw that it was a message from Jennie.

Okay, be careful, babe, the message said.

Victor didn't respond. He put his phone on the table in case he got a message from Richards. Had they already made it to the hospital? The closest hospital was fifteen minutes away, but Victor reckoned the ambulance would arrive much faster.

"This was... completely unexpected, huh?" Victor asked and immediately regretted doing so.

It was a dumb question, and he knew it, and Tara probably knew it, but he was just trying to make some small talk, get her mind off things. Tara kept quiet before shaking her head.

"She... she just... stabbed herself," she said through newly formed tears.

"Don't think about it. You did good calling Professor Richards and me right away. If you hadn't done so, Marie would have been dead now."

"What if... what if she's already... dead?"

"I'm not gonna lie. She may or may not be dead. But if you hadn't reacted the way you did, she would have been dead before the ambulance arrived."

Tara nodded reticently.

"Your Uber is almost here. Here, go home and get some sleep," Victor said as he pulled the wallet out of his pants.

He gave Tara the money for Uber and said goodbye to her. As for him, he returned to the security room. As much as he dreaded it, he had to continue monitoring patients one and three. He had to be there in case they got into trouble, too. The problem was, he had no keycard for the rooms. Professor Richards made a spare key and offered it to Victor, but Victor refused, stating that he may misplace it due to his lack of organization. He knew that the key still lay somewhere in Richards' office, but he didn't know where exactly.

I sure as hell hope Isabelle and Amanda don't do anything as crazy as Marie.

The first thing that held his eyes as soon as he arrived in the security room was the blood on CAM

5. The lights were on, and the red splotches were clearly visible, now dried on the floor – all but the big puddle near the kitchen. The women on cameras one and three were sound asleep in their beds. Victor was grateful for the soundproof rooms the professor provided. He wouldn't have the strength to comfort Isabelle and Amanda, as well as Tara.

He placed his cellphone on the desk and turned on the sound. He slumped down into the chair, and as he stared at the cameras, the adrenaline finally began to subside. Now his brain was starting to process the events – he saw clearly in his mind's eye the blood when he first entered the room, Marie lying on her back with her arm outstretched, her pleas for help, her guts hanging out of the hole in her stomach...

Victor rubbed his eyes. He was suddenly sleepy, but he knew that there was no way in hell he would be able to fall asleep. How could the professor let such a thing slip? He assured him that Marie was not at any risk. Did he lie in order to convince Victor not to meddle? Or was he simply not aware of how bad off Marie was?

Either way, the experiment would be canceled after this; Victor didn't see another way out of it. It was a shame, but better for the women. First, it was Marie, but who knew? Maybe tomorrow it would be Isabelle or Amanda. They looked okay for now and showed no signs of mental deterioration, but there was no doubt that these things could just sneak up on a person. There was another thing that worried Victor – the legal repercussions of Marie disemboweling herself.

The professor would face a ton of questions from the university, and most likely the police, too. But would Victor face the same treatment? He was a partner to Richards in the experiment, not a subordinate, so chances are he would be in trouble, too. He tried to push those concerns out of his head before they caused him to panic.

It was almost 4 am when Victor heard the entrance door opening and then slamming shut, followed by a tired pounding batter of footsteps. Victor tossed one final glance at the cameras to make sure Isabelle and Amanda were okay, grabbed his phone, and then raced down the hall and towards the stairs. Halfway down the staircase, he ran into Professor Richards' exhausted figure. He was still wearing his bloodstained lab coat.

"Ah, you're here," he said to Victor with a forced smile.

"Professor, how's Marie? Is she okay?"

Richards looked down for a moment before raising his head and nodding.

"She had to undergo surgery to have her intestines reinserted. She's stable for now and should recover without any consequences."

"Thank God," Victor breathed a sigh of relief, feeling like a ton of bricks just fell off his shoulders.

"How are the other two subjects?" Richards asked.

"They're sleeping. They aren't aware of anything that happened."

"Good, good," Richards nodded.

He turned around to go down the stairs, and Victor followed him. Now that the concern for Marie was no longer looming above his head, he had a different emotion that emerged – anger. Once they were on the first floor, Victor could no longer contain the sudden flood of aggression that enveloped him. How dare Richards risk the lives of the patients like that? How dare he not release the remaining patients immediately?

"Professor, we need to talk," Victor said, bursting at the seams.

Richards stopped to turn around long enough to glance at Victor before continuing down the hall towards his office.

"Of course. Let's talk in my office."

Victor forced a smile through gritted teeth. Richards opened the door of his office and allowed Victor to step inside first. Victor nodded and made his way in, before hearing the professor's voice behind him.

"Where's Tara?"

"I told her to go home earlier," Victor retorted.

As he faced Richards, he expected the professor to reprimand him, and he was just about ready to bite back. To his surprise (and disappointment), the professor nodded and said, "Good call. She must be traumatized beyond words."

He made his way past Victor towards the drinks cabinet, where he proceeded to pour himself a glass of his usual beverage – more in quantity this time.

"We should have seen this coming, Professor. You said that Marie wasn't at any risk," Victor demanded, trying his best not to shout, although he was raising his voice slightly.

"What happened to Marie was unfortunate," Richards said calmly as he imbibed.

He was staring at the cabinet in front of himself.

"Unfortunate? Professor, she nearly died!" Victor shouted "She literally eviscerated herself! This is going to raise a ton of questions!"

"Don't worry about the legal issues, Victor," Richards said as calmly as before, as he spun to face the assistant professor. "I have it all under control."

Victor wanted to grab the professor by the shoulders and shake him violently.

"Professor, do you realize what happened tonight? A woman that trusted us could have lost her life. She could have died!"

"She knew what she was getting into," Richards said sternly, which took Victor aback momentarily. "It's all in the NDA. In case of injuries or death, you and I are not responsible. Marie knew it, and she knew the risks. Do you think I forced these women to join the experiment, Victor?"

Victor gulped. "And what now? We just continue the experiment as if nothing happened?"

"Of course not. Marie will be dismissed, and we will make sure to monitor the remaining two subjects closely."

Victor was at a loss for words. The shaking he wanted to do to the professor earlier morphed into wanting to punch him in the face.

"Are you listening to yourself, Professor?" Victor asked. "A patient disemboweled herself, and you want to continue the experiment! Do you realize how insane that sounds?!"

"You want to stop the experiment? Now that we've gone through the initial phase? Now that the university has invested so much into the Fertility Project?!" Richards raised his own tone this time. "Don't be a fool, Victor! We are on the verge of something great here!"

"A woman almost lost her life! What needs to happen for you to see how dangerous the experiment is?! When you said that Marie was safe, I trusted you! And now look what happened!"

Richards' mouth contorted into a thin slit that expressed frustration and infuriation.

"Do not undermine my knowledge, Victor," he said. "I made a mistake, I admit it. But this is uncharted territory we're trekking on. Accidents are bound to happen. Instead of cowering at the first mishap, we need to embrace it, improve, and continue without stopping."

Victor took a deep breath.

"With all due respect, professor, but it's easy whacking a thorny bush with somebody else's dick."

"Excuse me?"

205

"It's not your life that's at stake here, professor. These women trust us, and they have no idea how dangerous the experiment is."

Richards downed his drink in one big gulp and slammed the glass on top of the mini-fridge before taking a menacing step towards Victor. He then suddenly seemed to calm down, as he said, "We have come too far to stop the experiment now, Victor. If you want out, I will happily let you leave and find a replacement for you. Is that what you want?"

Victor opened his mouth, but had no idea what to say. He looked down at his feet before feeling the professor's hand gently touching his shoulder.

"Victor," Richards leaned closer to him. "These things happen in experiments all the time. Marie's case was an unfortunate accident due to various unforeseen factors, but hers was the worst possible scenario. Think of the future, Victor. If you ask any of these women if they would be willing to take the same risk Marie took in order to have a child, all of them would give you the same answer. And if the experiment is successful, not only will you change these women's lives forever for the better, but you will make a name for yourself that will be etched in history."

Victor's anger began dissipating. Everything the professor said sounded appealing, now that the gory images faded from Victor's mind. Was the risk for these women really that high? Marie was unstable from day one and was probably already a walking disaster waiting to happen. But Amanda and Isabelle still showed no signs of mental deterioration. If they continued, then he would make sure to monitor both women closely.

"Fine," Victor finally said. "But the moment I see either of the remaining two women behaving strangely, I am going straight into the investors' office and demanding they shut down the whole project."

"Agreed," Richards nodded. "As I said before, I miscalculated with Marie. It won't happen again."

Chapter 12
63 days until disaster

Marie had recovered from her self-mutilation and was released from the hospital less than a week later. Richards had already called and told her that she would no longer be able to participate in the project, and she hadn't complained about it. When Victor asked the professor if she spoke about the incident, Richards shook his head dismissively and said that he didn't want to open up sensitive topics and cause her to potentially have another psychotic episode. Victor agreed that it was for the best.

With only two test subjects remaining, the professor and assistant professor focused on Amanda and Isabelle. Both women seemed to be doing okay for the most part, and Victor himself made sure to check the cameras from time to time in order to ensure nothing was amiss. When Tara returned to her night shift four nights later, Victor was surprised. He asked her what she was doing here, and she said that she was ready to come back.

"You were right, professor," she said with determination in her voice. "If it weren't for me, Marie would have been dead. But she's alive. I want to be here to ensure such a thing doesn't happen again."

Victor was both amazed and envious of her bravery. He himself dreaded going into the security room ever since that night, but the fact that cameras two, four, and five were off now made things easier. Two of the students, however, Uriel and Jackie had dropped out, and the remaining four had to cover for them until Richards found adequate substitutes.

Three days after Marie's incident, Professor Richards and Victor gave the women a pregnancy test. Both came out negative, and while Victor was discouraged, Richards told him to keep his chin up because this was only the first try, and they had at least five more to go before they gave up. According to Richards, there was no way the experiment would fail unless he failed to take into consideration something critical during the testing of the mice. Knowing Richards, Victor assumed that the professor would have double and triple-checked every factor before asking the university for the funds to conduct the experiment.

The following two weeks were monotone, with the same inseminating procedure being done on the two women and the daily checkups to make sure they were okay, both physically and mentally.

Victor had started missing Jennifer and Leah more by this time. It was already difficult since he had arrived, but now that some time had passed, it was becoming unbearable. He tried video chatting with them more often, but he was either really busy or dead tired. It was probably his imagination, but Leah seemed to be growing up way too fast while he was gone. There were moments when he wanted to ditch the Fertility Project, but he would then remind himself why he spent this long on the experiment in the first place. Now, even if he wanted to quit, he was too far in to do so, and dropping out would be for nothing.

Jennifer encouraged him by saying there wasn't a lot of time left in the experiment, but he could tell that she wanted him to come home from the way she constantly told him that she missed him and that Leah wasn't the same without him around. Victor had tear-jerking moments on the video calls a few times when he saw Leah's happy reaction upon seeing her dad's face, and during those moments, he missed cradling her, putting her to sleep, watching her playing, talking to her as he would to another adult, etcetera. He promised himself that he would dedicate a lot more time to his family as soon as the Fertility Project was over.

Days went by slowly, and then around two weeks after the second insemination, Richards gave another pregnancy test to the two women. Once the women were done, Richards took the tests and went into his office. Victor was tasked with escorting Amanda and Isabelle back to their rooms. He could tell that Amanda was especially nervous because she wasn't as chatty as usual. Victor tried striking up a conversation by saying how much he admired her calligraphy work, but she dismissively thanked him.

Knowing that there was nothing else he could do right now to make the women feel better, he left them in their rooms and returned to Richards' office. When he entered, he saw Richards sitting with his legs kicked up on the desk, a Cuban cigar in his hand, the smoke billowing up in the air. Richards puffed, the plume of smoke leaving his mouth as he looked at Victor with a stupid grin that he could not hide. Victor was tempted to start laughing right there and then because he knew what Richards' reaction meant, but he wanted to avoid giving himself false hope. As soon as Victor closed the door, Richards put his feet down and motioned for Victor to come closer.

"Here, have a cigar. On me," the professor said.

The assistant professor approached the desk and saw a lonesome cigar laid on the table in front of him.

"Professor, a little early for celebrations, don't you think?"

"We did it, Victor. We did it."

They stared at each other for a long moment before the two of them burst into uncontrollable laughter. Victor laughed so hard that his stomach hurt. Once they were done laughing, Victor prepared and lit up the Cuban cigar with the professor's help and drew the first whiff. He did it too sharply, and before he knew it, he found himself coughing his lungs out. The professor reminded him how to smoke a Cuban cigar and not to inhale the smoke into his lungs, which Victor, of course, already knew. The excitement was just taking control of him.

"So, the tests are positive?" he asked finally from the chair in front of Richards' desk.

Smoke, along with the stench of the cigars, filled the air around the desk. The professor always enjoyed the smell and taste of Cuban cigars, but Victor hated them – just like alcohol. Richards slid the two pregnancy tests to him and said.

"See for yourself."

Sure enough, both tests showed two vertical lines to indicate that they were positive. A smile stretched across Victor's face from ear to ear.

"We have to tell the patients right away, professor," Victor said as soon as he saw that only a stub remained of the professor's cigar.

"Hold on, my boy. Let's wait for the smoke to dissipate first, so we don't go there smelling like a bunch of hobos."

Victor agreed. He started feeling sick from his cigar less than halfway through, so he gave it to Richards. Richards extinguished it and told Victor to keep it as a gift. Although Victor had no intention of smoking the thing, and he sure as hell hadn't planned on bringing it home so that Jennifer could catch him with it, he wasn't going to decline the professor's generous gesture. Richards pulled out a drawer and fished out an air freshener. He sprayed it around in random directions before placing it back inside.

"Now, then," he stood up and grabbed the pregnancy tests. "Shall we?"

Victor pulled out his own chair and led the way towards the patients' rooms. He took the lead in swiping the keycards across the card readers of rooms one and three and pushed the doors open.

Richards summoned the women outside, visibly unable to control the grin on his face. The women, both looking stressed out of their minds, eyes bulging in anticipation, stepped outside and stopped next to one another, in front of Richards and Victor.

"Here you go, ladies. It doesn't matter which one is whose," Richards said as he handed the pregnancy tests to Isabelle and Amanda.

Amanda was the first one to look down at the test. She gasped and covered her mouth with one hand, while Isabelle jerked her head towards her in confusion. She then looked down at her own test and uttered a loud 'Oh, my god'.

"Congratulations, ladies. You are officially pregnant," Professor Richards said as he held his hands behind his back.

The women began screaming and shouting incoherent words of joy. Isabelle threw herself in Professor Richards' arms, while Amanda hugged Victor in response, forcefully enough to make him stumble backward a step. The hallway was filled with the sounds of joy and gratitude for a solid two minutes or so, and only when Richards raised his hand in a stop sign did they slowly cease.

"Now, hold on. This is just the initial step, okay? We still have a lot of testing to do and make sure everything is okay. The pregnancy tests have a ninety-nine percent accuracy rate, but there's still a one percent chance that-"

"Oh, shut it, professor! Don't take this away from us!" Isabelle chirped.

She and Amanda were embraced in a waltz-like stance and were gyrating around the hall, all the while giggling. Victor's mouth was stretched into a smile, and he didn't care how silly he looked. This right here, this joy that the patients were experiencing – that was the real reward of being a scientist, he realized.

"Alright, let's call your husbands then, shall we?" Richards grinned.

***

The days went by much faster now that Amanda got the news that she was pregnant. She was ecstatic 24-7, and nothing could ruin her mood. She and Isabelle were allowed to call their husbands and share the good news. When Amanda first called Wayne, he answered skeptically – he probably expected some bad news. And then when he heard Amanda's voice, he sounded happy, but still careful – they shouldn't have been in contact for about four more months.

Amanda could hardly contain her happy giggle when she told Wayne about the good news. He asked her if she was screwing with him, and when she confirmed that she wasn't, the line went silent for a moment before Wayne began screaming in joy and triumph, throwing expletives along the way. His voice was heard loudly enough through the speaker for Isabelle, who was next to Amanda, to hear everything, so Amanda shushed him.

When Wayne asked if Amanda would be coming back home any time soon, she said that the professor needed to run more tests and that she would probably not be home for at least two more months. Wayne insisted on coming to visit her, deeming it safe enough, but Amanda dissuaded him from it, quoting the professor that now is the most critical moment to be careful.

She asked Wayne how things were at home, and he proudly told her how he cooked for himself and managed not to break a single plate or glass. Amanda told him how much she missed him and that she couldn't wait for them to start their new life together with the baby. Eventually, she had to say goodbye to Wayne with a heavy heart, but not before telling him how much she loved him.

The checkups were conducted more thoroughly, and two days after the initial pregnancy test, the professor gave them another one to confirm that it was indeed positive. Amanda felt kicks in her stomach from time to time, but Richards confirmed that it was completely normal. He stated that the baby would grow much faster than it normally would while in the womb, and then upon birth would resume growing at the usual rate.

Amanda and Isabelle formed a motherly bond after they got the test. They discussed the three other former patients, all of whom had left the experiment willingly due to the stress and inability to cope, and although Amanda was sad for them, she couldn't help but feel a little bit of anger towards them, too. They had made it this far, and they had this gift bestowed on them, and they just threw it away. Still, she hoped that they'd find the happiness they were looking for outside of the experiment.

As she did.

Chapter 13
50 days until disaster

Now that the patients were pregnant, Victor found himself having less time to miss his family. Just two weeks after the first positive pregnancy test, he noticed the patients' abdomen growing.

Worried, he pulled Professor Richards aside and asked him what was going on. Richards laughed it off and said, "Rapid fetal development, Victor. The fetuses that get conceived in the way which you and I conducted here manage to synthesize the mother's nutrients much faster. Think of it as a baby on steroids. You've seen how much the subjects have been eating lately, haven't you?"

Victor nodded. The professor was right. Isabelle's and Amanda's appetite exponentially jumped just two days after the test, and the professor had multiple meals arranged for them every day, upping from three to five, plus some snacks in between. Both women managed to eat almost everything thrown at them with ease, without gaining an ounce of fat while their bellies grew.

"But Professor, isn't such fast growth dangerous for the patients?" Victor skeptically asked.

"Not at all, Victor. I wrote all about it in my report with the mice. You've read that part, have you not?" the professor furrowed his brow.

"Yes. Yes. I have," Victor briskly answered.

The truth is, he didn't read about that part in detail. Once he reached the part where the mice managed to conceive with the method Richards used, he skimmed through the rest of the research, too excited to read every single detail.

"So, remind me, how long until the patients give birth to the babies?" Victor asked.

The professor rubbed his chin, looking nowhere in particular, before saying, "It should be, by my estimation, around four weeks. Twenty-nine days, to be precise."

Victor tried to hide the shock on his face.

"And, the distension of the abdomen within those four weeks... it's not going to complicate things for the patients?"

"They may feel some pain here and there, but they will suffer no damage to the inner wall of their abdomen. There may be a chance that you and I will have to deliver the newborns with C-sections, but the patients have already been informed about that."

Victor felt his heart drop to the pit of his stomach at a sudden question that popped up in his mind.

"W-We are going to deliver the babies alone, Professor?"

The professor shot a stern look at Victor.

"Of course, Victor. As the scientists who inseminated the subjects with the solution we created, you and I are the only adequately trained professionals to deal with the delivery of the babies. This is no big deal, as you've already learned this in college, and you've had mock practice, right?"

"I mean, yes, but Professor, this was only practice. And it was years ago!" Victor started sweating bullets.

"Nothing to worry about, my boy. The mind never forgets. There is a birth simulator in the reproductive center that allows the students nowadays to practice life-like scenarios. I'll arrange for someone to bring it in here, so you can practice in your free time."

"I appreciate it, Professor."

Richards turned around to return to the exam room before looking back at Victor and saying, "Oh, and Victor?"

"Yes, Professor?"

"Do make sure to read through the notes again. There may be some critical info you may have missed along the way."

"Y-yes, Professor," Victor stammered.

He suddenly felt embarrassed at the fact that he clearly looked like a student who wasn't ready for a test. He wondered why Richards gave him equality in the Fertility Project and wondered if it was the right choice. Victor was clearly nowhere close to Richards' level and probably wouldn't be for many years to come – or ever.

No, Richards entrusted him with the project because he believed in Victor's knowledge and skills. Victor would not disappoint him. Instead of taking short naps or scrolling through social media on his phone, he would read Richards' notes, revise the books about birth and delivery that he already read, and practice with the birth simulator.

He wasn't looking forward to the birth simulator, though. It was essentially a very life-like mannequin that the university called Gloria, and she was essentially a highly advanced robot that could simulate childbirth, including all the obstacles that a woman could face during delivery. Victor only used the mannequin once and successfully managed to deliver the robot baby within an hour, but he saw the students having issues with it due to the pre programmed scenarios that Gloria could play.

Either way, real childbirth would be much nastier and more difficult than the simulation, so he decided he should get used to it as soon as possible – in order to eliminate the risks the women may face.

***

Victor wasted no time in gathering a myriad of books related to reproductive medicine that he could read through. He was a fast reader, so he reckoned he could finish one in two or three nights. Since he didn't have enough time to read every single book and practice the simulation along with that, he decided to make a plan.

He would practice the simulation for two hours every day, and he would prioritize reading the books about childbirth by sticking to one hour of reading after the morning checkups, two hours after lunch, and two more in the evening. It would be difficult for sure, but he only had a few weeks to do it. But he couldn't burn himself out, either.

He would take it easy during the final week when the women were estimated to give birth, in order to stay fresh and completely focused on the day of the delivery. He also cut back on time spent speaking to his family, and instead of chatting with Jennifer and Leah for a whole hour every day, he now spent thirty minutes – and sometimes he skipped speaking to them altogether. It was painful for him, but he had to focus on the job right now – he would have time to spend with his family once the experiment was done.

***

"Professor, can I use the simulation device for practice, too?" Tara asked when Victor led her into the classroom where Richards had brought Gloria.

"It's not a simulation device, Tara. Her name is Gloria. You need to treat her as a living human if you want to be able to deliver her baby properly," Victor winked. "And sure, you can use her in your free time, but you need to make sure to plug her in to charge as soon as you're done. Her battery lasts for only ten hours."

Gloria didn't look realistic. She had smooth, rubber skin and chestnut, shoulder-length hair, but her facial expression changed depending on the scenario. Right now, she lay in bed in her hospital gown with a blank stare up at the ceiling, but at the press of a button, she would begin to moan, scream or speak, depending on her condition. There was a monitor on a portable desk next to her that displayed her current status, heart rate, etcetera. It was off right now.

"Now that you're here early, Tara, do you wanna give it a go before your shift?"

"It may take a long time to deliver the baby, wouldn't it, professor?" Tara asked with a timbre of curiosity.

She seemed to have fully recovered since the incident with Marie, much to Victor's relief.

"We can always stop halfway through. Not like we need to deliver a real baby, right?" Victor shrugged.

He went over to the desk where a box of disposable nitrile gloves sat. He pulled out two for himself and two for Tara. Tara didn't have a lab coat, but since this was just practice, she didn't need it. They didn't need the gloves either, but Victor wanted to immerse himself in the experience more.

"Now, let's see here..." Victor said as he approached the control panel next to Gloria.

He pressed the button to power her up and immediately, the screen came to life, displaying Gloria's current state. There was a fetal heart monitor under Gloria's own heart rate.

"Doctor, I think I'm in labor," a feminine, yet robotic voice came from Gloria's mouth.

She stiffly turned her head in Tara's direction and locked eyes with her. Tara gasped before looking at Victor and nervously chuckling.

"Well, let's get this baby delivered, then," Victor grinned and positioned himself in front of the vaginal opening where the tip of the baby's smooth head protruded slightly.

***

"I need... I need to sit down for a moment," Tara said while panting.

She wiped her sweaty forehead with the sleeve of her shirt and slumped into one of the chairs she pulled out. Victor was cradling the robot baby that he wrapped inside a towel. The baby didn't produce crying sounds when it exited the mother's womb, but it did have a fake umbilical cord that needed to be severed. The baby also had attached sensors that indicated whether the delivery was a success or not.

The entire procedure lasted one hour, and Victor and Tara were met with shoulder dystocia (the condition where the shoulder of the baby gets stuck on the mother's pelvic bone). Victor had to perform the McRoberts maneuver to get Gloria in a position in which the baby would get unstuck from the pelvic bone, and that trick itself cost them over thirty minutes.

The delivery itself was successful, though, but it was a close call. Gloria's heart rate was close to critical, and Victor was sure that delivering Amanda's and Isabelle's babies like that would not be acceptable. Still, he couldn't help but feel somewhat good at the proper practice, and seeing the satisfaction on Tara's face made it all the better.

"You're already late for your shift, Tara," Victor said. "Brian is probably waiting to go home already."

"You're right, professor. I'll go there... in a minute," Tara said, a hand raised to indicate she needed more time to rest.

As Tara left, Victor was tasked with returning Gloria and the baby to their natural positions. He had to reattach a new, rubber umbilical cord – that came with Gloria – to her placenta and the baby's abdomen and reinsert the baby inside the womb. This was an easy task because the vaginal opening stretched further after the procedure was done to allow for easier insertion. Then, Gloria had to be plugged into the nearest electrical outlet to charge up. She would take less than an hour to charge what little energy she used, but it didn't hurt to keep her charging longer

It was past dinnertime and night checkup, and Victor felt exhausted. He still had some reading to catch up on, so he made a cup of coffee for himself and got down to business – tonight, he was reading *The Future of Embryology* by Professor Howard Richards.

***

Weeks had gone by, and Amanda and Isabelle now had incongruously large bellies – Isabelle significantly larger than Amanda, as if she were already in the third trimester. Richards explained that the uneven growth of the fetus was common in this sort of situation. Everything seemed to be going according to plan, and neither of the patients complained of anything major. Amanda experienced slight back pain, which was normal since the sudden gain of weight proved to be a shock for the body. Victor scrupulously monitored the patients in order to make sure they were okay. Partly, he didn't want to blindly believe everything Richards said (even though he didn't put a voice to that thought), but he also grew to care for Amanda and Isabelle and wanted to do everything in his power to help them have healthy babies.

Around three weeks after the first positive pregnancy test, Richards announced that they would be having their ultrasound. He had planned on doing it earlier, but there was too much work to be done. Now that they were technically in the third trimester and ready to give birth in less than two weeks, it was time to check if everything was okay with the babies.

Amanda and Isabelle were ecstatic about it and couldn't wait to see on the monitor what their babies looked like. It was done in the afternoon, and Richards had one of the students roll two ultrasound machines into the exam room. Amanda and Isabelle were brought into the room and told to lie on their backs. Victor was in charge of taking care of Amanda, so he spread a water-based gel on her stomach as the first step.

"Ouch, that's cold," she complained.

"Sorry," he said.

He grabbed the transducer – a probe attached to the ultrasound machine used for scanning – and slowly ran it across the belly, staring at the monitor for anything appearing. Immediately, blurry, white, and grey images appeared on the black screen. They changed their shapes as Victor moved the transducer around.

"So, how does the ultrasound work, Victor?" Amanda asked.

"Similar to a sonar," he said. "The gel allows the sound waves to travel back and forth, and as soon as this device detects a sound, it will pick up an- ah, there we go."

Victor slightly turned the monitor towards Amanda so she could take a better look. She looked confused, and rightly so because it was difficult to understand what was on the monitor. Victor pointed to the oval shape and said.

"This is the baby's face."

Amanda's mouth stretched into a smile.

"Oh, my god," she muttered to herself, her eyes glued to the monitor.

Victor continued moving the transducer around until he found a different shape.

"You said you wanted a girl, right?" he asked.

"Yeah?" Amanda skeptically said.

"Well, I'm no expert, but based on what I see, I think I can almost one-hundred percent confirm it's a girl."

Amanda put her hands over her mouth, still staring at the monitor. She muttered another 'Oh, my god', and her eyes filled with tears.

"Professor, can you come here for a moment, please?" Victor shouted across the room.

Professor Richards, who was performing the ultrasound scan on Isabelle, looked in Victor's direction before placing the transducer down, wiping his hands with a paper handkerchief, and heading towards Victor.

"Everything okay, Victor?"

"Yes, Professor. I just need you to confirm for me... this is a girl, right?"

Richards glanced at the monitor and squinted. He got closer to the monitor, and not even two seconds in, he nodded and said, "Yeah, a girl without a doubt. Congratulations, Amanda," he smiled heartily, before nodding and hastily returning to Isabelle.

"Oh, Wayne... I wish you were here..." Amanda said as she sniffled.

"You'll get images of the ultrasound, so you can show your husband as soon as you're back together. Have you already decided on a name?"

"A name?"

"You know, for the baby?" Victor chuckled.

"Right. Um, I actually haven't thought about it. I like the name Gabriella, but I'll have to see what Wayne thinks about it. Oh, I hope he's not disappointed that it's not a boy."

"I'm sure he'll be happy to know your baby is a healthy girl. I'm not seeing any deformities or anomalies, but I'll have to double-check with Professor Richards after this."

Victor removed the transducer from Amanda's belly, wiped the gel off of it, as well as the gel from her belly, and told Amanda she could get dressed. He clicked on various timeframes of the ultrasound, pressed a few buttons on the keyboard, and the machine instantly printed a reel of five ultrasound photographs.

"Here you go, Amanda," Victor said as he handed the photos to her.

Amanda took the photos gently, still smiling as tears of joy welled up in her eyes.

"Thank you so much, Victor. For everything," she said.

"Don't mention it. Let's get you back to your room for now, okay?"

Amanda nodded, and they made their way past Richards and Isabelle.

"Good, everything is good for now," Richards said as he stared at the monitor along with Isabelle.

As Victor was about to exit the room, Richards' voice resounded behind him.

"Oh, Victor?"

"Yes, Professor?"

"I'll be done in a moment here. Come see me in my office later," he took the keycard out of his pocket and handed it to Victor.

"Yes, Professor."

The way the professor conveyed the sentence seemed to carry with it a sense of urgency. Another lecture to Victor about not getting too close with the patients? If so, he would listen to what the professor had to say. Listen, but not necessarily obey. As Victor unlocked the door for Amanda, he had to guide her away from a wall that she was about to bump into, due to the fact that her eyes were glued to the pictures of her ultrasound.

"Thank you again, Victor," she said. "I'll make you some of my famous sandwiches as soon as I take a short nap."

"Save them for yourself, Amanda. Gabriella needs them more," Victor smiled.

Minutes later, Richards and Isabelle waltzed out of the exam room, Isabelle looking visibly pleased, holding the pictures of her ultrasound.

Victor unlocked room one for her and proceeded to return the keycard to the professor.

"Get some rest, Isabelle. We have another checkup in just a few hours," Richards politely said.

Once the door was closed, he turned to Victor, the smile dropping off his face like an anchor.

"Victor, come," he said as he turned around without waiting to see Victor's reaction.

They strode downstairs and into Richards' office. The professor wasted no time loping over to the drinks cabinet and pouring a larger glass of a differently colored beverage this time.

"Professor, is everything okay?" Victor impatiently asked.

The professor poured half the glass into his mouth in one sip and held his cheeks puffed-up before swallowing.

"No, we have a problem, Victor," he said, before proceeding to add more of the dark liquid to his glass.

"Professor, slow down. We can't have you drunk in the middle of the day," Victor raised his hands in a stop sign but made no attempt to take the drink away from Richards, even though he wanted to.

Richards took another sip before walking over to his desk and slumping into the chair. He loudly slammed the glass on top of the desk and looked nowhere in particular as he scratched his cheek. He suddenly looked ten years older from the worry.

"Professor, you're killing me. What's going on?" Victor let out a nervous, uncontrollable chuckle.

"Subject one's baby is not okay," Richards finally said and locked eyes with Victor.

Victor stared at the professor for a long moment before taking a seat opposite his desk.

"What do you mean?"

"I mean, the baby has congenital abnormalities. A myriad of them."

Victor ran his hand through his hair. This complicated things immensely.

"You haven't told Isabelle, have you?" he asked the professor.

"No. I haven't," Richards shook his head.

"How serious is it?"

"Enough to have it visible at birth. I still need to consult my colleagues who specialize in this area, but you don't need to be an expert to see such prominent deformities."

"Professor, the patient has to know."

"I know, I know. But you have to understand, Victor. This is a delicate situation. There are no physical deformities in the patient's family history, so if we tell her that there's something wrong with her baby, she's going to blame us. She might even sue us."

Victor leaned back in the chair.

"Does she have any right to blame us for the deformities?"

Richards sighed.

"Professor. Are we to blame for her baby being the way it is?" Victor insistedly questioned.

"There is no way of telling. One of the downsides of the Fertility Project procedure is the heightened risk of abnormalities. But that risk is negligible compared to the risk in normal pregnancies."

"I didn't see any of it mentioned in your research, Professor."

"One out of five mice gave birth to deformed offspring. Those mice have been eliminated from the cycle of the experiment and therefore not recorded."

"Are you saying you knew the risk of this happening and still took it, Professor?"

Richards shook his head before grabbing the glass and emptying it into his mouth.

"The subjects who signed up for this experiment knew what they were getting into. I explicitly mentioned in the NDA the potential risks of deformities during the procedure."

"I see," Victor nodded.

He felt somewhat angry at the professor but then quickly realized that he had no right to blame him. Richards informed the patients of the risks, and they took it. That meant that he and Victor were legally safe from any lawsuits. But what about the trauma Isabelle would have to endure as a mother with a sick child?

"What do we do now, Professor?" Victor asked.

"Abortion obviously isn't possible at this stage. But lying to her will only make it worse. I will talk to her about it tomorrow, let her know that there is something wrong with the baby. It's nothing major, mind you, nothing nearly as serious as autism, but some people cannot stand the thought of their children being deformed in any manner."

"Maybe we should wait until you consult your coworkers first, Professor. Maybe it's not as bad as you think."

Richards looked away and lethargically nodded while pressing his lips together tightly. A moment later, he leaned back in his chair, which squeaked in protest.

"What about subject three's baby?" he asked.

"I think everything is okay. At least, I didn't see any congenital deformities."

"I'll send the footage to my colleagues at Harvard and see what they say. In the meantime, don't say anything to subject one. Her baby is due in less than two weeks, and we can't have her stressing, or god forbid, doing something crazy, now that we're so close."

Victor agreed.

"Either way," the professor continued. "No matter what the results are, even if the baby happens to have deformities, this is still going to be a huge accomplishment, Victor. We will be the first scientists in history who actually managed to help infertile women become fertile. When the two remaining subjects walk out of here, with or without healthy babies, they will be able to conceive without our help later on in life."

The professor was right. The risk of getting unhealthy babies was high, but it was a tradeoff. Victor hoped that Amanda's baby was still okay, though. However, if she happened to have something wrong with her, at least she would be walking out of this facility knowing that she could conceive with her husband again in the future.

He hoped that the patients would see it that way, too.

Chapter 14
36 days until disaster

Isabelle's and Amanda's bellies continued to grow. Isabelle had visible stretch marks across her stomach with prominent blue veins under the skin. It looked as if her stomach would explode if someone poked it with a needle. She complained of frequent stomach aches, and the professor made sure to get everything ready for when she went into labor. There was a room in the basement specifically made for that, with all the medical necessities, including an incubator for the baby. Victor had only seen the room once since there was no need to go there – yet.

He continued practicing with Gloria and read more and more books, but since he was starting to feel somewhat burnt out, he took it easy for a few days. Isabelle's baby was due any day now, and he couldn't afford to be distracted. Besides, practicing and reading just before the actual procedure would do no good. It was like studying for a test; cramming worked, but trying to study an hour before the test did nothing except heighten cortisol levels.

Although Isabelle complained of the pain in her stomach, she looked great. At the back of his mind, Victor was afraid that she might start going crazy like Marie, but both remaining patients were doing okay. There was still one problem, though –

Richards didn't tell Isabelle about the congenital deformity. And then one afternoon around 4 pm, the professor burst into Victor's room without knocking, startling the assistant professor who had been in a half-asleep state.

"Victor. It's time," the professor said.

***

As soon as Victor walked out of his quarters, he saw Richards racing up the stairs with the keycard in his hand. Victor sprinted, comically thinking that he probably should have worked on his stamina and not just scientific knowledge. As soon as Richards unlocked Isabelle's room, the screams began permeating the air, as if someone unmuted a TV. The professor violently burst inside the room and turned right.

Victor followed his gaze and saw Isabelle lying on her bed with her hands gently held around her belly. Isabelle's face was contorted into a painful grimace, and she'd either scream with her eyes closed or exhale in short, labored breaths.

"Victor, help me take her to the delivery room, hurry!" the professor motioned towards Isabelle.

Victor immediately went around the bed's right side while the professor went left. They grabbed Isabelle under her arms and tried helping her up, but as soon as she moved an inch, she screamed even louder.

"I can't!" she shook her head. "I can't!"

"We have to try, come on!" the professor insisted.

Richards and Victor tried moving her again, and again, she cried out loudly. The professor's forehead was already sweaty from frazzle, but the determination on his face was as present as ever. He looked at Victor and said, "Victor, we will have to do the delivery here. Go down to the delivery room and get everything we need! You'll probably have to make multiple trips! Tell the new student to turn off camera five and assist you!"

"I'm on it, professor!" Victor shouted before turning on his heel and sprinting out of the room.

The new substitute student who worked today was out in the hall with a concerned look on his face.

"Professor, what can I-"

"Come with me!" Victor interrupted him.

They raced down into the basement and opened the first door on the right. The whole time Victor wondered why in the hell the professor didn't put the delivery room closer to the patients' rooms. Once he burst through the door, he looked around for the essential items first. There was a bin where they kept the medical protective clothing he and the professor needed to wear. The set included surgical caps, masks, gloves, and surgical gowns. There were also shoe covers, but Victor doubted they had enough time to put everything on.

"Grab two pairs of everything from that bin!" Victor commanded the student, pointing to the bin.

Victor himself went over to the portable medical table for tools that had a protective cover over it. He already knew that the tools under the cover were ready to be used after sterilizing, so he pushed the table out of the room. Getting it up the stairs was easier than he expected since the table was lightweight, however by the time he climbed up on the second floor, he was already winded.

Definitely gotta work on my stamina, dammit.

The student was close behind him by the time they reached Isabelle's room. The screams were now intermittently getting louder and quieter while Richards spoke words of comfort to Isabelle. He was positioned in a crouching position in front of the bed. During the time they were gone, Victor noticed that Richards managed to help Isabelle get undressed below the waist.

"Professor, we brought the protective clothing!" Victor shouted to make sure the professor would hear him over the caterwauls.

"Good," Richards stood up and went over to the student.

Both Richards and Victor donned the protective clothing, and only when Victor had everything on did the reality of the situation hit him. Isabelle was in labor, and he was one of the only two people available in the building to help deliver the baby. The realization was so strong that he suddenly wanted to back out, get out of the building, and pretend this never happened. But then he remembered Jennifer and Leah and how they were counting on him. He had to do this. He had to give Isabelle the life she deserved. As soon as that thought came into his mind, his fight instinct kicked in.

"Professors, what should I-"

"Wait outside!" Richards was the one who sternly interrupted the student this time.

The student disappeared immediately out of the room. Isabelle was in the second stage of labor, which meant the delivery itself could last up to two hours. Victor was already prepared for this. Throughout the labor, Victor thought he saw tiny bulges appearing on the surface of Isabelle's already tormented stomach. He dismissed those as a normal occurrence – after all, this entire experiment wasn't something that could be considered normal. He couldn't tell how much time had passed when Richards exasperatingly shook his head and turned to Victor.

"Victor, the contractions aren't strong enough. We need Pitocin to help her push. There's some down in the delivery room! Go!"

Victor nodded and immediately rushed out of the room. The new student was still waiting there, still with the same concerned look on his face. As soon as he saw Victor, he took a step towards him.

"Professor, what should-"

"Go home!" Victor shouted.

The student nodded, then rushed down the stairs and out of the building without a word. Poor guy was probably rethinking his education choice. Victor raced downstairs, chanting the words *Pitocin* in his mind over and over, as if he would forget the name of the medication.

Pitocin, Pitocin, Pito-

The word abruptly stopped in his mind when he felt his foot miss a step. It all happened so fast. He stumbled forward and began tumbling down the stairs. He felt the back of his head hitting against something, and his vision instantly started going dark. As a sense of vertigo began overtaking him, he tried raising his head but wasn't sure if he even managed to do so, from the ceiling spinning around him.

Pitocin, was the last word that formed in his mind before everything went black.

***

He drifted in a limbo, neither awake nor asleep. Gradually, his senses began forming. Victor shot his eyes open and sat upright with a jolt. Immediately, he became aware of the throbbing pain in the back of his head. He gently placed a hand there, and upon bringing it in front of himself, he saw no blood. He could have still suffered a concussion, though. Then, he suddenly remembered what happened before he lost consciousness.

Pitocin!

He hoped that he hadn't been out long. He clambered up to his feet and rushed into the delivery room. His head hurt like hell, but he gritted his teeth and ignored it while he looked for the Pitocin. He found one vial in the medicine cabinet and grabbed the other necessary things, like an IV bag, stand and syringe. He raced up the stairs to the second floor and-

The professor stood in the middle of the hall in front of room one. His head hung down, and his gloves were stained with fresh, dark blood. The first thought that went through Victor's head was that he was too late. He ran to the professor, who didn't raise his head in response.

"Professor, I'm here, I... I got the Pitocin!" he said with hopefulness.

Richards looked up at him with weary eyes before yanking his gloves off. They came off with a rubbery sound before he pulled his mask down.

"Professor, what happened? Are Isabelle and the baby okay?" Victor asked, even though in his heart, he knew the answer; he just refused to acknowledge it.

"I'm sorry, Victor. They didn't make it," Richards said in a somber tone. "Can you please bring a stretcher here? We need to wheel out the bodies."

Victor felt like he had been hit by a truck. His legs got wobbly, but he remained on his feet with what little strength he had left.

"What happened, Professor?"

Richards sighed.

"Isabelle managed to give birth to the baby, but they both died shortly after."

Victor was dumbfounded. A cold sweat washed over him and he felt like he was going to collapse again.

"How... how long have I been away? I... I fell down the stairs and lost consciousness, Professor. I'm so sorry..." he had no words to describe the guilt he felt at that moment.

"Don't blame yourself, my boy. Even if you had made it in time, the Pitocin wouldn't have helped. Isabelle was already dying, and there was nothing we could do to stop it. And the baby... the baby was stillborn," he put one hand on Victor's shoulder, his eyes filled with tears. "Victor. I'm so sorry."

He turned away to wipe away the tears.

"It wasn't your fault, Professor. You did everything you could. I just... I don't know what we should do now."

"I'll take care of the bodies. And I'll inform the husband. Please, just bring me a stretcher," Richards sniffled and said, still facing away from Victor.

Victor complied and rolled in a stretcher from the exam room. Richards returned to room one – insisting on going alone – and came out a few minutes later with Isabelle's body wrapped in a bloodied bedsheet. Squeezed next to her on the stretcher was the smaller body of her baby, also wrapped in a sheet. Victor was grateful that he couldn't see their dead bodies. Without a word, Richards wheeled the bodies downstairs towards the morgue in the basement.

Victor hadn't even realized that he was crying until Professor Richards left. The guilt that he felt a few minutes ago was alleviated but still present. However, a profound sadness now began to creep in. Was Isabelle really dead? His mind tried convincing him that it wasn't too late, that he could still do something to prevent such a morbid outcome, but of course, that wasn't possible.

As much as it pained him, he had to see what happened during Isabelle's childbirth. It was like a car crash; he knew it would be gruesome, but he couldn't help but have a morbid curiosity over it. Maybe it would help convince him that it really wasn't his fault, and that's what he desperately needed right now –to not feel guilty.

***

Upon entering the security room, he was faced with an empty chair and a monitor that displayed two rooms. CAM 3, where Amanda was, showed the woman sitting on the bed and gently caressing her stomach. CAM 1 showed a bed stripped of sheets and a few prominent droplets of blood on the floor. Victor sat on the chair and pulled it closer. He fiddled around with the program, trying to remember where the access to the previous footage was. A few minutes later, he found it and entered CAM 1's recording from 3 pm to 4 pm. The video player automatically entered full-screen, and Victor heard loud screaming coming from the computer. He quickly plugged in the headphones and put them on.

On the camera, Isabelle was writhing in pain on her bed. There was a large splotch on the floor near the kitchen, probably from her water breaking. Victor fast-forwarded the video and saw himself and Richards bursting in. He knew what would happen in the next ten or so minutes, so he skipped a few minutes until he heard Richards in the video asking him for the Pitocin and then Victor leaving the room.

With only Richards and Isabelle left in the room, the professor urged the woman to push while he stood in front of her spread legs. Isabelle's screams intermittently went from loud and long to low and short. This went on for a solid five minutes or so before Richards shouted, "I can see the head, keep pushing, Isabelle!"

Indeed, Victor saw the tip of the blood-covered head protruding out of Isabelle's vagina, and slowly, very slowly, the head surfaced more and more. It took minutes for the tip of the head to come out, and then the rest of the baby rapidly began emerging, with Isabelle's screams intensifying tenfold. She was screaming bloody murder, never reaching a crescendo, but the tone rather perpetually increasing. The baby plopped out, and Isabelle's screams stopped immediately. Her head slumped to the side, her eyes fluttering momentarily before she ceased all movement. Her chest wasn't heaving at all, in contrast to doing so violently just a second ago. But what really caught Victor's eye was the baby.

The face looked deformed beyond recognition. Both eyes were covered by bulbous, fleshy tissues, the nose was basically two tiny holes, and the mouth was crookedly stretched on the left side of the face. The extremities were equally deformed, with one hand being a stump and the other having three, unequally placed, crooked fingers. One of the legs was emaciated, while the other looked too bulky, and Victor was sure that the few toes he saw were elongated and twisted. On top of all that, the newborn had a sickly chartreuse color, unlike anything Victor had ever seen before.

That was no fucking human baby.

"What the fuck," he silently muttered to himself with wide eyes.

Richards grabbed the nearby scissors and snipped the umbilical cord, cradling the baby. He hadn't even looked at Isabelle, who clearly either fell into a coma or was already dead. The professor used one hand to touch the baby in various spots, probably checking to see if it was healthy, and a moment later, the vigor seemed to dissipate from him as he stared down at the unmoving body of the baby.

"Shit," the professor muttered on the camera with an exasperated sigh.

He cast a glance in Isabelle's direction before placing the baby's body on the bed next to its mother. He leaned on the bedframe and hung his head down. He stayed like that for a few minutes before eventually turning around and leaving the room.

What the fuck did I just watch? Victor's mind screamed a million questions.

He rewound the video and watched again as the baby plopped out, his mind trying to find a logical solution as to why the baby looked like that and why Richards hadn't assisted Isabelle. Maybe she could have been saved, for Christ's sake. Victor exited the video and blankly stared at the screen for a few minutes, his mind trying to communicate to him what he had just seen, but either he was too tired or too confused to understand fully.

When he finally came to his senses, he ran his fingers through his hair and leaned forward towards the monitor. He browsed through the videos of CAM 5. There wasn't much scrolling to be done since the camera has been off ever since the day Marie left. He remembered that the incident with Marie happened in the middle of the night and that it was around 2 am, so he started with the 2 am to 3 am footage. His heart thumped rapidly, and cold sweat immediately enveloped him.

Although he knew the gist of what happened, he didn't want to question Tara afterward for details. Victor fast-forwarded through the video until he saw Marie stumbling out of bed and towards the bathroom. She came out a minute later and grabbed onto the kitchen counter. She took a knife and plunged it into her stomach before dropping it on the floor with a loud clatter. Marie dug a hand into the tiny hole in her stomach, and by now, a large pool of blood had already formed around her.

She dug her hand deeper and deeper, and then, she yanked her guts out. But there was something else there, too. Something that fell out of her stomach along with the guts she pulled out. The tiny, lumpy mass fell on the floor with a wet splotchy sound, but Marie didn't pay attention to it. She was staring at her extracted intestines, and as if just then realizing what she did, she screamed.

Victor fast-forwarded the video until he saw himself and Richards entering. In the video, Victor didn't see the small fleshy lump on the ground. He stepped on it and slipped, almost falling on the floor in the process. The fleshy substance disappeared under his foot as a red stain. There was even a squishy sound the moment his shoe crushed it. Squinting, Victor rewound the video a few minutes back. He zoomed in on the thing on the ground, trying to discern what the fuck it was. It was too pixelated, but he started to make out its form. It was round, uneven, but he couldn't tell more. Victor let the video play with the lump on the ground zoomed in.

It moved. Holy hell, it moved.

Victor continued playing, practically holding his breath in the process. It moved again, ever so slightly, and it was then with a horrifying realization that he understood what he was looking at.

A fully-formed fetus.

He jumped when he saw a foot stepping on the fetus like it was nothing and slipping, only to leave a splotch of blood and bits of flesh. Victor wanted to vomit. He rewound the video and watched. *Did it really move?* Yes, it did. There was a malformed fucking arm on the thing, and it moved feebly, along with the oversized head that seemed much too heavy for the fetus to even begin lifting. Victor zoomed out and watched again, and he paused the video just before he saw himself stomping the fetus into nothingness.

He turned to the side and retched, but nothing came out. He had to hold onto the desk to avoid falling face-first. Over and over, he muttered 'What the fuck', panting and shaking like a leaf in the wind. Minutes later, when he finally felt good enough to at least straighten his back in the chair, he faced the monitor again. There was one final thing he needed to check.

246

Victor entered CAM 2 recording, which was meager compared to the other two he'd just checked. He remembered the exact date when the two women left and navigated to find it in the saved videos, but it was nowhere to be found. Victor clicked on the last video from CAM 2, but it only showed the footage up until 9 pm. After that, there was nothing. He entered CAM 4, and again, was faced with the same thing. No recordings after 9 pm. No, wait, there was one. Victor realized that the video showing 3 am to 4 am was there, only for some reason, it was buried among the other videos, not chronologically displayed.

He clicked it and saw Regina tossing and turning in her bed. Her forehead was glistening from sweat, and she moaned in pain every so often. Victor fast-forwarded and saw her getting into a sitting position at the edge of the bed. She sat like that for a few minutes and-

Suddenly, a projectile of vomit shot from her mouth and onto the floor. Regina called out for help as she stood up, but suddenly lost balance and fell on her side. She began shaking epileptically, more vomit oozing out of her mouth in the process mixed with her foaming at the mouth. No, not vomit.

Blood.

Seconds later, she stopped shaking and ceased all movement entirely. Her eyes were still wide open, vacantly staring in front of herself. Everything was still for a minute until Richards came into the frame. He knelt next to Regina and felt her pulse, woefully shaking his head a moment later. He then proceeded to lift Regina up and place her on the bed, where he wrapped her in the bedsheet. And then, he carried her out. The video showed the empty, vomit, and blood-covered room until the video ended.

Victor was dumbfounded. The professor lied to him. He knew all along how dangerous the Fertility Project was, and he lied. Professor Howard Richards, the most renowned scientist in the country, the person who was like a father to him, hid things from Victor on purpose. Why? Because he knew Victor would go to the police? Because he was so desperate to make a name for himself, even at the cost of innocent women's lives? This had to end, and it had to end now. Victor would go to the police. But no matter how much this treason stung, he would first tell the professor that he found out everything. He would tell him that he would report everything to the police – he at least owed him that much. Would the professor be willing to kill him to keep the secrets of the project hidden?

Victor would come prepared into his office.

Chapter 15
36 days until disaster

When he first knocked on the office door, Victor got no response from the professor. He knocked again but was met with silence once more. He decided to try the door, and sure enough, it was open. As soon as he stepped inside, he saw the professor's silhouette seated in the dark at the far end behind the desk. He saw the unmistakable glints of the liquor bottle and glass.

"Professor?" Victor called out.

"Come in, Victor," the professor responded somberly.

Victor flipped the lights on, causing the room to be illuminated immediately. Richards shielded his eyes momentarily from the light before blinking and looking at Victor.

"You shouldn't be drinking, Professor. What if Amanda's water breaks?" Victor asked.

The professor dismissively waved before saying, "We still have a couple more weeks before Amanda goes into labor."

Victor sat in the chair opposite the professor and sighed deeply.

"So, what happened back there?" he asked.

Richards had the chair turned sideways and was facing away from Victor.

"I already told you, the baby was stillborn."

"And Isabelle?"

Richards took a long sip directly from the bottle before saying.

"Victor, we need to talk."

Victor leaned back in the chair, trying to look as calm as possible, even though he was on the verge of shouting at Richards, insulting him, and calling him a murderer.

"Talk about what, Professor?" he asked, wondering what kind of bullshit story the professor was going to concoct this time.

"I know you, Victor. I know you don't trust me as much. Probably not at all. Not since the incident with Marie," he swiveled his chair to face the assistant professor.

"You're right, Professor. And I tried telling myself that the suspicions I had were not justified. But now I am sure that I was right to be suspicious of you."

"Yes, you were. I would have been disappointed if you let it slip. I am your mentor, but that doesn't mean that you shouldn't question the things I do. In fact, I have to say that I'm proud of you for doing so."

Victor would have felt flattered and honored to hear those words from Richards in any other situation, but right now, he felt nothing but disgust. He leaned forward and looked Richards dead in the eye.

"I know what happened to Isabelle, Professor. And I also know what happened to Marie. She wasn't crazy, was she? She had something inside of her, and she managed to pull it out. If she hadn't, she would have ended up like Isabelle."

Richards stared at Victor reticently as he tapped the desk repeatedly with his nails. Victor raised his tone as he said, "I also know about Regina. I've seen the footage. I've seen how she died from the seizure. Camera two's evidence is gone, but you failed to remove the evidence of camera four."

"No, I didn't fail to remove it, Victor. I deliberately left it there. I kept it hidden until today when it became visible in the folder again."

"Are you saying you left it there for me to see it?"

"That's exactly what I'm saying, Victor."

"Why? Why would you do that? I could just go to the police now, and you'll be in prison for the rest of your life."

"You could. But you might change your mind after hearing me out."

Victor guffawed at the absurdness of Richards' statement. There was no way in hell Richards was fooling him again. The professor pulled out a drawer and reached into it. Victor put his hand in the pocket of his lab coat, ready to pull out the scalpel he had stowed away earlier, and fight back. He expected Richards to withdraw a gun, but instead, the professor slammed a folder on top of the desk. The folder's cover was blank, and after staring at it for a moment, Victor looked up at the professor.

"What is this?" he asked.

"The real report of the Fertility Project," Richards answered.

***

There were documents and photographs inside, disclosing information about the Fertility Project that Victor had never seen before. There were regular mice with gaping holes in their stomachs and deformed mice, so misshapen and malformed that some of them were hard to even recognize as mice.

"What the hell is this, Professor?" Victor asked as he rapidly darted his eyes across each line of the document.

"I haven't been fully honest with you, Victor. The Fertility Project is not as pure as I made it out to be. It's dangerous, very dangerous. In fact, the mother's chances of surviving the pregnancy are extremely low. Hell, even for the body to accept the formula we inseminated the women with is not entirely safe and can cause sudden deaths."

"Is that what happened to patients two and four?" Victor looked up from the document long enough to shoot daggers at the professor.

"Yes," Richards said with slight hesitation. "Their body rejected the formula, but since the insemination causes a symbiotic relationship between the mother and the fetus, the mothers could not survive."

"Then why the hell did you do this, professor? To prove that you can make infertile women fertile? When everyone hears about this, they'll lock both of us up, and we'll be known as mad scientists in the scientific community – and the whole world!"

"Go to the next page, Victor," Richards commanded.

Victor turned the page and saw a picture of a perfectly healthy mouse pup. As he read the text of the page, he became increasingly baffled. He looked up at Richards once he was done reading, wanting to say something but not knowing what.

"You're, of course, familiar with parthenogenesis, Victor?" the professor asked.

"Of course. It's a natural form of self-reproduction in asexual animals, some plants, etcetera. It essentially helps certain species procreate without the fertilization of the male sperm. But I don't understand what this has to do with the experiment."

"During the test, the offspring that the tested mice gave birth to had adopted a parthenogenetic form of reproduction, meaning they were able to give birth to their own offspring."

"But the offspring were deformed."

"They were, and due to their extremely rapid growth, they continued to give birth to more and more offspring at an impressively rapid rate, and then those offspring gave birth further to more generations of self-reproducing mice. Due to this, these first generations of the parthenogenetic mice were dubbed The Mothers, and their sole purpose has always been to simply give birth to as many new mice as they could. Most of the mice would be defective, but... every so often, they would give birth to a perfectly healthy, non-parthenogenetic mouse!"

"It says here that the chances of a healthy offspring being born are less than ten percent," Victor rebutted.

"Yes, but when the rare, healthy mouse spawned, it was not only as healthy as healthy gets. It was *superior* to the other mice in terms of intellect, physical prowess, and other capabilities. For some reason, in those rare cases when the good mouse spawned, all the deformities of the previous generations would be ignored, and instead, the mouse would adopt only the good traits."

"So you think we could create a perfect human with this experiment?"

"I don't *think*, Victor, I'm *sure* of it. I haven't only tested it on mice. Listen, the Germans tried creating the perfect Aryan race during World War II in the Lebensborn project. They tried pairing 'pure' women with SS officers to breed."

"But they were on the wrong track. They were only looking for people who were not Jewish and had blonde hair and blue eyes. There's no evidence to support that those traits are superior in any way to other colors."

"Precisely. They were working on creating the perfect race, but they weren't taking other important factors into consideration – like the history of illnesses, a genetic inclination towards certain skills, etcetera. These women I chose, they were all carefully hand-picked because they had the valuable genetic traits which could be passed on to create a perfect child."

Victor's mind was buzzing a hundred miles an hour. He was trying to process everything the professor just told him. It was all so much information.

"So the Fertility Project," he asked. "It was never to help the women become fertile, was it? It was to create the perfect babies."

"Precisely. I know how you feel about this, Victor. This discovery is still only in the experimental phase, and it doesn't work ideally. But think where it will be in twenty or fifty years. Future generations may perfect it until they can create a whole generation of genetically flawless children without having to go through the deformed ones. If this succeeds, Victor, we will be revered in the scientific community. Everyone will regard us as the fathers of reproductive medicine who have sped up and maybe even perfected the evolutionary cycle of humans. They will all rush to fund us so that we can continue perfecting the project. We can choose which direction we want to go in, Victor, until we are able to create a world full of perfect humans!"

Victor leaned back in the chair, thinking about the whole thing for a long time. He gave another once over to the document. A world full of perfect children. Children who would grow up to contribute to the world – scientifically, medically, technologically... This could fast-forward the advancement of human civilization as they knew it!

"What about the mothers who give birth to the first generation? To... the patients?" he asked.

"They cannot survive, I'm afraid. They are here simply as vessels to bring the parthenogenetic children into the world. Remember what I told you, Victor. Sacrifices have to be made in the name of science."

Victor sighed and stared at the folder on the desk. He couldn't wrap his mind around everything he just learned. Parthenogenetic human creatures? Rare breeds of babies with perfect traits? Although genes played a huge role in certain things humans did, the practice also needed to be taken into account. Those people who had no talent in what they did but worked hard, would reach a certain barrier that they could never break past. But those with the right genes for that particular activity... if they practiced and worked hard, they could become the best in what they did.

Victor imagined a world full of scientists, doctors, athletes that broke new records... He then thought about Leah. One day, not too long from now, she would grow up and start dating. Victor would want his daughter dating only the best man on the planet. If the Fertility Project successfully managed to be accepted by the world, the old would be replaced by the new and better. They wouldn't kill off the non-perfect humans, no, but as the old generations died, more and more parents would flock to the solution of getting the perfect child.

It'd already happened before. A scientist in China genetically modified a newborn in a controversial experiment, before facing charges. He was regarded as a monster for experimenting on a baby, but thanks to him, that baby was now immune to various diseases that the world didn't even have a cure for, yet.

Victor leaned forward to grab the folder before leaning back and placing it in his lap. He listed through the findings one more time, trying to find something that would convince him that the project was a big mistake, but there was no lying to himself; he had already decided in his mind that he would go through with it until the end. This was big, much bigger than he was initially told when he started the experiment.

"You're sure there's no way to save the patients, Professor?" he asked, already knowing the answer.

"Trust me when I say I did everything in my power to save the mice who gave birth, Victor. Even with a successful C-section, the mother dies almost as soon as the umbilical cord is severed. There is nothing we can do. The mother dies either when the connection is severed, or... well, you can see there."

He gestured to the attached photo of the dead mouse with a huge hole in its stomach that looked like it had been opened from the inside.

"So, how did Marie survive, then?"

"Marie's case was... unconventional. Her body rejected the fetus, and the fetus was undeveloped, weak. She was slowly dying and had she not dug the fetus out when she pulled out her intestines, she would have been dead."

"Why do the fetuses kill the mothers that reject them?"

"They're trying to survive. When no nutrients are provided to them, they begin eating the only thing that remains."

"Their mothers."

"Precisely. It's a fight against the tide where the fetus tries to consume nutrients to survive, but ultimately kills the host and itself in the process."

"Victor ran his fingers through his hair and said, "I don't understand how anything genetically superior can be born from this monstrosity, Professor."

"It's something I don't fully understand, either. But if we successfully manage to do this, we will have more than enough time to research that."

A minute of silence filled the room while Victor reread the interesting parts of the project.

"Won't we go to prison for putting these women's lives in danger on purpose?"

"Not if we... fabricate the results. We thought we had it figured out, but unfortunately, a number of unforeseen circumstances caused the women to die tragically – an outcome they all knew was possible when they signed the agreement. You understand what I'm saying here, Victor?"

"The university doesn't know anything about this, do they?"

"Of course not. They would never have funded it in the first place."

"Why did you lie to me, Professor?"

"Because you would never have agreed to do this. You know I'm right about that."

He was. He knew Victor too well – at times, even better than Victor knew himself.

"And how do I know you're not lying to me again?"

"You don't. But you know me well enough by now to figure that when I lie, I lie with a purpose. Any information I withheld from you was all done so in the name of science, and to get you to join me."

Victor closed the folder and slowly placed it on the desk. He felt Richards put a hand over his. The professor looked at him solicitously and said, "Victor, you are like a son to me. If this project is successful, I want us to reap the rewards. Together."

He released Victor's hand a moment later and leaned back in the chair. Victor took one final glance at the closed folder and shook his head.

"What about the students?"

"We'll tell them that the Fertility Project is over, and their assistance is no longer necessary. We'll tell them that Amanda and Isabelle will be taken to the hospital for further evaluation and give the students the extra score we promised them."

Victor ran his fingers through his hair, still staring at the folder. Then, he looked up at the professor and, with determination, said, "Alright, Professor. Let's do it."

Chapter 16
22 days until disaster

"She left? And her baby is okay?" Amanda asked with concern.

She was in the exam bed, getting ready for an ultrasound.

"Yes, she and the baby are perfectly healthy," Victor grinned as he gently spread the gel on Amanda's stomach.

"Well, where are they now?"

"They've been transferred to a hospital for further care. Our work with them is complete, and now the rest is up to her."

Amanda chuckled, tears of joy filling her eyes. She usually wasn't so emotional, but her hormones were probably out of control right now.

"I'm so happy for her," she said. "She really deserves it. She and her husband have had such a difficult life. Her parents-in-law never accepted her, and her parents died in a crash when she was just seventeen. Her aunt had to take care of her. I'm so glad that she can finally start her own family the way she deserves it."

Amanda wiped her tears. Victor gave her a weak smile before taking the transducer and beginning to move it across her belly.

"You're such a good person, Victor. Both you and Professor Richards. I wish I could repay you for your kindness," she said.

"Oh, no, no. It's okay. The professor and I are just doing our jobs," Victor said.

His tone was not as lively as usual. Amanda suspected that he was simply tired. He has been working hard lately, not just with the project, but he mentioned once reading a lot and practicing with a pregnancy simulation device every day.

"Are you okay, Victor? Maybe you should take a few days off."

Victor briefly looked at Amanda before giving her another aloof smile and turning to face the monitor.

"I can't. You're due any day now, anyway. I'll take a break as soon as you and your baby are healthy."

His face turned more and more grievous as he silently stared at the blurry images on the screen. Amanda turned her head to see what he was looking at, but she may as well have been looking at hieroglyphics. She thought from time that she saw something that resembled a head or an arm or foot, but she couldn't tell for sure.

"Is everything okay with the baby?" she asked.

"Uh, yeah. Everything is fine. I'm just double-checking it here."

Realizing that Victor wasn't talkative today, she went silent. A few minutes into the ultrasound, Professor Richards took over and finished up. He told Amanda that everything was fine and that she should go to her room and get some rest. She thanked him and went back to her room. She felt a kick inside her stomach, this one a little stronger than usual, making her stop momentarily and yelp in pain.

"You're a strong one, aren't you?" she asked as she gently stroked her stomach.

***

With only one patient left, Victor had less work to do. He stopped reading books and practicing with Gloria. Neither of those would help him in what he was doing, anyway. Instead, he spent a lot of time catching up on some sleep and chatting with his family. He had just finished examining Amanda and eating lunch before slumping into bed. He knew that Jennifer wouldn't be doing anything right now, so he called her. She picked up almost immediately. His wife and daughter came into view on the video after just two rings, sitting next to each other on the living room couch.

"Look, it's Daddy!" Jennie said as she pointed at the screen.

Leah confusedly looked at the camera before flailing her arms up and down with an excited smile on her face.

"Hey, baby girl! You taking care of your mom for me?" Victor asked.

Leah produced an incoherent sound and looked at her mom.

"How's everything over there, babe?" Jennie asked.

"Ah, you know. Same old stuff," Victor said brusquely, trying to avoid talking about work.

"How is the final patient doing? Is her baby okay?"

"Yeah, so far, all is good. Her baby is due any day now."

He hadn't told Jennie anything about the other patients. He didn't tell her about Marie digging her guts and fetus out, or the other two patients dying, or Isabelle and her baby meeting such a tragic end, or the fact that Amanda would be dead any day now. He felt like shit about it, but he tried to focus on the big picture. Once he was a famous scientist, Jennie and Leah would understand; he was sure of it. Even so, he doubted he would ever tell them that he knowingly sacrificed Amanda.

"And the other patient? Isabelle?" Jennie asked.

"Probably okay. I haven't actually been in touch with her since she left the experiment."

"Aren't you interested in knowing how she and her baby are? You did help her give birth to the baby, after all."

"Yeah. I just wanna focus on the project right now, honestly."

Leah got louder – either from excitement or boredom – and it was hard to speak over her. Jennie leaned out of the camera's sight and came back a second later with a t-rex toy. She promptly pretended to make a roaring sound and bounced the dinosaur up and down towards Leah. Leah seemed to find this amusing, and she grabbed the toy immediately. Jennie turned back to the camera and said.

"You know, this is a big achievement, Victor. You changed one couple's life forever. Even if she's the only one successful, what you did is *huge*. I'm really proud of you, honey."

Victor felt a knot forming and twisting in his stomach. He forced a smile and muttered a 'Thanks' to Jennie. He quickly stood up from the bed and pretended to look around the room, facing away from the camera.

"Hey, how about we take a vacation once you're back?" Jennie asked. "You, me, and Leah could go somewhere. You always wanted to go to New Zealand, right? We can book a trip there."

That sounded like heaven. He did always want to visit New Zealand, but with the hustle and bustle of raising a child and working, it just wasn't possible. He doubted that it would be possible even after finishing the experiment. There would still be a lot of work to do regarding the parthenogenetic offspring. He suddenly got the urge to tell Jennie everything. He had to tell her because that way he'd be able to proceed with the project with a clear conscience.

"Hey, Jennifer, listen, I need to tell you something," Jennie nodded and closed her mouth, listening with rapt attention, while Victor's heart began beating like crazy. "There's someth-"

"Leah!" Jennie shouted.

Leah was biting the dinosaur toy, and Jennie quickly took it away from her and instead gave her a different toy that didn't have so many ridges and sharp edges. Victor's mind began clearing up. The moment had passed and all he could think was, 'Holy shit, I just dodged a bullet.'

"Sorry, you were saying, babe?" Jennie asked.

"Nothing. I was just saying, let's talk about the vacation when I return, okay?" Victor said.

"Are you okay, honey? You've been kinda distant lately."

"Yeah, sorry. I've probably just been working too hard. It's nothing you need to worry about."

Jennie gave him a suspicious once-over before nodding.

"Okay, if you say so," she said. "Just don't push yourself too hard. Amanda will need you to be fully rested for her delivery."

"Yeah. Jennie, listen, I gotta go. Let's talk again soon, alright?"

"Okay, stay safe there, babe. Leah, say 'Bye, Daddy'!" Jennie told Leah as she pointed to the camera.

Leah confusedly looked at her mom and then at the camera. Victor waved at the camera, and Leah raised one hand. She probably tried mimicking her parents' gesture, but it came out as clumsy flailing of the arm with the fingers contracting and extending dissonantly. Victor chuckled before ending the call. As soon as the video was off, he sighed deeply. Immense guilt suddenly enveloped him. On the one hand, he felt that he made the right call not telling Jennie about the real purpose of the Fertility Project. There's no way she would support it – not right now.

Right now, Victor needed someone to tell him that he was making the right choice, and the only person that would do that was Richards. After they were done with the experiment, things would be different. Those who would have doubted and shunned them would have a change of heart, Victor was sure of it.

The following two days went by slowly as Amanda waited for the baby to be born. And then, one morning at 10 am, while she was writing the name Gabriella in bilius font on a piece of paper, Amanda's water broke. She hadn't even realized what it was until she felt something wet between her legs and heard the dripping onto the floor. She thought that she had inadvertently peed herself at first until the realization struck her. She quickly waved at the camera and called the person monitoring her to get the professors immediately. In less than a minute, Victor and Richards were at the door with a stretcher, transporting her downstairs to the delivery room. She didn't like that the delivery room was in the basement since there might be some humidity that could be bad for the baby, but she assumed that the professors made sure the room was entirely safe for the delivery.

Amanda wasn't going into labor yet, but about an hour after she was laid on the delivery bed, the immense pain started. It felt like stomach cramps, but a lot worse than she had ever experienced. The pain soon grew in intensity, and Amanda, the woman who was too shy to scream in front of anyone – screamed at the top of her lungs.

Professor Richards and Victor were buzzing around the room, exchanging medical mumbo-jumbo while prepping Amanda for the delivery. Either way, no matter how bad the pain was, it would soon all be over. She would have her baby delivered, and she and Wayne would live happy lives with their new child. With Gabriella. But then a terrifying thought crossed her mind. What if there were some complications during the delivery? This was a new type of experiment, and things could easily go wrong. But everything was okay with Isabelle, right? Professor Richards came up to her with a syringe.

"Turn on your side, please," he said.

Amanda did so as best she could and then felt a sudden prick in her back. She yelped before the professor helped her roll back into the previous position.

"What was that?" she asked.

"Something to help you relax," he turned away with the empty syringe, while Victor came next to her, preparing an IV bag.

"Victor," she grabbed his hand, and he jerked his head towards her. "If anything goes wrong, please... just save the baby. Save Gabriella."

"It'll be fine, Amanda. We'll save the both of you," Victor smiled vaguely.

He stared at her with a look of concern on his face before giving her a nod of approval. Professor Richards returned to the delivery bed with a full surgical outfit, including a mask over his face.

"Amanda, we are going to have to perform a C-section. You're going to feel some tugging and pressure down there, but everything will be okay," he said.

"Is the baby okay, Professor?" she asked with concern in her voice.

"The baby is fine, Amanda," Richards nodded reassuringly before looking at Victor. "Victor, let's start."

Amanda lost the feeling in her abdominal area (including the labor cramps) and lower body parts. The professors placed a medical sheet just below her neck that blocked her view so that she couldn't look down even if she wanted to. From there, they began doing something she couldn't see. Just like the professor said, she began feeling pressure and a slight pulling sensation down there, but no pain. She held her breath, fearing that the strong pulling from the professors might injure the baby. But then again, they were professionals. She trusted that they knew what they were doing.

She couldn't tell how long had passed since the delivery first started, but at one point, maybe around thirty minutes after it started, she saw Professor Richards straightening his back and cradling a tiny figure. She heard a baby's cry – potent and energetic, just like she expected her daughter to be. She heard a snip of the scissors and smiled out of relief. She muttered something about seeing her baby, but it only came out as a weak mumble.

The last thing that went through her mind before she got sleepy was how she couldn't wait to start her new life with Wayne and Gabriella.

**

Victor stared at the monstrosity that Richards cradled. The baby's face looked humanoid, but more verging on the traits of a Neanderthal. The huge forehead, the jutted-out jaw, the tiny, pig-like eyes... All the hopes that Victor had of Amanda giving birth to a normal baby went down the drain when he looked at the face of the newborn. There was no way this baby was ever going to have a normal life.

He looked at Amanda, who mumbled something incoherent. Her eyes inadvertently shut, and her head slumped to the side. Victor took a step forward, but he felt Richards' restraining hand on his shoulder. The professor was staring at him with a grievous expression on his face.

"It's too late for her, Victor. I'm sorry."

Victor continued staring at Amanda's probably lifeless body, trying not to think of what he had just done. And then the professor's words came again, sternly this time, snapping him out of his stupor.

"Victor, if we don't hurry up, the baby is going to die, and the experiment will have gone to hell."

They went outside the room and strode down the hall to the final door at the end. Victor had never gone this far down, so he was surprised to see that the door had a card reader on the side. Richards pulled out his keycard and swiped it across the reader. It beeped, and the sound of the lock resounded. He pushed the door open and told Victor to flip the lights on. Victor fumbled for the switch until he felt it on his fingers. Once he flicked the switch on, the room was illuminated by a bright, surgical light.

Victor stopped with his jaw dropping at the sight in front of him. There were vertically lined-up tube-like glass chambers on both sides of the long room, each of them big enough to hold a human inside. Each of the tubes looked like something straight out of a horror movie about a mad scientist's experimental monsters. He also noticed that at the base of the tubes were control panels with buttons that Victor wouldn't dare play with, out of fear of killing someone's life support. He imagined the tubes being filled with green liquid and all sorts of deformed monstrosities resting inside. At the very end of the room was an incubator-like device, but it seemed far too large for any baby.

Richards strode over to the giant tube on the left of the enormous incubator and pressed a button on the base. The front of the tube's glass parted ways at the center, and Richards removed the baby from the towel it was wrapped in, and placed it inside. Now that it was entirely exposed, Victor saw the deformities of its body, as well as its face. They weren't horrible, but still visible nonetheless. The baby was calm at this point and had stopped crying. Richards pressed a button on the panel, and the glass closed again. At the bottom of the tube, where there were numerous tiny holes, transparent liquid began spurting out, filling the chamber's inside. Victor gasped, worried for the baby's safety, no matter how deformed it was.

"It's okay, Victor," Richards said.

The liquid was now above the baby's head, and the more it filled, the more the baby floated. Once the tube was entirely filled, the baby floated in the center of it, and it seemed to be completely calm – or dead, Victor thought.

"This will help the baby grow strong and healthy," Richards said. "This panel will display how the baby is doing."

Victor looked down at the panel. There was the word 'OK' displayed in green letters at the very top of it.

"What is this, professor? Isn't the baby going to drown?" Victor asked.

"No. This is a formula of regenerative chemicals that will help the baby grow strong. If anything were to go wrong, the liquid inside would immediately drain, and a loud alarm will let us know that something is going on. I also have it attached to my cellphone so that if something goes wrong at any time, it will inform us."

Silence permeated the room for a long moment while Richards and Victor stared at the incubator. Richards had the look of a proud parent, with a conniving smirk on his face. Victor, on the other hand, stared at the baby in disgust. Not because of its deformities, though, but because this innocent newborn was put into a test tube like an animal specimen to be studied purely for scientific purposes. One question ran through Victor's head over and over as he stared at the rows of empty tubes that would soon be occupied.

What have I done?

Disaster Night, Part 4

A towering figure grabbed the doorframe and stepped inside. It was so tall that it had to duck to avoid slamming its head on the top of the door entrance. The flashlight illuminated the creature, and Survivor saw it clearly. It stood at least eight feet tall, with a hunched back, an incongruously large stomach, and elongated, emaciated arms that went down almost to the ground, where its oversized, ape-like hands hung limply. The legs were spread widely and as emaciated as the arms, the knees slightly bent and crooked, and the feet were disproportionately long and thin, with an uneven number of deformed toes.

Most notable was its face, though. The head had patches of oily, dirty hair wetly sticking to the scalp. The forehead was too high, with one black eye visible under it, and a tumorous blister covered the other eye. The nose was wide and squished, the tip almost reaching down into the mouth full of crooked teeth. The jaw of the creature jutted forward in a comical witch-of-the-bog manner, with wrists hanging limply and legs deformedly standing in an X position.

Despite its meager humanoid features and the wrinkled skin that somewhat resembled that of a human in color, Survivor saw no intelligence or sentience in the creature's eye. He heard one of his team members shout 'Open fire!' and he squeezed the trigger. The recoil was almost non-existent, and he expected the monster to fall, but to his dismay, it simply flinched and reared back with a roar.

It then went for the closest victim it could find – the guard. It grabbed the guard by the arm with its oversized hand and lifted him up like he was nothing, despite the emaciated extremities and the barrage of bullets the creature endured. There was no blood anywhere, but Survivor saw tiny holes in the creature's skin – it was acting like some sort of armor.

The guard – Lopez - was screaming and flailing but to no avail. The monster raised Lopez higher and then brought him down with immense force. A loud crack resounded in the room, and the guard's legs went wobbly like pudding. Lopez screamed in pure, agonizing terror – or pain, or both. Survivor saw fragments of bones jutting out of the guard's legs, but the creature didn't stop there. It smashed Lopez on the ground once more, with such force that he instantly went quiet. Another crack resounded, and this time the guard's back twisted at an unnatural angle.

The entire time, bullets were pelting the creature's body, but to no avail.

"I'm reloading!" Talker shouted.

Survivor was almost out of ammo and would need to reload, too. Suddenly, the creature clasped one hand over its eye and shrieked in pain. It began flailing its arms, and Survivor realized that its eye had been shot. Blinded, the creature charged in a frenzy. Everyone sidestepped – everyone except Cougar. The creature picked Cougar up by the waist and chucked him forward. Cougar's screams echoed loudly as he was thrown through the already broken window, and disappeared out of sight, but the loud gunshots drowned out the impending thud.

"Cougar!" Bulldozer shouted.

The creature continued flailing around as if trying to swat away the bullets, randomly circling around the room. And then, it turned to face Survivor. Before he had the time to sidestep, the creature lunged at him, picking him up like he weighed nothing. He dropped his gun and clawed at the creature's bony wrists, but it was too strong. It brought him against the wall and held him up, its face so close to Survivor's, that he could smell its putrid breath and see every pore in its skin. Even though its eye had been damaged beyond repair, he felt its blind gaze on him.

It was normal in those situations to have an instinct kick in that tells the body it's over and to give up – but the brain always defied that thought. Survivor was trained to keep going, even when there was no hope of surviving, even when his body was crying that it wanted nothing more than for him to stop. He pulled the knife out of its pouch on his chest, and as if on cue, he saw something about the creature – a spot on its chest that looked somewhat different than the rest.

The area around the pectorals looked less thick, and more smooth and soft. With no other hope of trying anything better, Survivor thrust the knife forward. It embedded itself in the creature's chest, and the monster immediately released its grip on him, dropping him to the floor. It flailed it's arms rabidly, and Survivor quickly shot up to his feet. He knew that it was risky, but there was no time to think – he ran up to the creature and shoulder-bashed the hilt of the knife, causing the blade to dig itself in deeper.

The shooting had stopped by now, and the remaining two team members held their guns trained at the creature, whose screams and flailing were abating with each passing second. Within moments, it fell to its back, kicking and flailing, while the piteous shrieking continued, but then its motions slowly stopped. Its chest continued heaving up and down, but Survivor knew better than to give it a moment of rest. He ran up to the creature again, grabbed the knife by the hilt, and yanked it out. It came out with ease, causing the creature to shriek once more. Survivor brought the knife down into the monster's chest again, and then again, and again, until the monster on the ground ceased all movement altogether.

The entire time, Bulldozer and Talker kept the weapons trained on the creature. Survivor sifted through the room until he found his MP5. Once he grabbed it, he pointed it at the monster as well. It still wasn't moving.

"Un-fucking-believable," Bulldozer said. "It has a weak spot?"

"On the chest. See how different the skin looks there?" Survivor pointed.

One glance at Lopez's mutilated body answered the question all of them had in their heads – the guard didn't make it.

"We gotta check on Cougar," Talker said.

Survivor walked over to the broken window, stepping across the shards of glass that crunched under his boot, and peered down. Cougar was lying on his back on the concrete in front of the entrance. His leg was at an unnatural angle, and his head slumped sideways. Survivor didn't want to get any hopes up that he was still alive.

"Fuck," he muttered.

"Guys, you okay over there?" Squarepants' voice came through the radio.

"We're fine, Squarepants. But Cougar is down," Talker said.

"Tell Squarepants to meet us in front of the Genetics Center," Bulldozer commanded.

Talker spoke up again.

"Squarepants, get your ass in front of the Genetics Center."

"Roger that, Talker. On my way."

Survivor could tell by how light his MP5 was that he only had a couple of bullets remaining, so he removed the clip and replaced it with a full one, putting the almost-empty one in the magazine holder. He made sure to communicate this to his teammates so that they knew not to reload at the same time. Once he was done, Talker reloaded, and then Bulldozer.

They made their way downstairs and through the entrance – luckily not running into any of those freaks along the way. Once outside in the cool night air, Survivor saw the body of a nude child near the entrance.

"What the fuck is that?" Talker asked.

He and Survivor got closer to the body to examine it, while Bulldozer went up to Cougar's body. No, it wasn't a child. It had the features and size of one, but it was definitely not human. It had an oversized head, deformed face and extremities, and the skin looked thick like it did on the big one, but only up to the forearms.

"Juveniles," Survivor said. "This must be the child of that big thing we killed."

"Jesus fucking Christ, how many of these are there?"

They glanced in Bulldozer's direction and saw him checking Cougar's pulse. He forlornly shook his head before standing up and uttering 'Shit' to himself.

It was then that they started hearing distant gunshots coming from the direction of the Genetics building. The distinct loud echo of the single-bullet firing told Survivor that it was Delta sniping hostiles. Bulldozer gestured with his head for the two teammates to follow him.

"HQ, this is Alpha team," Survivor pressed the button on his microphone and spoke into the radio. "We're heading to the Genetics Center. We believe Professor Richards is there."

"Roger that, Alpha. Be advised that there are hostiles around the building, and Team Bravo has gone silent in there. Use extra caution."

"Copy that. What about Delta?"

278

"They're in positions around the Genetics Center. They'll provide sniper support for you."

"Roger that, HQ. Alpha out. Delta Team, do you copy?"

"We hear you, over," Another voice came through a few seconds later.

"Have you encountered any of the big guys?"

"Yep. Tough sons of bitches to kill."

"But you managed to kill 'em?"

"Yeah. But we have to use piercing ammo to kill them, 'coz the other stuff don't do shit."

"Got it. If any of them get close to you, their weak point is probably their chest."

"Copy that, Alpha. Thanks for the heads-up."

The distant gunshots ceased moments later.

***

"Fuck, man, we're all that's left of the team?" Squarepants asked.

He was already in front of the Genetics building when Survivor, Bulldozer, and Talker arrived. There were dozens of the children-monsters' bodies splayed around the concrete entrance, along with three of the big ones. Survivor glanced up at the rooftop of one of the nearby buildings and saw the glint of the sniper's scope.

"Alright, let's move," Bulldozer said.

They breached the front door, and with the newfound confidence that they could take down the monsters now that they knew their weaknesses, they kept their flashlights on. In this building, they had to search every nook and cranny because Professor Richards could have been anywhere in there.

Most of the rooms were empty, save for a few bodies of the juveniles and two dead Bravo members that they encountered. As they further explored the first floor, they found an empty office that screamed Professor Richards' name on it. Unlike the other quarters they encountered, the office was spacious and even had a drinks cabinet on the right. Survivor took a mental note to reward himself with a bottle of vodka as soon as the mission briefing was over.

"Professor Richards, are you in here?" Bulldozer called out as he scanned the room with his gun raised. "We're with The Company, we've come to rescue you."

The team checked the few meager hiding spots that the room had and found no one inside. Squarepants was already leaning on the desk and staring at the screen of the open laptop. It was plugged into a charger, and the brightness of the screen illuminated Squarepants' face, casting ominous shadows under his eyes.

"Huh, look at that. It's not secured," Squarepants said.

"Anything useful on it?" Bulldozer asked.

"Yeah. There's something. Want me to read it?"

"Read it aloud," Bulldozer commanded.

Chapter 17
4 days until disaster

The first generation of parthenogenetic humans has successfully been delivered. It has grown significantly in size since day 1. The newborn started with 5 lbs, 7 oz in weight and 21 inches in height. It has since grown to an impressive 230 lbs and 9' 7" feet in height. The newborn, dubbed the Mother, has stopped growing around twelve days after birth. It is consuming up to 12,000 kcal a day, and its muscle mass appears to be improving with the growth, indicating that there may be a deficiency in myostatin and excess production of the growth hormone. Further tests needed.

The Mother *has given birth to exactly eight parthenogenetic offspring, all of whom have adopted the mutated genes, causing them to have congenital disorders. The offspring have since been dubbed The Rejects.*

The Rejects *have shown impressive physical abilities (approximately 3 times stronger and faster than the average athletic human), however, their cognitive abilities are lower than expected, and a lot of their offspring are either stillborn or die shortly after birth. Tests needed to prove the theory.*

One common trait that the Mother and the Rejects have adopted is a form of scleroderma – the hardening of the skin. It begins at the fingertips and toes and gradually moves up until it reaches the pectoral area. Fully grown Rejects' skin is so thick that penetrating it with a needle is impossible. Unlike the typical scleroderma, the parthenogenetic creatures' organs and capabilities are not affected by the skin's hardening. More so, it seems to act as a natural shield for them.

The Mother continues to give birth to the Rejects at an impressive rate (approximately 1.4 rejects every day). Even more fascinatingly, she appears to be able to communicate with her children like a queen bee without using body language or speaking—suspected communication using either vibrations, sounds, smells, or pheromones.

Since the Rejects seem to be controlled by the Mother, they may still prove to be useful in certain areas. If the Mother was to be controlled by an external source, then that source would be able to command her and the Rejects.

Conclusion: *Since the perfect baby, dubbed The Immaculate has been born, the Fertility Project will officially end in four days. I will dispose of the evidence (and the witnesses) until the cleaners arrive to transport the Mother and the Immaculate to the new facility for research.*

- Report of the Fertility Project, Professor Embryologist Howard Richards

Chapter 18
Hours until disaster

Victor woke up with a jolt at the sound of his alarm. Hastily, he shut it off. He was covered in cold sweat and panting heavily. He had just woken up from a nightmare where he was stalked by deformed-looking babies. He tried fighting them off, but there were too many of them, and eventually, they swarmed him until they covered every inch of his body. It was almost 4 pm. He hadn't even planned on sleeping this early, but he guessed that the stress must have gotten to him.

In the past few weeks, he'd been wracked with guilt, stress, and worry. On the one hand, he was glad that the Fertility Project was almost over and that he would begin transitioning into accepting the honorary (and monetary) rewards from the prestigious and well-known communities. That's what kept him sane. On the other hand, however, he was plagued by the guilt he felt for lying to Amanda. She trusted him, and he betrayed her. He tried to push those thoughts out of his mind as he told himself that it was for the greater good.

He got dressed and headed outside the room. The building felt empty as it was, but right now, with only him and the professor being the only ones left, it felt like a graveyard. Victor made his way towards Richards' office when the professor himself stepped out and said, "Ah, you're here,

Victor. Good. Come on, Amanda's husband will be here any minute."

Victor nodded. He and Richards strode to the front of the building, where the scary-looking guard with the foreign accent stood. A car pulled up in front of the building and killed the engine. A moment later, a man around Victor's age stepped outside. In the afternoon sun, he looked gaunt and broken. His hair was disheveled, heavy circles loomed under his eyes, and his unkempt beard clearly showed that he hadn't been taking hygienic care of it for days. With haggard steps, he shuffled towards the entrance, where Richards greeted him with a handshake.

"Mr. Weaver. Allow me to express my condolences over the loss of your wife," he said it so somberly that even Victor almost believed that there was actual sorrow in his words.

Wayne Weaver didn't respond but rather stared at Richards with unfocused, dreary eyes. Seeing this, Richards gestured towards the entrance.

"Let's speak in the office, shall we?"

***

"I just don't understand how this could happen," Wayne said from the seat on the other side of Richards' desk.

He sniffled as tears began rolling down his cheeks. Victor and Richards sat opposite of him, deafeningly quiet. Victor hung his head down and refused to look the man in the eye. He was afraid that if he did so, he might break down and tell him the truth.

"There were... unfortunate complications during the procedure, I'm afraid," Richards said. "Amanda and the baby were perfectly healthy, but... there were unprecedented complications during the delivery. I'm so sorry."

Wayne sobbed for a bit before looking up at Richards with sudden anger in his bloodshot eyes.

"You killed my wife! This is your fault! I'm gonna sue your asses for this!" He shot up from his chair so vigorously that it fell backward.

"Calm down, Mr. Weaver. It wasn't anybody's fault," Richards said. "My associate and I did our best to save both Amanda and the baby, and when things got bad, we tried to honor your wife's final wish – to save the baby. But we failed. And I do not have the words to express the sorrow we feel for our failure."

Wayne broke down again, sobbing uncontrollably with his face buried in his hands.

"Amanda, I'm so sorry..." he muttered. "We never should have come here. We should have simply adopted a kid. It's... it's not such a terrible option. Oh god..."

Tears welled up in Victor's eyes, and he blinked them away. He wanted to tell Wayne how sorry he was for the pain he was going through, to admit to him that he and Richards never planned on saving Amanda's life and that his daughter was alive but deformed. As Victor opened his mouth, he felt Richards' hand on his thigh.

"Victor, can you please bring some water for Mr. Weaver?"

Victor nodded, making his way out of the room as hastily as he could without looking suspicious. As soon as the door was shut behind him, he allowed the tears in his eyes to flow freely. His vision blurred from them, and he sniffled a few times, but the sobbing fit that he expected never came – instead, he felt sick to the stomach. He hurried to the nearest bathroom and threw up the half-digested lunch into the toilet. He felt another wave of his food climbing up to his throat, and he vomited again, feeling the acid burning his throat. He spat and remained on the floor above the toilet, like a drunk teenager in a night club on the weekend, for several more minutes since he wasn't sure if he would vomit again.

"Calm down, Victor, calm down," he told himself over and over, trying to convince himself that he was okay and that this was the right choice. "You're going to get through this, and you're going to become a famous scientist. Leah and Jennifer will have everything secured for them so that they never have to work another day in their lives. It's not gonna be like it was for you when you were growing up. No, you're gonna make sure Leah has absolutely everything she needs."

With that, he began feeling much better. The nausea was almost entirely gone, but he still felt wobbly, so he gave himself a few minutes to recuperate. Once he freshened up, he got outside and saw Richards returning from the direction of the entrance. He saw Victor, so he waited for him to catch up.

"Everything okay, Victor?" the professor asked.

"Yes, Professor. I just felt a little sick. Where is Wayne?"

"He left. He threatened to sue us, so I offered him a handsome compensation, which I didn't have to do. I was hoping to avoid any unpleasantries, but since he refused, I'm afraid Mr. Weaver may find all the charges dropped if he tries to pursue them."

"How so?"

"He has no legal basis on which to sue us. It's all in the contract. He and Amanda agreed to participate despite the risks when they signed the NDA. There is nothing he can do to blame us now."

"I see," Victor nodded.

He turned to leave, but Richards called out to him.

"Victor, are you feeling okay? You've been acting strange lately," he said.

"I'm fine, Professor. Just tired, is all."

Richards nodded.

"You're not having second thoughts about all this, are you?"

Victor waited a moment before answering.

"No, Professor. Like you said, sacrifices need to be made in the name of science. What we're doing here will help the world."

Richards smiled vaguely.

"I'm glad you think so. Get some rest and meet me in front of the incubation room tonight at 8 pm. I have something to show you. And then, it will be time to conclude the Fertility Project."

***

Victor didn't like going into the incubation room, but he had to do it almost every day. He hadn't stepped in there for at least five days now, though. He didn't have almost any work to do ever since the final patient gave birth, but he wished that he did, to pass the time faster. At 7:55 pm, Victor went down to the basement. Despite the meeting with Amanda's husband earlier, he felt good. The project would be over soon! He saw Richards already waiting at the end of the hall in front of the incubation room.

"Good to see you, Victor," Richards said and gave a nod of approval.

He looked somewhat distressed, though. His shoulders were tense, his lips somewhat stiff, and his eyes too focused.

"Everything okay, Professor?" Victor asked.

"Yes. Come. I have something to show you," the professor said as he unlocked the door.

As he stepped inside and flipped on the light switch, Victor was greeted with the incubation room, now much different than it was the first time when he stepped inside. The tubes, all of them, were now filled with a transparent liquid, and inside them were the Rejects. Each of the humanoid monstrosities had grown to its adult size, looking like something straight out of a horror movie. Most of them had normal-colored skin like humans, however, many of them were too pale or going in the opposite direction, taking on a sickly gray or olive color.

All of the Rejects were taller than the average human, ranging from six and a half to eight and a half feet. Their faces had some semblance of humanity, either from an intact nose here, or a visible eye there, ear, mouth, patches of hair, etcetera, but none of them had a fully intact face. The bulbous and cancerous-looking growths on their faces reminded Victor of the abominations from the movies *Wrong Turn* and *The Hills Have Eyes*.

Their bodies were no better, either. A lot of them had crooked, kyphotic, and scoliotic spines, bony chests with incongruous ball-shaped bellies, elongated, disproportionate extremities, as well as long, ape-like bony fingers and toes; either too many of them or not enough.

There were juvenile Rejects in the tubes, too. They were usually separated from the adults by draining the regenerative liquid from the tube, and then picking up the deformed babies and putting them in a separate tube. Since the liquid rendered the Rejects unconscious, it was safe for Richards and Victor to separate the babies from the parents. Right now, there were so many juvenile Rejects that many of them had to be put together in one tube. Over the last few days, they had grown to multiple sizes, ranging from babies, to toddlers, to the sizes of little children.

The Mother, the first parthenogenetic creature, Amanda's child – Gabriella – was at the far end of the room, inside an incubator much larger than the other ones. She had grown significantly since her birth. She was now around nine feet tall and didn't look any different than her Reject children, except in size. She had patches of hair on her large, bald head, a forehead that jutted forward, tiny eyes that were closed due to the incubation, a crooked mouth stretched slightly to the left, revealing her human-like teeth slightly, and a jaw too small compared to the rest of her face.

Her body seemed more congruous than her children, with her arms and legs being equal in size and length, although her entire body did look somewhat emaciated, save for the bulging stomach which occasionally produced a Reject. One thing that Victor noticed the Mother and the Rejects had in common were the wide hips, with the femurs placed widely apart, ideal for giving birth.

"Come, Victor," Richards said as he strode through the room between the tubes.

The first few times he walked between the filled tubes, Victor felt vulnerable and expected any moment for those creatures to break the glass and lunge at him. After a while, he became desensitized. When they reached the Mother's incubator, Richards turned around and smiled at Victor.

"Victor, it has been an honor working with you on such a groundbreaking project. I could not ask for a better partner."

"Thank you, Professor. But I still don't understand. You said that the project is over. But why?"

"Here's why. Look."

Richards gestured towards an incubator on Victor's left, and Victor loudly gasped at the sight in front of him. In the incubator, floating right in the middle was a perfectly healthy, non-deformed human baby. Victor stared in awe at the newborn's flawless features, the face that unmistakably resembled Amanda's, the tiny hands and feet that had the right number of fingers and toes, even the small vagina that visibly showed the baby's gender. *This* was the baby Amanda desired.

Gabriella.

Victor smiled and approached the incubator. He placed one palm on the glass, feeling a warmth enveloping him inside. This baby was his creation. And it was the most beautiful baby in the world.

"She's... she's perfect," he said.

And then he heard some sort of mechanical sound behind him that sounded foreign and yet not unfamiliar. He shot around and saw the professor holding a gun pointed at him. Startled, he widened his eyes.

"Professor? Wha-what are you doing?"

Richards sniffled, and his face contorted into one that expressed sorrow. A tear flowed down his cheek as he spoke.

"I'm sorry, Victor. You were supposed to be my successor. But you are not fit for it."

"Professor Richards, what are you talking about? Please, put the gun down!"

Victor's heart began racing in fear and confusion. He couldn't comprehend what was going on.

"You've been having doubts, Victor. About the project. I know it."

"I... I have, but I agreed to go through it with you, professor. I already told you I would not go to the police!"

"The police don't concern me," Richards sniffled. "It's... *them.*"

"Them? Who's 'them', professor?"

"We've been watched very closely this whole time, Victor. They wanted to make sure the experiment would be a success. But they also wanted to make sure neither of us would go rogue. I tried to convince them that you're on their side, that we could just pack and continue the third phase of the experiment..." he sniffled again, still holding the gun pointed at Victor. "But they insist that I be the only one to participate."

"Third phase? Professor, I don't understand anything, please."

"I lied to you, Victor. The motivation of the Fertility Project was never to achieve scientific greatness and create a society of perfect humans."

"So, what was the motivation then?"

"Money," Richards responded coldly.

Victor looked down at his feet, feeling duped like an idiot once again. He looked up at the professor and asked.

"Who funded the project, Professor?"

Richards didn't respond.

"Professor! Who?!"

"You were like a son to me, Victor. Forgive me."

Richards closed his eyes. With nothing better at hand and no time to think, Victor reached into his pocket and pulled out his cellphone. He chucked the phone at the professor. It must have been some crazy luck because the device hit Richards directly in the center of the forehead.

A loud bang exploded in the room, right next to Victor's ear. A glass-shattering sound ensued, followed by a watery splash that Victor felt on the back of his legs. He turned around and saw the perfect baby's incubator glass shattered and the baby lying on the floor. She had a big, red hole in the middle of her chest.

"NO!" Richards shouted, dropping the gun on the floor, running to the baby and pushing Victor out of the way.

He lifted the head of the baby and cried out in despair. And then, a hum filled the room. It was so steady and loud that it was hard to tell where it was coming from, but both Victor and Richards looked around in confusion. The hum ensued once more, causing the entire room to vibrate with intensity. Victor looked at the Mother's incubator – her eyes were open!

The two tiny, black dots stared directly at Victor, with such tenacity that Victor screamed. Another hum filled the room, and then a dull thud. And then another, and another, like the battering of the rain on a rooftop. Victor pivoted around and realized with horror that all the Rejects were suddenly awake and banging on the glass of their incubators.

Crack.

One of the incubators spider-webbed from the impact of the Reject's slam, and then a shatter of

293

glass ensued. A blood-curdling scream filled the air before it got drowned out by more and more shatters of the glass, followed by more screams, some higher-pitched, some guttural, none of them sounding human. Victor saw one of the tall Rejects stepping out of the incubator and onto the shards of glass on the floor with its bare foot. It took an unsteady step forward, staring directly at Victor with a snarl. It was all Victor could take.

He bolted towards the exit, ignoring the sound of the other incubators breaking and the Rejects who already stood outside of them. He heard the professor's scream behind him, not one of horror, but pure, unadulterated agony. He sounded like he was being flayed alive. There was a loud snap, and the professor's screams soon turned into whimpers, but Victor didn't stay to listen to them.

He burst through the door with his shoulder, closed the door, and ran down the hall, hoping the electronic lock would hold the monsters back. His hopes died when he heard loud banging on the door that vibrated throughout the entire building, followed by a high-pitched scream behind him, and he knew that there was no way he could outrun these monsters. He turned left into the delivery room and, with no better hiding spot, slid behind the bed.

A patter of footsteps followed inside the room not even two seconds after Victor hid. They stopped, and a guttural noise escaped the creature's throat. Victor firmly closed his eyes, praying for the creature to go away. He heard the creature's slow and soft thudding of footsteps as it explored the room. And then another set of footsteps resounded outside the room.

"Oh, my god. What the fuck are those?!" It was the guard from outside the building.

Loud gunshots filled the hall, and a scream from the delivery room caused Victor's eardrums to hurt.

"HQ, this is armed security guard Dalton! We have a code red! I repeat, code red! Send backup immedi- AGH!"

The guard's voice was cut off by something. More screams ensued, followed by rabid, frenetic footsteps all around the building – now even on the floor above. Victor curled behind the bed, feeling more afraid for his life than he'd ever been before.

As the sounds of those monstrosities drummed around him, he closed his eyes firmly and thought about Leah and Jennie.

Disaster Night, Part 5

"Wow. What a dick," Talker said when Squarepants stopped reading Richards' journal.

"So, the professor conducted an experiment, but he didn't tell anyone what the true purpose of what it was, huh? And then he decided to get rid of the involved people?" Squarepants said and whistled.

"Not our problem," Bulldozer retorted briskly. "Our mission is to extract him."

"Why should we risk our lives for a piece of shit like him?" Squarepants scoffed.

"Because that's our mission. Besides, Richards is probably paying The Company handsomely to keep him safe. So if we fail to get him out alive, it'll be our asses on the line."

Squarepants frowned but said nothing.

"Alright, let's check the basement first," Bulldozer said.

He led the way back to the staircase and downstairs into the basement. Almost as soon as they reached the basement, Survivor heard Talker gasp and mutter 'Jesus' under his breath. The mutilated body of a security guard lay at the bottom of the steps, his face literally torn off, revealing bulging eyes that stared upward and blood-smeared teeth. A gaping hole was in his torso, showing a broken ribcage and organs splattered to his side, like moist food dropped on the floor. A putrid smell filled the air, but Survivor wasn't bothered. Just like the smell of gunpowder, the smell of death was normal.

Along with the security guard's body, there were four bodies of juvenile Rejects in various positions on the floor, apparently shot to death. Bulldozer stopped in front of the door on the right and waited for his team to take up positions.

***

Victor had no idea how long had passed since he first hid in the delivery room, sitting in the dark. He tried being as quiet as possible while the footsteps and screams reverberated through the building for god-knows how long. He was tempted to make a run for the stairs and bolt to the exit, but every time he stood up and approached the door, he thought he heard someone just outside.

And then, some time after staying hidden in the room, he heard gunshots. At first, he was relieved. It must have been the police, and they would be coming to rescue him! He didn't even care if he had to go to prison; he just wanted out of this building. But then, the gunshots got mixed with distinctive, human screams. Soon it turned into a cacophony of not just human screams, but monstrous ones as well, until only the latter remained.

He thought about Jennifer and Leah. Would he ever get to see them again? If he did, would it be behind a thick pane of glass in prison during visits? Or would Jennie be informed by the police that her husband tragically died in the experiment gone wrong? As much as he preferred staying in

297

good memory with Jennie and Leah, he was too much of a coward, and he wanted to see them again, even if it meant seeing them during prison visits. But would Jennie even want anything to do with him after this? Or would she cease all contact with him after finding out that he willingly sacrificed an innocent woman? The horrific realization that Leah might grow up without a father terrified him – or worse yet, that she might grow up knowing that her father was a monster who ended up in prison for murder.

He wanted to scream. He wanted to go out there and kill those monsters with his bare hands and go home and hug his wife and daughter. He didn't care about the experiment or scientific greatness anymore. After this, he doubted he would ever even do his job, even if he had the chance to. Moving into the countryside and having a happy, cozy life with the family on a farm suddenly seemed so much more appealing. Hell, they could even adopt a dog. Victor smiled at the thought of Leah as a toddler running across the vast, green fields under the afternoon sun while he and Jennie sat on the porch. His eyes filled with tears at the life they would most likely never have.

That thought was interrupted when the door creaked open. Victor gripped the scalpel he'd been holding in his sweaty palm for the past hour, and shrunk in his spot, trying to take up as little space as possible in the hopes of not being noticed. His heart began thudding loudly, and he held his breath while soft footsteps resounded on the floor.

He listened and tried to determine where the sound was coming from.

He saw the silhouette of one figure appearing on his left next to the bed. Victor's survival instinct kicked in, and he knew what he needed to do. He would not die in here. And if he did, he would go down fighting - not like a coward. The figure took a step forward, and Victor gripped the scalpel more firmly. He scrambled to his feet and lunged at the intruder.

***

Since the lights were on inside the hallways of the building, the team didn't need their flashlights. Talker was the first one through the door with Survivor closely behind him. Out of the corner of his eye, Survivor saw a figure jump from behind a delivery bed with something in his hand and rush towards Talker. Talker was faster and managed to hit the assailant across the face with the butt of his gun, knocking him down instantly. Everyone in the room pointed their weapons at the figure, shouting at him to put his hands up. The meager light from the hallway revealed the face of a timid young man in a lab coat.

"Wait!" he shouted, raising his hands, much like in the same manner security guard Lopez back in Richards' office did.

Usually, civilians cowered just at the sight of armed forces, especially one as armed to the teeth as The Company's Intervention Unit. On some rare occasions, though, it was a trick to buy time and strike from behind.

"That him? That the professor?" Squarepants asked.

"Are you Professor Richards?" Bulldozer asked.

The young man scanned the faces of the unit members with wide eyes, darting in various directions.

"Talk, asshole!" Talker shouted.

"N-no, I'm not! But I worked with him! I'm Assistant Professor Victor Lukanski!" the scientist recited quickly in one breath.

"Where's Richards?" Bulldozer asked.

"He-he's dead. Please, don't kill me," the scientist pleaded.

Bulldozer stared at the man for a long moment before briefly glancing at Survivor.

"Give me your radio," he said.

Survivor unplugged his wired microphone from the radio and took it out of the holder before tossing the radio to Bulldozer. Bulldozer caught it skillfully and spoke into it.

"HQ, we found someone who worked with Richards. He says his name is Victor Lukanski."

HQ's voice came through a moment later.

"He's the scientist who closely collaborated with the professor. What about Richards?"

"Lukanski says he's dead."

"Make sure that that's really the case, Alpha. If Richards really is dead, then your primary objective is to evacuate Lukanski out of the hot zone."

"Copy that, HQ."

Bulldozer tossed the radio back to Survivor, who grabbed it and placed it back in the holder. He didn't bother plugging in the microphone.

"Alright, genius. Time to get you out of here," Talker said as he took a step towards Lukanski.

The guns were lowered and Lukanski put his hands down tentatively.

"You're... getting me out of here? Are you with the police?"

"Don't talk, just move. And do everything we tell you, or you'll end up dead. Got it?" Bulldozer said.

"Wait, wait! We can't leave just yet!" the scientist pleaded with wide eyes.

"Why?" Bulldozer reticently asked.

"We can't go until the Mother is dead."

Survivor and the other unit members exchanged glances with each other. Bulldozer looked like he was losing patience, even though he didn't show it in any way except stare at the scientist.

"Look," Lukanski said. "The Mother is what gives birth to all these creatures. If we leave it be, it'll continue making more. And they grow up really fast. Those big things you saw out there... they're only two weeks old."

"Shit," Squarepants scoffed.

Bulldozer continued staring at Lukanski solicitously before jutting his head towards him and asking, "Where's the Mother?"

"Down the hall and through the door. That's where I last saw Richards, too."

Bulldozer sighed.

"Talker. Stay with the scientist. The rest of you, follow me."

"Oh, come on, why do I have to babysit the nerd?" Talker grumbled.

"Enough talking," Bulldozer spat. "Squarepants, get your C4 ready."

"Hell, yeah," Squarepants grinned widely.

Disaster Night, Part 6

Although the hallway was quiet, Squarepants, Bulldozer, and Survivor proceeded carefully towards the door at the end. Although a card reader was next to it, the door was busted open, with a visible dent on the side. Bulldozer stopped in front of the door while Survivor pulled out a stun grenade. He removed the pin and chucked the grenade inside, and a moment later, a loud bang resounded, followed by a bright flash.

The team made their way inside and immediately saw three adult Rejects flailing their arms and covering their eyes, along with a whole bunch of juveniles. The unit opened fire, focusing first on the big guys. Two went down easily, but the third one covered its chest with its massive hand and sauntered towards them. Halfway through, it stopped and made a grimace. Its elongated fingers contorted, and Survivor saw something peeking from between the monster's legs. At first, he thought that the monster was taking a shit in the middle of the floor, but then he realized that the shit actually had the features of a baby, as deformed as they were.

The baby slid out of the monster with a meaty sound, covered in some gooey substance, and plopped on the floor with a wet thud. Immediately the baby began moving around, producing some sort of moaning sounds. Survivor fired a single bullet into the baby's forehead, and upon realizing that its offspring had been killed, the adult Reject screeched loudly and rushed towards the team with its arms spread. That was a mistake on its side because it left its weak spot uncovered, giving Bulldozer enough time to take down the creature with four clean shots.

Taking care of the juveniles was easy enough, but their numbers were the problem. They ran on all fours like feral animals towards the team while screeching, some of them even trying to circle around, but they dropped like flies against the barrage of bullets. Survivor was sure that had he been alone here by any chance, he would have been swarmed by the Reject children.

"Clear!" Bulldozer called out when the final Reject took a bullet to the chest and fell backward with a screech.

As Survivor scanned the room, he just then realized how fucked up it was. There was an array of test tube chambers with the glass broken, lined up on either side of the room, all the way to the far end of the room. At the very end was a larger, rectangular aquarium of some sort, with a tall figure inside it.

The Mother, Survivor immediately realized.

The team made their way across the floor covered in a wet substance that smelled like chlorine, their boots crunching on the broken shards of glass that covered it. They scrutinized each corpse on the way, just to make sure they didn't get ambushed. As they got closer to the

Mother, Survivor was able to discern more and more details on the figure in the aquarium.

It was dormant, floating in a transparent liquid with its eyes closed. By the looks of it, it was very similar to its offspring, as deformed as they were, but much larger. It stood at least nine feet tall, and even from twenty feet away, it looked intimidating.

"Looks like we found Richards," Squarepants pointed to the floor left of the aquarium.

There was a dead body – too mutilated to be identified as a man or woman – in a red-soaked lab coat splayed on its back. The face that was turned left was bashed in, making it look like an extremely life-life rubber doll that had its face dented. One of the arms looked as if it was holding onto the elbow socket by just a few tendons, as if something powerful had tried yanking the arm off the person. A piece of the femur bone sharply stuck out in the upper thigh. Whatever happened to Professor Richards, it wasn't a pretty way to go.

"Shit," Bulldozer said with the shake of his head. "That's karma for you, right there."

"HQ, we found Richards. He's dead," Survivor contacted base.

"Copy that, Alpha. Extract Lukanski out of the hot zone back the way you came," HQ said.

"Roger that, HQ. We're finishing up over here and will be at the extraction point soon. Alpha out."

"Squarepants, set the explosive," Bulldozer jutted his head towards the Mother's aquarium.

"Roger," Squarepants immediately approached the Mother's aquarium with hurried steps, before adding. "You are one ugly motherfucker."

He pulled out the C4 from the holder in his vest. The explosive looked like a simple block of plastic. The good thing about it was that it was extremely stable. There was essentially no way of accidentally detonating the explosive by shooting it, heating it, setting it on fire, or doing anything else. There had to be a shockwave, for example, when a detonator inserted into it was fired.

Squarepants cut open the cover of the C4 and shaped it into a cone before sticking it on the glass of the aquarium with a dramatic slam. He pulled out the remote detonator, and a grin stretched across his face.

"Get ready for some fireworks," he said.

Survivor, Bulldozer, and Squarepants backed away and ducked between two test tubes around halfway through the room – Squarepants on the right, the other two on the left. Squarepants opened the lid on top of the detonator, which disengaged the safety. He grabbed the handle and looked at his teammates.

"Fire in the hole!" he shouted.

***

Victor stood buried in one spot in anticipation. The armed forces guy in front of him didn't look like he fit the job, at least not facially. Although he was in his late thirties or early forties, he looked way too handsome to be risking his life on a suicide mission like this one. In fact, with that face and wearing a uniform, armed to the teeth, he looked more like a cosplayer than an actual task-force member. Victor imagined that under the helmet, he had lush, long hair that every balding man envied. Prettyface stood in front of the closed door in a wide-legged stance, firmly gripping his rifle, staring at Victor incessantly.

Victor felt uncomfortable. He averted his gaze and pretended to look elsewhere, but whenever he looked back at Prettyface, he'd find him staring at him with an unblinking gaze. Victor wanted to move through the room, turn his back on him, but he half-expected the guy to point his gun at him again. Either way, Victor at least felt much safer with these guys around. They were trained professionals and not only that, but he heard what they said on the radio. Since Richards was dead, their job would be to escort Victor out safely. But why? Because he's a civilian? So they could prosecute him properly in court?

"So, are you guys with the police?" Victor asked, even though he saw no emblems or anything distinguishable on the guy's uniform.

"No," the guy said.

That wasn't good. If they weren't with the police, then why were they here? Suddenly, a terrifying thought crossed Victor's mind. What if these were the guys that financed the Fertility Project, and they were here to either collect or destroy all evidence – and kill any witnesses?

"Wh-what are you gonna do to me?" Victor asked, suddenly feeling a lump forming in his throat.

"You heard HQ. Gonna get you out," Prettyface shrugged.

"You're not... gonna kill me?" Victor knew that it was a stupid question, but at that moment, he panicked and didn't know what else to say.

"Aren't scientists supposed to be smart? If we wanted you dead, you'd be dead before you even got the chance to see us. But you're still standing, so... no, we're not gonna kill you," he shifted his weight from one leg to the other before adding. "Unless HQ orders us to. Which I think would be fitting for a piece of shit scientist like you."

Fair enough. But if these guys knew already what was going on and weren't with the police, what would happen next to Victor? Who the hell were these guys, anyway? Before he could ask any more questions, gunshots and screams came from down the hall. Prettyface didn't even bother glancing in the direction of the noise and still maintained the calm facial expression. A thought crossed Victor's mind that his phlegmatic reactions to such dire situations were what caused him to stay so handsome at this age. Prettyface must have noticed the worry on Victor's face because he said in the next moment.

"Don't worry so much. You'll get wrinkles too early," he winked and grinned, flashing his pearly, Hollywood-actor perfect teeth.

***

"Fire in the hole!" Squarepants shouted a second time, and then a third time.

The next shout was supposed to be 'Detonating!', but that never came. His sentence abruptly got interrupted, and he stumbled forward. It took Survivor a moment to realize in the dark that a juvenile had jumped out of nowhere on top of Squarepants, knocking him forward. The detonator slid across the floor, and Survivor was immediately on his feet with his gun raised. He shot the juvenile, knocking him off Squarepants and backward effectively, but it was too late. Squarepants grabbed at the missing chunk of his neck, coughing, while blood gushed out of the bite-shaped wound. And then, just a moment later, he stopped moving, and his eyes stared vacantly nowhere in particular. The juvenile Survivor previously shot stood up and screeched, blood and spittle flying from its mouth. Bulldozer cut the creature's screams short with a bullet to the eye.

"Squarepants... dammit," the team leader shook his head.

He found the detonator and bent down to pick it up when a loud hum filled the room. Both he and Survivor immediately became apprehensive, looking around the room for the source of the sound. The hum was long and caused the entire room to vibrate. It lasted for a few seconds before stopping, but then resumed again after a pause.

"What the fuck is this?" Bulldozer frenetically pointed his gun around.

Survivor looked in the Mother's direction, and just then realized it – the Mother was awake!

Its black eyes stared directly at Survivor, and now, no longer dormant, it had a hateful look in its eye – a look thirsty of revenge that only a parent yearning for the deaths of those who killed so many of its children could have. The hum filled the room once more, and when the Mother raised one deformed hand, the sound stopped. It brought the hand forward, instantly shattering the aquarium and causing the liquid inside to flow out.

The Mother stepped out of the aquarium.

***

Victor felt a very low vibration in the room, and instantly, the hairs on the nape of his neck stood straight. Prettyface felt it too, because he looked around with a frown. He put a finger up to his ear and spoke.

"Guys, everything alright over there?"

Distant screams reverberated through the building – they almost seemed to be coming from the building itself. But then came the unmistakable sounds of footsteps pattering above, and Victor knew what this meant.

The Mother was summoning her children.

"We have to get out of here!" Victor shouted at Prettyface in a panic.

"We're not going anywhere until my squad is back," Prettyface retorted, albeit a bit less reticently this time.

He cracked open the door and peeked through. The screams got much louder almost immediately, and he stepped back and slammed the door shut, now much more apprehensive.

"Get back!" Prettyface shouted to Victor while grabbing the doorknob. "Bar the door and stay low until I get back here."

"Wait! Where are you going?!"

"I'll be just outside, gonna make sure none of those freaks get through," he said as he opened the door.

The screams were much closer now, and Victor hoped the building simply carried them that way, giving the illusion of proximity.

"You're gonna get yourself killed!" Victor shouted.

"If I stay inside, those things are gonna get my teammates. And then you'll be on your own, doc," Prettyface said as he stepped outside and faced the stairwell.

He raised his gun just a little higher, the screams so loud now that Victor could almost distinguish how many different voices he heard.

"Howdy, gentlemen," Prettyface said in a relaxed manner as he fired the first round.

***

For a long moment, Survivor and Bulldozer stared in silence at the Mother menacingly towering above them. Survivor couldn't tell if the Mother simply looked angry due to the deformed face it had, but if she could make an expression that expressed anger, he was sure she would.

The tall creature took a step forward, the glass loudly crunching under its massive foot. The step itself seemed to send microscopic tremors through the ground, even though Survivor knew it was impossible, despite the size of the monster. The Mother took another step, massively closing the distance between itself and the unit members. Another hum ensued, much louder this time, and then the familiar screams of the Rejects came from somewhere in the building – no, from *everywhere* in the building.

"Bulldozer, we're running out of time here!" Survivor called out.

Without uttering a word, Bulldozer opened fire. Survivor did the same, and the Mother began taking more rapid and determined steps towards them. She didn't even flinch from the bullets, even when they shot her in the chest. She raised one hand with long nails and swiped the air when she reached Survivor. Survivor was faster and ducked under her sweep, rolling forward so that he got behind her. She focused her attention on Bulldozer, who slowly backed away while firing.

The Mother slightly bent her knees and unhinged her jaw, letting out an ear-piercing screech, spittle flying out of her massive mouth. She sprinted towards Bulldozer and, with ease, grabbed him with one hand. She held him by the waist up in the air in front of her face, as if examining him curiously. Bulldozer continued shooting until his weapon was out of ammo. He dropped the gun and screamed in pain, probably from the Mother's vice-like squeeze.

Survivor saw the cone of the C4 Squarepants made lying on the ground in front of him. The detonator, however, was right next to the Mother. He would need to get past her to grab it, and not to mention that the cone would need to be attached to her somehow. Bulldozer screamed louder now and thrashed against the Mother's grip. Survivor quickly pulled out a stun grenade and tossed it in the Mother's direction.

"Heads up!" he shouted before jumping behind one of the tubes for cover.

He put his hands over his helmet and squeezed his eyes shut. The bang came a moment later, and at this proximity, it was much louder than when a wall separated you from it. He heard a screech, and upon getting out of the cover, he saw Bulldozer on the ground, crawling towards the detonator, and the Mother flailing her arms confusedly in random directions.

Survivor picked up the cone and saw Bulldozer standing up with the detonator and motioning for him to toss the C4 to him. Survivor did so, and for a tense moment, the cone flew through the air before Bulldozer easily caught it. He strafed around the Mother, who was still spinning in circles, blinded and confused. When he found the right moment, Bulldozer jumped and slammed the C4 onto the Mother's chest with a loud cry, where it remained stuck like an ice cream cone. The team leader barely ran a few steps away from her when he pressed the handle on the charger and caused the loud, fiery explosion to knock the Mother down. That was the good thing about C4 – if shaped the right way, the explosion could be concentrated in one area and completely diverted from the other.

The Mother screeched louder and writhed on the ground. But she was still alive. A moment later, she clambered up to her feet and shrieked louder than before. Survivor saw an open wound on her chest and fired into it. This time, she recoiled, and that only intensified when Bulldozer joined in shooting from his sidearm.

Less than a dozen bullets later, she was on her back again, her crooked mouth open, and her body no longer moving. The two of them got closer to examine her one more time before hearing a cacophony of screams and gunshots down the hallway. Bulldozer made a grimace.

"Shit. Talker!" he said.

***

Victor managed to push the delivery bed against the door, but he also pushed a medicine cabinet against the bed just to be on the safe side. He didn't even need to bother being quiet with the gunshots and screams being so loud just outside the room. He had no effective hiding spot right now and could only hope that Prettyface would be successful in holding off the Rejects.

The screams coinciding with the gunshots seemed to last forever, with the shrieks slowly decreasing in intensity. It sounded like there were fewer and fewer Rejects until suddenly, both the gunshots and the screams subsided. Deafening silence ensued while Victor held his breath in anticipation.

A bang resounded on the door, slightly kicking the bed away from the door. Victor gasped but couldn't find the strength to scream or say anything. Another bang and the bed moved further. The door was now ajar enough for a thin person to squeeze through, and Victor wanted to push against the bed but was too frozen with fear.

Bang!

The cabinet slid from the bed and fell on the floor with a loud, shattering sound.

Bang!

The door burst open. Victor backed away and gasped loudly, seeing the tall figure that stood in front of him.

"What do you think you're doing?!" It was one of the special forces guys.

***

Survivor and Bulldozer went through the door and into the hallway. Right away, Survivor saw that something was wrong. The hallway was littered with the dead bodies of juveniles and two adult Rejects. Among them, there was a uniformed body that Survivor recognized immediately as a member of the Intervention Unit. He suspected the worst as he and Bulldozer made their way forward, guns raised in case any of the Rejects suddenly decided to get the drop on them.

"Talker... dammit," Bulldozer said once they got close to Talker's body.

He was slumped on his back, four juveniles around him, and one on top of him. Bulldozer kicked the juvenile off Talker, revealing a large gash in his chest. He looked peaceful other than that, almost as if he was simply asleep, and one thing that Survivor thought Talker would have appreciated was the fact that his face was intact, even in death.

Bulldozer tried the door to the delivery room, but it wouldn't budge. There was a tiny gap, though, so it wasn't locked. Bulldozer kicked the door, widening the gap slightly. Relentlessly, he kicked over and over, and each time he kicked, the gap got wider. A loud crash resounded in the room after one of the kicks. When the gap was wide enough for a person to squeeze through, Bulldozer and Survivor stepped inside. It became apparent that a bed and medicine cabinet were blocking the door, and a frightened Lukanski stood on the other side of the room. By the look in his eye, he may have pissed his pants.

"What do you think you're doing?" Bulldozer sternly asked,

***

"I... he told me to block the door," Victor confusedly said.

The uniformed guy standing in front of him had a stern look on his face. Victor expected him to either backhand him or just outright shoot him.

"We're getting out," he said a moment later, as he stepped out of the way for Victor to move. "Don't fall behind, doc."

Victor nodded fervently. He couldn't help but notice that besides Sterny, only one other uniformed member remained. He looked so average that Victor almost didn't even notice him back when four armed guys were in the room.

"Move it!" Sterny shouted.

Victor loped towards Average Guy, who took the lead out of the room, with Sterny at the back. They moved quickly even though they weren't running, and Victor had to up his pace from fast walking to light jogging. He heard the pattering of Sterny's boots at his heels, which spurred him not to stop, but at the same time, he didn't want to bump into Average Guy in front.

They climbed up the stairs, and as soon as they were on the first floor, Average Guy stopped and pointed his gun at something. Victor felt a hand on his shoulder from behind, forcefully holding him back. The loud gunshots startled him, coming from Average Guy, who had just fired into one of the juvenile Rejects. The creature flew back with a scream and hit the floor, where it stopped moving altogether. Two more came out, and Average Guy took care of them as well.

"Clear!" he called out before they proceeded to the exit.

"Alright," Sterny said from behind Victor as they exited the building and into the cold night air. "Let's get the doc to-"

A loud slam resounded just behind Victor. Both Victor and Average Guy turned around, and if Victor could scream, he'd do so. But he could find no voice to produce more than a whimper.

***

"Alpha, watch out!" someone from Delta team shouted before a sniper shot ensued, loudly echoing in the air, but Survivor didn't focus on them.

He couldn't believe it. The Mother was alive. She was holding her colossal hand on top of Bulldozer's broken body, her clawed fingertips digging deep into his flesh. Based on the fact that Bulldozer's neck and back were literally twisted like a pretzel so that he basically lay on top of his own legs, Survivor deduced that the Mother slammed into him from above, breaking his neck and spine. Immediately, he reacted as he was trained to – to protect the VIP. He pushed Lukanski out of the way and squeezed the trigger.

He barely managed to fire two shots when the Mother backhanded him, causing him to fly backward at least a dozen feet and knocking the wind out of him. He was overcome with pain and vertigo, and once his vision stopped spinning, he realized that the Mother was slowly making her way towards the scientist, while he was scooting away from her backward on all fours.

"Alpha, our ammo ain't doing shit to this thing!" one of the Delta snipers shouted over the radio.

Survivor had dropped his MP5 when the Mother backhanded him, and upon trying to stand up to retrieve his weapon, his knees collapsed, and he slumped back on the concrete, unable to stand up. He felt sharp pain in his chest and realized he probably had a few broken ribs from the slap. He pulled out his sidearm and unloaded into the monster from the ground. The mother didn't even flinch. He kept shooting, even hitting the exposed wound on the chest, but it did nothing to hurt her. He changed the clips and continued, squeezing the trigger over and over, and then-

The pistol clicked to indicate he was out of ammo. And the Mother was right on top of the scientist.

**

As Victor stared up into the Mother's eyes, he realized that Professor Richards was wrong, and always had been. The Rejects were cognitively

318

challenged, yes, but the Mother was not. Her eyes possessed intelligence that may have even surpassed that of humans – and right now, they were full of rage and hatred. Hatred for prying her away from her human mother, for taking away her children and testing them, and eventually slaughtering them like pigs. Hatred for the injustice done upon her.

As the Mother stopped above Victor, she stared down at him, perhaps trying to determine if he was even worth her time – or maybe figuring out a more suitably painful death for the last remaining person responsible for her pain.

"Gabriella..." Victor somehow uttered the name against the lump stuck in his throat.

He hadn't expected the monster to react at all, and yet against all odds, it did. Its eyes widened with compassion, a glint appearing in them. A low hum escaped its mouth, and this was it, Victor thought – he managed to pacify it. She stared at him, and he felt compelled to continue speaking to keep her soothed.

"I'm so, so sorry for all of this, Gabriella. If I could turn back time, I would do things differently. But I can't. I can't bring back Amanda."

At the name of her mother, Gabriella opened her mouth and screamed a ferocious scream. This could only be the scream an animal made, in order to intimidate its prey just before hunting it – or maybe it was just a scream out of pure anger. The Mother raised one hand above her head, the clawed fingers wet with fresh blood glinting in the moonlight. As Victor closed his eyes, he thought that a quick death like that wasn't bad at all.

***

Survivor saw the Mother raising a hand high above her head. She was going to impale the scientist. Survivor tried to shout to Lukanski to move out of the way, but what came out instead was a wheeze of air. He tried to think of one last, desperate move he could make before the mission became a failure.

A piercing explosion filled Survivor's ears, making them ring. It took the cloud of dust around the Mother a moment to settle before he realized that she was reeling, her body arched backward, until she staggered back to balance. Another bang, causing the Mother to stumble backward a few more steps this time. Survivor heard the sound of an APC approaching from his left. Then, a voice over the radio.

"Firing RPG! Danger close!"

"Danger close, get back!" someone else shouted.

Survivor was on his feet, the adrenaline coursing through him. He rushed to Lukanski and effortlessly threw him over his shoulders, running away from the danger zone. Another explosion resounded a moment later, the impact causing Survivor to lose his balance and stumble. He somehow managed to stay on his feet. The APC roared and came to a halt right next to Survivor and Lukanski, and immediately, the rear door opened. Five Juggernaut-armored guys carrying RPGs and heavy machine guns dropped out and made their way past Survivor.

The Fat Guys unit.

Gunshots and more explosions resounded, coming from the Fat Guys, armored vehicles, RPGs, and snipers. At this point, Survivor placed Lukanski on the ground behind the APC and turned around. He stared at the Mother as she screamed, more and more of her skin getting blasted off and revealing the soft, red tissue underneath. She desperately tried moving forward against the barrage of bullets, but she may as well have been trying to move against a tsunami. The lower part of her leg was blasted off, and she fell forward, yet still continued to crawl with indescribable fury.

"Firing RPG!" another voice resounded from the Fat Guys.

He was standing far back, since the blast from an RPG could kill a person even when standing twenty feet behind. Another explosion, and by this time, Survivor was effectively deaf from the loud sounds around him. When the cloud of dust settled, the Mother was motionless, half of her head missing, the skull visible with one remaining eye. Her mouth was contorted in a comical grimace.

"Cease fire! Cease fire!" someone ordered.

Silence ensued, and it was music to Survivor's ears. The entire ordeal must have lasted less than twenty seconds, and when he looked back at Lukanski, he saw him on the ground, panting and staring in the direction of the Mother's mutilated body. Survivor picked him up – not so gently – and shoved him forward.

"This the VIP?" one of the Fat Guys asked when he approached them.

He had a bulletproof visor on his head, but a balaclava was covering his face under it. Survivor nodded.

"Where's your team?" Fat Guy asked.

"Dead."

"All of them?"

"Yeah."

Fat Guy guffawed.

"Surprise, surprise," he said. "Survivor survives again. I'm beginning to think you made a pact with the devil. Their lives for yours."

Survivor stared at him but didn't respond. He had already gotten used to the petty remarks from the other units; he killed his own team, he left his team for dead, he used voodoo to stay alive, he wasn't human, and many others. Fat Guy seemed to lose interest in toying with Survivor, so he grabbed Lukanski by the shoulder and spun him in the direction of the exit.

"Where are you taking me?"

"Shut the fuck up," Fat Guy said, before turning to Survivor and saying. "We'll take the VIP from here. No other civilians were involved, so we just gotta wait for the cleanup crew. As far as I'm concerned, you can go back to HQ for debriefing. Mission accomplished, Survivor."

Epilogue
1 day after disaster

"I want to speak to my lawyer," Victor said as sternly as his sleep-deprived and stressed out condition allowed him to.

He was sitting in a small eight by eight room with nothing but a desk and two chairs inside, and a door with opaque glass near the top. Although there was no one-way mirror, there was no doubt about it – this was an interrogation room. Across from Victor sat a man in his forties. He had a buzz cut, and his face looked like he was irked – that was when he wasn't reticently staring at Victor. He wore a white shirt and jeans, and although he fit the description of a detective or interrogator, Victor knew by now that he wasn't being held by the police. That's what terrified him even more.

"I'm afraid I can't grant you an attorney, Mr. Lukanski. It would seem that this situation is much more difficult than we initially thought," the man said as he skimmed through the pages of a folder that he had turned away, so that Victor couldn't see the contents.

"What do you want from me, goddammit?" Victor snapped.

It had been a whole day since the Fertility Project incident. He was put into a military vehicle with fully armed soldiers as his escorts and driven somewhere. Whenever he tried asking questions, the soldiers would tell him to shut up. Victor didn't let up until one of the soldiers told him he would kick his teeth in if he spoke up again. He didn't look like he was joking, and Victor didn't speak up again.

When the truck stopped, they put a bag over his head and escorted him out – escort meaning dragged him through wherever he was. At first, he felt a cold breeze on his skin but soon was overcome with a warm feeling, which must have meant he was taken inside. He heard the echoing of the soldiers' boots on something that sounded like a metallic surface, but Victor couldn't be sure. There were also murmurs of other people, and they distinctly sounded like they were in a big hall of some sort.

Then, the air went silent, and he was thrown onto a seat and ordered to keep his hands on the table. He heard the door closing and stayed like that for at least an hour until the door opened once more. The interrogator in the white shirt pulled the bag off his head and apologized for the soldiers' rough handling.

"What *we* want, Mr. Lukanski, will depend purely on what *you* want," the interrogator briefly looked up at Victor with bemusement before looking back down at the folder.

"You want a confession, is that it? Huh?! I'm not giving you one. I had *nothing* to do with this shit!" Victor slammed his fist on the table.

He didn't have a short temper, so his own reaction surprised him. He must have been fed up with all of this. The interrogator didn't so much as flinch, let alone look up at Victor. He casually flipped to the next page and leaned back in the chair, clearing his throat.

"You have a family, is that right, Mr. Lukanski?" he asked.

Victor didn't respond.

"Wife Jennifer and daughter Leah, is that right?" He looked up, and Victor thought he detected a barely visible smirk on his face.

Victor continued staring at the interrogator but couldn't find the words to say anything. He felt his chest tightening immensely.

"Whe-where's my family? Are they okay? Are they safe?"

"Relax, Mr. Lukanski. Your family is safe. For now. But that can quickly change. So how about this?" The man closed the folder and leaned across the table, crossing his fingers. "You cooperate with us, and I'll see if I can't arrange a supervised phone call with your wife."

"What do you want from me?"

"First, I want you to tell me what happened in the experiment you and Professor Richards co-hosted."

"I... I don't know. I was just his assistant," Victor blurted out unconvincingly.

"Really?" the interrogator asked.

He and Victor were locked in a staring contest for what felt like an eternity until the interrogator looked down at the folder. He slid it across the table to Victor before leaning back.

"Open it," he said politely, even though it sounded like an order.

Victor stared at the closed folder for a moment before meeting the interrogator's incessant gaze once more. He was staring at Victor silently in anticipation. Victor opened the folder. The first thing he saw made him gasp, not so loudly, he hoped. There was a file of one of the patients – patient number two, Daria. A photograph was attached to it, and that's what made Victor wince. The picture was of her dead body, apparently taken in a morgue. She had dried blood caked around her mouth, but other than that, she seemed peaceful.

"Turn the page," the interrogator said.

"I really don't think I need to see this."

"Please. I insist," the interrogator gestured to the folder with a vague smile.

Victor knew that this wasn't a polite request, and he wouldn't be left alone until he did everything these people wanted. He turned the page and was met with patient four's page. Another gruesome picture was attached, but again, there didn't seem to be any morbid details visible, and for that, he was grateful.

Victor turned to the next page and saw Marie's file. Here, there were multiple pictures attached, some of them from the camera footage of when she cut open her stomach. Victor looked up at the interrogator, who continued staring at him unblinkingly. As Victor turned the page, he saw Isabelle's file. There were pictures of her dead body on the bed in her room, post-delivery. Aside from Isabelle's pictures, there were also pictures of her stillborn infant. The deformities were even worse when taken with the flash of a camera close up.

Victor quickly flipped to the next page, which was only worse than the previous one. It was Amanda's file. Pictures of her were attached, before, during, and after pregnancy. The picture of her body lying on the delivery bed with a C-section cut with Richards and Victor in the room staring at her newborn made Victor feel sick. He slammed the folder shut and looked up at the interrogator.

"Okay, I get it. You know everything."

"Professor Richards was trying to make the perfect human. And he made it. Briefly. Before the accident took place, correct?"

Victor looked down at the folder silently. The interrogator leaned forward.

"Mr. Lukanski, I can assure you that the people I work for will not take your refusal to cooperate so lightly. I want to help you and your family, but I can't do that unless you talk to me."

Victor knew the guy was bullshitting him. For all he knew, his life was over – either he was going to be imprisoned or killed. But right now, they had him by the balls, and he could only hope to at least have them spare his family. They didn't know anything about the project, and he could use that to try to convince this asshole that his family was not a threat.

"I thought Richards wanted scientific greatness," Victor said. "But in truth, he wanted money. He said that the experiment was about to move to the next stage, but he never told me who he worked for."

"He worked for us. But I'm afraid Richards didn't know what the true purpose of the experiment was, either."

"What do you mean?" Victor frowned.

"Richards was one of the finest embryologists in the country. When we heard about him, we gave him a monetary offer he simply couldn't refuse. The purpose of the Fertility Project was never to create perfect humans. It was to create perfect *soldiers*. Bred weapons of war. But I'm afraid they were inefficient. The Rejects are highly capable candidates for physical prowess, yes, but they can't be commanded; thus, their cognitive abilities render them useless to us. The Immaculates, however... they are the ones we want. And not to create perfect mankind, or whatever bullshit Richards believed or made you believe. No, we simply want to have the upper hand in the market."

"You're the ones who funded the project?"

The interrogator didn't answer, but leaned back without a word.

"Why are you telling me all this?" Victor asked.

"You were right about one thing, Mr. Lukanski. The project was about to initiate a new phase. And we ordered Richards to dispose of you since you were a liability. However, you ruined our plans and the entire experiment. You got Professor Richards, the scientist who ran the whole thing, killed, and we had to get the security company to clean the whole place of any evidence."

"So, no one will know what happened there?"

"No."

"What about the families of the involved people?"

The man gave him an aloof smile that portrayed confidence. Victor hung his head down.

"For what you did, the punishment is usually severe. But, it's your lucky day, Mr. Lukanski," the interrogator said.

Victor thought he was toying with him, but he looked up in hopefulness nonetheless.

"Richards' death puts us in a difficult position. He was the only one who knew what to do in the experiment. Except, of course, one other person."

"Me," Victor finished his sentence.

"That's right. So, my company wants to give you a proposal, Mr. Lukanski. A very convenient one, at that. You will continue to live a normal life as a loving father and husband. How does that sound?"

"What's the catch?"

Just then, the door opened, and a woman in formal attire walked in with a paper and pen. She placed them on the table in front of the interrogator, who thanked her. She left the room without a word, not even glancing at Victor, and closed the door behind her. The interrogator slid the paper and pen toward Victor.

"You will work for us and continue Professor Howard Richards' legacy."

Victor scoffed.

"You want me to continue the Fertility Project?"

The interrogator didn't respond. His silence was the answer.

329

"And if I refuse?" Victor asked daringly.

The interrogator grimaced and shrugged.

"Nothing. Your case will be given to the police, and they'll do with you what they see fit."

"How do I know you won't just kill my family and me once the project is over?"

The interrogator let out a mocking laugh.

"Our company values great minds like yours, Mr. Lukanski. The Fertility Project is only the beginning. You wanted to achieve scientific greatness, right? What better way than this?"

Victor looked down at the paper. He didn't even need to read what it said to know what it was, but he still skimmed through it. He looked at the bottom of the paper where the blank spot for his signature was. He grabbed the pen and clicked it. He felt like he was in some sort of dream and that he would wake up at any moment. This couldn't possibly be happening; it couldn't...

He had just made it out of the Fertility Project alive, and now these shady people, possibly terrorists, wanted him to work for them, to sacrifice more women and create a super-army for them to use for their own purposes? As if in a flash, he thought about his entire life up to this point. How did one bad decision lead to such a chaotic butterfly effect that completely altered his life?

Victor thought about Leah and Jennie. He saw his wife cradling his daughter, speaking to her softly about her daddy, both of them smiling, anxiously awaiting his return.

Without any further hesitation, Victor brought the pen down sharply and signed the paper.

THE END

Final Notes

Thank you for reading my book. If you enjoyed it, I would appreciate it if you left a review on the **Amazon Product page**. Your reviews help small-time authors like me grow and allow us to continue expanding our careers, and bring you – the readers – more stories like these.